TERMINATION ORDER

Books by Philip Friedman

Rage
Act of Love, Act of War
Termination Order

TERMINATION ORDER

a novel by
PHILIP FRIEDMAN

The Dial Press/James Wade
New York

Published by
The Dial Press/James Wade
1 Dag Hammarskjold Plaza
New York, New York 10017

Copyright © 1979 by Philip Friedman

Manufactured in the United States of America

First printing

Library of Congress Cataloging in Publication Data

Friedman, Philip, 1944–
Termination order.

I.   Title.
PZ4.F89886Te   [PS3556.R545]   813'.5'4   78–31945
ISBN 0–8037–8625–5

For
Sylvia and Sam,
who had nothing to do with it.

Some things can be known; others can only be surmised.

In deducing what must be from what is, a writer sometimes comes uncomfortably close to describing the personal reality of someone he has never met or seen. In a sense, this is the ultimate success; in another sense, it is unfortunate, because it can lead a person to believe, quite erroneously, that he is reading his own life story.

Because I have reason to think that *Termination Order* comes very close indeed to some truths of which I claim no first-hand knowledge, it seems particularly important to say that none of the characters in these pages is based on any real, living individual.

If there is reality in what follows, it is largely because of the help I received from several people who gave generously of their time and their special knowledge. For reasons that will be obvious, I cannot name them, but I want to acknowledge their contribution and offer them my sincere gratitude.

P. F.
New York, 1979

1

Released from the pressure of their classrooms, children bubbled along the sidewalk under a sign that shouted *SCHULE DER STADT WIEN*. Across the street, Gregory Moore drew warmth from their energy, then let his eyes swing back up the block.

In contrast to the bulky stone schoolhouse, the building that held Moore's attention was small and reticent. Its ground-floor windows hid behind steel shutters or wrought-iron gratings. One wing, surrounded by a narrow lawn and an iron picket fence, was shrouded from the street by a row of trees. Even the brass plaque next to its door was discreet—pedestrians had to strain to learn they were passing the Soviet Embassy.

The Viennese schoolchildren, in colorful parkas and contrasting knapsacks, walked past the embassy hand in hand with their mothers, oblivious to the building's purpose, or uncaring. Moore himself excited more curiosity—a thin-faced man of medium height, with dark hair and eyes of a brown so deep they seemed almost black, his hands plunged into the pockets of a camel's hair overcoat, standing alone on the cold and windy corner.

When the last of the children was gone, the street was again bleak and empty. The massive wrought-iron door of the embassy swung back. A stocky man in a

Russian fur hat and a gray overcoat came down the walk. The television camera mounted prominently over the front door methodically registered his progress.

When the Russian reached the gate and opened it, Moore stepped forward. The motion caught the Russian's eye. He stopped.

Moore nodded a greeting and smiled briefly.

For an instant, a puzzled frown touched the Russian's almost Mongolian features, then he turned away and pulled the gate closed behind him.

Moore followed at a moderate distance, making no attempt to conceal himself. The Russian stopped next to his car, a bright red Lada—one of the Communist-Bloc-built Fiats. Moore watched him get in, start the engine, and drive off.

For most of that evening Moore waited in a middle-aged Mercedes parked in a dark plaza. Atop a stone pedestal next to the car, an eighteenth-century Austrian emperor sat astride a prancing bronze horse.

Across the plaza and the street that bordered it loomed the Palais von Hildebrandt, once the seat of a minor branch of the House of Hapsburg, now a mélange of commercial and residential apartments. Its oversize wooden doors were the symmetrical halves of a fifteen-foot-high archway, each with a carved lion's head prominent in its center.

A dark rectangle opened under one of the lions—a door within a door. The Russian emerged and set off along the face of the building toward the corner.

Moore flicked a switch and caught the Russian in the glare of the Mercedes's headlights. Startled, he turned; he stared at the car for a long moment before resuming his walk. Moore watched him until he had turned the corner, then started the Mercedes and drove it back to the garage.

Moore spent the rest of the week preparing for an international consumer electronics convention and exposition that was coming up at the end of April. Teletronics, Inc., where Moore spent the official working day, did almost half of its business in Europe. As one of Teletronics's three assistant vice-presidents in the European marketing section, Moore had the job of planning and overseeing the company's convention program—presentations by the sales and marketing departments, booths at the exhibition halls, and a series of social events for customers and suppliers.

Nights, he got home late, had a beer, and went to bed, where he would lie awake for half an hour, staring at the ceiling and thinking about how he planned to handle Alexander Rukovoi.

Saturday morning, Moore went for a walk along the Danube Canal. It was another sunny day; it was still cold, but for the first time Moore could believe spring was coming.

He was passed by a man in a warm-up suit, jogging. Three gray-haired women stood gossiping, with their faces toward the sun. Moore sat down on a wooden bench. A man in a loden coat came around the curve of the walkway, stopped to talk to a much younger woman in jeans while their dogs circled and sniffed each other. Across the canal, one of the pale Baroque buildings bore a bright patch of color—laundry hanging out to dry on a balcony.

Moore waited. In spite of the chill in the air, his palms were sweaty.

Two old men sat down on the bench next to him. One took a miniature chess set from a pocket of his overcoat. The men began to play, talking idly about a minor scandal at the university. Moore got up and walked to the next set of benches, just beyond a small playground.

He was ready to quit, sure he had miscalculated somehow, when he saw the figure he had been waiting for. Medium height, only slightly taller than Moore but far broader, with thinning red-brown hair cut so short he looked bald. At the man's side was a steel-gray Borzoi pup, its gait an odd mixture of grace and ungainliness.

When the Russian and his dog were about fifty yards away, Moore stood up and walked slowly toward them. Rukovoi did not recognize him at once. When he did, he glanced at the canal to his left and the steep hill to his right as if he wanted to turn aside.

As the distance between them closed, Moore kept to the center of the path, his dark brown eyes straight ahead. The two men brushed against each other briefly.

Moore kept walking; his pace increased. Having made the transfer, he was more keyed up than before. He spent an hour walking off the energy.

———

There were two dark letters in the flashing yellow sign that should have said STANBUL CAFÉ. Moore pushed the frosted glass door open and went inside.

The air was almost impenetrable with cigarette smoke. Three workmen sat at the bar drinking beer, and two of the booths were occupied—in one a man sat reading a newspaper, in the other a young couple talked intently. A brawny man with dark hair and a thick moustache was hunched over a table, a tall beer glass in front of him, his coat and trousers still powdered with the dust of his day's labor.

Moore walked to one of the vacant booths and sat down facing the door. After a few minutes, a slim young man came toward the booth, wiping his hands on a soiled dishcloth tucked under his belt.

"*Bitte?*"

"*Lager. Ein Viertel.*"

The dark young man went away and came back with a mug of beer.

Rukovoi was five minutes early. He stood in the doorway a moment, surveying the room. He was wearing heavy work shoes and coarse trousers, grimier than any in the room. His three-quarter-length coat was black vinyl and far from new.

He saw Moore, walked to the booth, sat down. Neither man spoke.

Finally the Russian said, "All right, I am here." His English was clear, with only a slight accent.

"Take off your coat, Alexander Ivanovich. Have a drink."

The Russian took a breath, preparing for an angry response, but something in Moore's face made him stop. He took off his coat, put it on the bench next to him, and sat down again. He left the knitted navy watch cap on his head.

Again, he waited for the American to speak, and again his impatience got the better of him.

"I do not like it, to be in such a place." He looked around. No one seemed to be paying any attention to them. "I prefer to be outside."

Moore said nothing. He looked toward the bar and waved for the waiter.

"*Noch ein lager,*" Moore told him.

"*Tee, bitte,*" Rukovoi said. "*Und ein Wodka.*"

Moore smiled. "*Auch ein Wodka für mich.*"

The waiter made notes on a small pad and went back to the bar.

"How are things at the Foundation?" Moore asked.

"I did not come here . . ." Rukovoi snapped. He sighed, shook his head. "It is the same as always." He paused, looked around again. "Will we have company here?"

"No. No one I know."

"Good. I, too, am alone."

"I hope so."

"I am alone. I am sure."

They fell silent again.

"I do not understand . . ." the Russian ventured.

Moore held up his hand. "In a minute."

Their waiter brought tea and vodka. Moore raised his glass.

"*Na zdoroviye.*"

"*Na vasha.*"

They drank. For Moore, there was a feeling of ceremony about it.

After a moment, Rukovoi said, "You are not just a forty-year-old marketing executive for an international electronics company."

Moore reached under his worn tweed jacket, took out a long white envelope, and laid it on the table.

"And you are not just a fiftyish mathematician who specializes in systems analysis."

Rukovoi hesitated. He said, "I admit no such thing."

"No games, Alexander. We're here to do business."

Rukovoi looked at the envelope. When he began to speak, he chose his words carefully.

"I assume you have asked me so theatrically to come here because you want . . . to make arrangements . . . to transfer information. To me."

Moore shook his head slowly.

Rukovoi was nonplussed. "But . . ." He motioned at the envelope.

Moore tapped the envelope lightly with his fingers, his intense brown eyes always on the Russian's.

"I want you to work for me."

Rukovoi sat back with a start.

"Preposterous." He shook his head. "What made you think I would do such a thing?"

"I've done some research about you, Alexander Ivanovich. I know more than you think."

"And this research tells you . . . I am a traitor?"

"No. But it tells me you're too smart to assign simple labels to complicated matters—labels like 'traitor.' "

"How else am I to take such a suggestion?"

"I haven't asked you to betray your country. You can't know that I plan to, or that I will."

"Anything I did for you would betray my country."

"Not necessarily. There are things that might be . . . mutually helpful."

"Even if that were true, it would not matter. For me to have contact with you is impossible." He shook his head again. "This conversation is pointless."

Moore opened the flap of the white envelope and

took out a single photograph, a little bigger than a file card. He slid it across the table toward Rukovoi. In spite of himself, the Russian looked at it. Looked closer, then at Moore.

"My son . . ." he said, perplexed.

Moore did not respond. His eyes held Rukovoi's.

"You have been following my son?" the Russian asked.

Still Moore said nothing, his eyes unwavering, using silence to build the pressure.

Rukovoi's anger broke through. "How dare you! You drag me here to make ludicrous propositions and to tell me you are following my son. If this is a threat of some kind, you will have much to regret."

Moore remained unmoved, unmoving, still staring at Rukovoi.

When the Russian sputtered to a halt, Moore took a second picture from the envelope and slid it across the table. This one was face down.

Compelled by Moore's manner, Rukovoi turned the picture over. He looked at it blankly at first, uncomprehending. Then, making an animal noise in his throat, he covered the picture with both hands, leaned across the table toward Moore, livid, his neck muscles corded, his eyes bulging.

"You . . . You . . . filth!"

For the first time, Moore's expression changed, relaxed to show compassion for the Russian.

Rukovoi turned the picture over so he would not have to look at it.

"Who has seen this?" he asked, defeated for the moment.

"You. And I. And the photographer. And one other, who is not important."

"No one else?"

"No one."

Rukovoi drained his vodka.

"The stupid, ungrateful . . ." he grated. He looked at Moore, sharing for an unguarded moment his bewilderment and his sense of betrayal. "His mother tried to be so good to him, while she lived. For what? For this?" He reached out for Moore's vodka, paused.

Moore nodded, and Rukovoi swept the glass into his hand and drank. When he spoke again, his tone was almost dispassionate.

"I do not understand. You have wounded me, yes. Of course. But to what purpose? This . . . this disgusting business will not make me into a traitor. He is my son, and he has caused me great pain, but . . . we are more enlightened than that. In the end this will mean very little, in terms of my own life, my career. Certainly, it is not enough to turn me against my homeland." He looked closely at Moore. "I would ask you not to disclose it, for the boy's sake if not for mine. But if you do . . ." He shrugged expressively. ". . . you do."

"There's more," Moore said.

He took out three more pictures and slid them across the table, face up. Two of them showed a slim, pale youth in a leather jacket.

Rukovoi looked at them.

"What does this mean? I do not know these others."

"The boy in leather is one of your son's . . . friends. He's at Moscow University, a visiting student. The other one, the one in the third picture, is one of *his* friends. A Frenchman who does business in Eastern Europe, as a cover for his real work. He's an operative for the *Deuxième Bureau*. And a notorious pederast. The French find it amusing that he learns so much from his activities with young boys."

Rukovoi's eyes widened. He could see what was coming.

Moore went on, slowly, without emphasis. "I have an itinerary of where you have been over the past three months, and where your son has been. I also have itineraries for the French operative and his protegé: Paris, Moscow, Vienna, Bonn. It's fascinating how much traveling you have all done. It wasn't easy putting it all together, but it was worth the time and the expense. There are some remarkable coincidences."

"But I never . . ."

Moore raised an eyebrow. "Perhaps not. But who will believe you?"

Rukovoi sat staring mutely at the three pictures. Moore slid another across the table. It showed the first-ring anteroom of the Vienna State Opera at intermission. A glittering crowd was circulating between the refreshment table and the display cases along the wall. At one end of the congested oval of promenaders was a small group of young people, more casually dressed than the others in the room; among them stood the pale young man in his leather jacket. Half the room away from him was Alexander Rukovoi, a flute of champagne raised to his lips.

"You see?" Moore said.

"It is all fabrication."

"No. It is all real."

"But what you make of it is unreal. A vicious illusion. My son is not a spy. I am not a spy. I have never seen these others before." He motioned at the pictures. "How did you find such things?"

"Hard work and money. My own money, some of it. . . . A few years ago, I began to think about how to recruit someone with a real future in the Soviet Union. I didn't do anything about it at first. Made some lists of people I ran across, thought about how I'd manage it, what I'd ask for. I had something long term in mind —a relationship that would grow over the years. Little by little, I got more serious about it. I began to accumulate information on the people on my list, looking for something I could use as a lever. . . ."

"A lever?"

"Sure. Give me a long enough lever and a place to stand, and I'll move the world, as the old Greek saying goes."

"The world. Or Alexander Rukovoi."

"Right. You were on my list. Not at the top, but you were there. I knew who you were, in a vague way. We've been in the same places from time to time over the years. Bonn. Berlin."

"Yes. I know."

"Ah. I wondered if you did."

"My government is very protective of its citizens when they are far from home. I was told repeatedly whom to be careful of. Over the years my briefings about American intelligence agents have frequently included some mention of you. At first they were not sure of what you did. You were a 'possibility,' not a known operative. Then they became sure. If I understand correctly what I have been told, you have an excellent reputation. They say that you are thorough and also that you are imaginative and not so bound by the rules as many of your colleagues. But I understood you had been . . . released from your employment."

"Fired."

"Yes. With hundreds of others."

"I was," Moore lied. "You see—I'm just a marketing executive after all."

"That is preposterous!" Rukovoi's indignation was mixed with amusement. "If that is true, why are we here?"

"I may not be on the payroll anymore, but I still have the old instincts. This isn't something for today: I want to stay with you for a long time. And whatever changes there are in Washington, they'll always be happy to have access to someone at the top levels of the Party."

"You will use me to get your job back."

"Not exactly, no."

Rukovoi shook his head, then leaned forward. "You said you kept a list and I was not at the top. Why did you choose me?"

"It was luck, really."

"Perhaps for you it was luck." Rukovoi grimaced. "How did it happen?"

"It was when I was still in Bonn—you had left by then. I was offered some information about homosexual groups in Soviet Bloc universities. I didn't see what use it was, but it was cheap enough, and the agent who was offering it had been useful on other things, so I said all right, I'd buy. At first, all I got was sketchy descriptions of locked rooms in basements —Western music, coffee and wine and smuggled drugs, and desperate young men. It was more sad than anything else. And then, just before I left, my agent said he had something better. It was a handful of pictures, very seamy. None of the people looked familiar to me. They were bad prints, photographs of photographs, and they'd been handled a lot, but you could see the originals must have been very good. Still, not much more than academically interesting. I paid him for them, and that was that. Or so I thought. But one of the pictures kept bothering me, and one day I figured out why—I had seen one of the boys in it before. I went through my file of possible Soviet recruits, and there he was, in a family picture I had of you. Your son."

"Go on," Rukovoi said.

"It gave me a place to start. From there it was a matter of sweat and time and ingenuity. When I got fired, I thought of dropping it. But I couldn't: it was too good. And it paid off, in the end. The homosexuality was a kind of slim reed, by itself. I didn't really think it would be enough to move you. But when I found out that one of your son's playmates was involved with a French intelligence officer, I knew I had something. The picture in the opera house was the capper. I took it myself. When blondie came to Vienna on a vacation, I got one of the people from my old network to follow him. My man didn't like the job much, and one night—it was pouring—he got a message to me that he was too sick to stay out; he was on his way home. So I said what the hell and I went out and followed the kid myself. I damn near fell over when I saw that you were at the opera, too. . . . I've never been more worried that a roll of film wouldn't come out."

"How strangely our fate overtakes us." Rukovoi's

glance took in the room around them. "In a Viennese café for Palestinian laborers." His blue eyes came to rest on Moore. "Who else knows of this?"

"No one. I've been very careful. I've got backup papers, of course, and copies of the photographs, for my own protection. If I die, the whole kit goes to someone who will use it with far less sympathy than I would. But for now there's no one else who has all the pieces. This is just between you and me."

"You did not report it at all? Any of it?"

"At first it was like a hobby for me; there was nothing to report. After I was fired, there was no one to report to."

Moore drank some beer; his mouth was dry. "Understand, sooner or later I'm going to have to report a lot more of it. I don't take it on myself to decide what's important or not, and once we get going I won't be able to handle you on my own. We'll need support and money. But still, there's no point in being careless with what I know about you."

"Do you expect my gratitude for your silence?" Rukovoi asked harshly.

Moore paid no attention. "It means I can assure you this will all stay between us."

"How can that be? You will have to involve others, as you said. When you do, they will want details, and you will have to respond."

"No. You have my word."

"Your superiors will insist. They will want to polygraph me."

"We can get around that."

"Surely it is not within your control to refuse to give my identity."

"I'll admit it will take work to keep the others away from you. But it can be done. There are people who will listen to me. Important people."

Rukovoi shrugged. He was not convinced. "Why are you expending so much effort . . . for me?" He finished his tea and pushed the cup away.

Moore stared into the bottom of the Russian's cup. There were a few black, sodden crumbs of tea in it, hardly big enough to be called leaves. For a moment, he studied Rukovoi with the same care. His Mongol-warrior face and sailor cap gave no hint of the speed and power of his mind.

"You know, Alexander, you're kind of an anomaly to us. We don't expect to find anyone who's got both your kind of scientific stature and a bright political future, too."

Rukovoi smiled, mirthlessly. "Because in your country the politicians are all lawyers."

"And in yours they are all bureaucrats."

"So then what is odd about Alexander Rukovoi? Systems analysis, decision theory, information theory—these are the delight of our bureaucrats."

"I had no idea they were so capitalistic these days."

"One does not have to believe in exploitive competition to see that linear programming can help optimize production decisions. Your mathematicians insist on telling stories about poker games and treacherous prisoners to illustrate such techniques, but that is merely the product of your capitalist neuroses. For us, the mathematics itself is sufficient. . . . But we did not come here to engage in dialectic."

"No."

"So we can return to the question of why you have expended so much effort because of me."

Moore waved toward the bar. They waited in silence until there was another round of vodka on the table.

Moore said, "Once I focused on you, I wanted to know more about who you were and where you were headed. I was very impressed. You're in a remarkably good position to move up. You're not fifty yet; you've got time to climb very high, if you get the right breaks. It seemed to me you could be a unique asset, as long as no one pushed you too hard, too soon."

"You assume I will agree to work for you at all."

"You have no choice. If I expose what I know you'll be ordered home at once. Even if you had done nothing, your son's connections would make you too vulnerable to rely on. And no one will believe in your innocence. You'll lose your precious countess. Your career will be destroyed. Your family will be disgraced. Even if you don't go to the Gulag or to an asylum or a rest home, your life will be miserable. Maybe if you're lucky they'll make you assistant plant manager at a steelworks in Novosibirsk."

As he spoke, Moore watched Rukovoi closely. At the word "countess," the Russian's eyes had narrowed and the fingers of his right hand had twitched as if he had been about to make a fist.

"When I was first working it out," Moore said, "I wondered how I'd make the approach if I found somebody like you. I tried to put myself in the place of the man I was going to recruit. The first thing I'd worry about was that I'd make a deal and then, once I was seriously compromised, somebody else would step in and change the terms, force me to do things I would never have agreed to at first."

"Yes. And I will not accept that risk. I would rather

take my chances now, if I have to. Waiting will only make it worse."

"Exactly. So I am guaranteeing you that won't happen. That's why I want to keep everyone else out of this."

"And you expect me to believe you?"

"Yes."

"And if I refuse, you will use all this, these pictures, to make it seem that through my son I am already a spy for this vile Frenchman. You will ruin not only me but my Volodya, and my daughters as well."

"Yes."

"I am that important to you?"

"Absolutely."

Rukovoi drank his vodka and sat staring into the smoky café. It was more crowded now, and there was an undertone of spirited conversation in unfamiliar languages. "What will you ask me to do?"

"To give me information."

"Yes. Of course. But . . ."

"I won't abuse the fact that I have you as a source. But there will be times when information from the levels you're going to reach could be very important."

"Such information could be used to gain great power."

Moore shook his head. "I'm not interested in conquest. Just information. Information to protect my country's interests, and maybe to keep people from wasting lives and money stupidly."

The Russian regarded him closely. "But our politicians aren't so rational, isn't it so?"

Moore felt suddenly as if he were wearing a cloak made of lead. The sounds of the café grated on his ears; the smoke-heavy air caught in his throat. He wanted to be outside, where it was cool and dark and quiet.

He said, "That's another reason I don't trust anyone else to know about you." He picked up his glass, put it down. He'd had enough to drink. "I won't mislead you. Nobody's going to give you the Lenin Prize for what you'll be doing. . . . But I won't ask you to give me the keys to the Kremlin, either."

"And all this is to be based on trust," Rukovoi supplied. "Trust for a man I do not know."

"But you'll learn about me. Quickly."

"No doubt. . . . But still . . ."

"It's your choice—trust me, or see your life in ruins."

Rukovoi sat motionless, studying Moore as if trying to look into his soul. "You are right, of course. I cannot say no. But neither can I say yes. I must think about this. I must learn more about you. And we must talk again."

It was a little after noon the next day when Moore, on his lunch break, unlocked a tall green door and walked down a familiar multiarched passageway. It was dark and cold in the passageway, but ahead of him he could see sunlight streaking the worn gray tiles of a courtyard and the white walls of the building surrounding it. He stopped at the mailboxes and put a key in the one labeled J. ROBBINS. As he took the mail from the box, the door to the street opened and closed; there was a momentary wind in the passageway. A tall man, younger than Moore, with a firm stride and thick blond hair in calculated disarray, walked up and stopped at Moore's side.

"Perfect timing," Moore observed.

"Wonderful. We're both late," Jordan Robbins said.

They crossed the sunny courtyard and went up a narrow staircase to the second floor. Robbins unlocked the door.

"How did it go with Rukovoi?" he asked when they were inside.

"Useless." Moore locked the door. "I told you it was going to be a waste of time."

They hung up their coats and went into the sitting room. Moore sat in a wingback chair, the only one in the room he found comfortable: The furniture had been carefully chosen to look as if it had been installed fifty years before.

"We're not having much luck lately," Robbins said.

"Maybe we should be more selective about whom we approach."

"He seemed like a good candidate."

"A mathematician?"

"With a taste for Western women," Robbins added.

"Sure. But he has to have permission for that."

"Maybe. Who knows?" Robbins shrugged. "Want a beer?"

"Fine."

Robbins left the room and came back with a pair of Gold Stars.

"I don't see how he gets away with it." Robbins perched on the edge of a nineteenth-century writing table. "Hell, we'd never get permission to go laying local countesses, and Langley's supposed to be a lot more liberal than Moscow."

Moore turned the cold amber bottle in his hands. "I've got other things to do, Jordie. I'm falling behind with some of my own people."

"The man's an anomaly. Even if he was only some

kind of mathematician or whatever, like it says on his visa, this would look funny. But we're pretty sure he's KGB."

"So what?" Moore stood up. "An affair with a countess is hardly something he could keep from his superiors. So either they approve or it's part of his job. One way or the other, it's not much use to us." He went to the window and gazed absently down into the street. "Unless we have some special interest in what goes on in the International Foundation for Systems Analysis."

"Not particularly. But he's not going to be there forever. He's too smart and ambitious, and his credentials are too good. Hell, why am I making a case for you? It was your reports that got us interested in him in the first place."

"I know," Moore said, not happy about it. "But I still say we should leave him alone."

"You're supposed to be our expert on turning Soviet deep-cover operatives."

"But I'm no expert on wild goose chases. Let's drop it."

Moore carried his beer to the small typing table in the dining room and sat down to write a report.

Robbins came into the room. "I almost forgot. Something for you." He held out an envelope. "Love letter from the home office."

"What is it?"

Robbins flipped the envelope onto the table next to the typewriter. Moore let it lie there.

"They want you back on the farm," Robbins said.

Moore's hands were paused over the typewriter keyboard. They stayed there, frozen, for an instant, and then he went back to his typing.

"Not a chance."

"What are you talking about, 'Not a chance'? It's not an *invitation*, you know."

Moore pushed himself away from the desk and swung around to face Robbins.

"Look, Jordie, this convention I'm working on for Teletronics is right around the corner. I can't just walk out on it. Besides, even if I didn't have the convention, I'm in the middle of something else. For the Agency. Something that could turn out very big. I can't drop it just like that, or it'll fall apart on me. . . . In a month or two, maybe."

"Don't tell me," Robbins said, intrigued. "You've bugged the Kremlin men's room. All the way from downtown Vienna."

Moore went back to his typing. He could feel Robbins staring at him, willing him to say more, but he held his peace.

Robbins said, "They won't buy it, you know. The orders are very clear. They want you in Washington. Now."

"They'll have to wait."

Robbins watched Moore type for another moment before he turned and went about his own business.

2

Rukovoi hesitated with his hand on the chrome knob, then pushed the door open.

Natalia von Hildebrandt's office at the International Foundation for Systems Analysis was as spaceship functional as the rest of the building, but she had added some touches of her own: accessories of cloth and leather to soften the metal, a few small but old and valuable paintings, vases of fresh flowers.

She was at her desk, going over a stack of invoices, a slim gold pencil poised to strike at any discrepancy. Even at work, she looked aristocratic to Rukovoi: Her clothes were immaculate and tasteful; her makeup was stylish but conservative, complementing the clear, soft skin that was her most remarkable feature, amazing in a woman who, many said, had to be at least fifty.

She kept working for a moment, then pushed her reading glasses into her red hair and looked up.

She smiled warmly, but her voice was formal and proper.

"Good morning, Dr. Rukovoi."

"Good morning, *Gräfin*."

"How are you this morning?"

Rukovoi grimaced and shook his head. "I am fine, thank you." His words were for the benefit of any microphones which might be there. "I thought perhaps if you were free we could take lunch together."

"I have no other plans." She stood up and came around her desk.

"Good," he said. "Shall we meet in the entrance foyer at . . . half one?"

He took her briefly in his arms. As he released her, his lips brushed her cheek.

"It's such a pretty day," she said. "Perhaps we could eat in the park." Her green eyes were full of concern for him.

"Yes. I would like that." He kissed her forehead and turned to leave.

"Twelve-thirty, then," she said.

————

It was not yet the season for music in the Stadtpark band kiosk, and the café between it and the Kursalon was a barren field of red chairs and white tables. But across the lawn from the long building, which always made Rukovoi think of a wedding cake with a green top, there were no empty places on the park benches. As he and Natalia walked along the curved row of people sitting with their faces tilted toward the sun, three Japanese men in dark suits stood up and started off toward the statue of Strauss.

"Aha!" said Rukovoi and pounced on the bench they had vacated.

Natalia sat down next to him and spread a napkin between them for their food. She had bought fresh rolls and some cheese at a bakery on *Johannesgasse*, and he had a thermos of coffee from the Foundation's cafeteria.

As they ate, he told her about his meeting with Moore. He kept his voice low, his words aimed directly at her. Whenever anyone passed close to them, he stopped or talked about the weather.

"What will you do?" she asked him.

"I don't know. I can't go along with him."

"But what if he does as he threatened? It means you will be called back . . . to Moscow. In disgrace. Volodya, too. Both of you could be put on trial for espionage, or treason. And your daughters, and your son-in-law. They would all be affected."

"No more than if I actually became a traitor," he snapped.

Startled, she pulled back.

"I am sorry, Natalia. What you have said is true. I cannot resist him openly, because of what he can do to me. Because of what he can do to us. And so I must convince him I am doing as he asks."

"What if he finds out that you are pretending?"

"It is not simply a matter of pretending. Pretending alone will not fool him."

He stopped. A short woman in a brown tweed suit was approaching them. She walked past their bench and onto the grass behind them. Rukovoi turned to watch her. Her attention was focused on a peacock sitting on the lawn. She cooed at it and dug into a bag for breadcrumbs, but the peacock stood up and walked away, its iridescent blue neck crooked into an improbable, boneless curve.

"Do you really think you can fool him?" Natalia asked.

Rukovoi watched the woman, bent over, still cooing, offering breadcrumbs to the bird as she walked. The peculiar twosome had gone a dozen yards together before the peacock turned, looked warily at the woman, then began to take food from her hand.

He turned back to Natalia. "Yes. If no one contradicts me."

She touched his cheek, an unusually intimate gesture for her in public. "I am frightened, Alex."

"I wish . . ." Rukovoi began. He shook his head, drank coffee.

"What do you wish?"

"It is not important. Wishing is not for adults." His tone was unintentionally harsh. "There is Nevelsky to worry about as well."

"When is he coming?"

"I am not sure. I think he will be here soon."

They sat in silence. A cold wind began to blow. She brushed a few strands of coppery hair off her face, drew her sweater closed, and gathered up the remains of their lunch.

"There is no way I can help?" she asked.

He wanted to put his arms around her. "Do not say such a thing. You have already helped. I would be lost without you. You know that."

"You are so *gallant*. But I haven't done anything."

"Ah." He forced a smile. "That is not so. Already, you have turned your back on your social circle—indeed, your entire class—and risked the scorn of all your friends, all for love of a scion of drab and styleless communism. An applied mathematician, not even someone with the glamour of pure theory."

She laughed. "Yes," she said, trying to match his bantering tone. "But I was a poor, innocent countess. I didn't know what I was doing. And by the time I did, it was too late to stop."

"It was too late for me, too."

She smiled, a little ruefully, remembering. "So it was, for both of us. But you must admit, you had no shame at the beginning, leading me on as if you were a Czech or something else perfectly acceptable, knowing

I would never have looked twice at a Russian." She stared across the empty café at the ornate, white Kursalon. "It is so foolish, to worry about such things. Childish."

"It is not childish," he said, somber again. "You fell in love with a Russian, and now you can see where it has led you."

———

Moore drove slowly, watching for any sign that he was being followed. At Baden, he got off the Bundestrasse and headed east along back roads until he hit the last major road before the atomic power plant at Siebersdorf; there he turned south again. The trees along the narrow strip of blacktop were still bare, but when, a half hour later, he stopped at another crossroad and got out of the car, the air was as soft and fragrant as if spring had already arrived.

He checked his watch. Five after two: three more minutes.

Thirty seconds late, the red Lada sped by. Moore stayed where he was for five minutes. Two other cars passed, the first more than a minute after the Russian.

As Moore got back into the Mercedes, a large blue truck blasted down the road toward him. He let it get well out of sight before he pulled away.

Rukovoi was waiting a mile down the road, the Lada barely visible along a dirt path among the trees.

Moore stopped, and Rukovoi got into the Mercedes.

"I have been thinking about our conversation," Rukovoi said as Moore drove on. "There are problems we must discuss."

Moore glanced at him. "All right. Go ahead."

The Russian twisted in his seat so that he was facing Moore. "Must I take it on faith that you are not recording what we say?"

"On faith, or on my word. I'm not, and nobody else is. I went over the car twice when I took it out today." He reached over and switched on the radio. "If that will make you feel better . . ."

Rukovoi turned the selector to FM and adjusted the dial until he had the state radio station that billed itself as playing "music on the assembly line"—pop songs, mostly American.

"You said there were problems," Moore prompted.

"Yes. You are right that I do not intend to remain a mathematician all my life. There is much need in Moscow for men who understand modern systems techniques, men who can assist the politicians and the economists in their policymaking. Perhaps make policy themselves. A man with such skills, an expert in the field, could aspire to the Central Committee. Even to the Politburo."

"You're talking about somebody with an impeccable Party record," Moore offered. "Let's say, a man with rank and experience in the KGB."

Rukovoi let the comment stand.

"There is a man called Nevelsky," he said. "Major General Gherman Nevelsky."

"Major General of what?"

"The Committee for State Security. KGB, as you call it."

"A friend of yours?"

"He is my colleague. General Nevelsky and I have worked together many times in the past. At the moment, it is not incorrect to say that he is my superior officer. However, General Nevelsky is . . . thinking in terms of the past."

"Old-fashioned?"

"Yes . . . or perhaps 'reactionary' is the word I mean. It is unfortunate, because he is a man of great skill and intelligence, except for the limitations imposed by his viewpoint."

"I gather you don't get along."

"We disagree frequently. More than once, he has spoken against me, and he has been proven wrong. Recently he has become more circumspect. He cannot afford to have it happen again."

"And you think he's out for your head?"

"You are very direct. I admire it."

"Most don't. . . . I don't know this Major General of yours. Has he been in the West much?"

"No. He dislikes the West. He works in Moscow when he can. . . . But he is coming to Vienna."

"Why?"

"He will tell me when he arrives."

"How long will he be around?"

"I have no idea."

"And he'll be looking over your shoulder the whole time?"

"Yes. I do not see how I can communicate with you while he is here."

Moore had been following the country road without thought, driving automatically as he and Rukovoi talked. Now the road signs indicated a decreasing speed limit and a major intersection ahead; they were getting closer to Wiener Neustad. Moore braked and shifted to a lower gear.

"What do you propose?"

"That we postpone all of this until after Nevelsky has gone."

Moore stopped at the intersection. A large blue truck rumbled by. Moore's stomach felt suddenly hollow; it took a moment for him to realize that it was not the same truck. When the intersection was clear, he drove across; his hand trembled slightly on the shift lever.

"We can't wait," he told Rukovoi. "I have pressures of my own to deal with. We have to start right away."

"What sense is there in compounding the danger?"

"I don't want to compound anybody's danger if I can help it, but we've got to get going. I told you—I have pressures of my own. Something has come up since we met in the café. You'll have to make a decision. Yes or no. In or out."

Rukovoi stared out the car window at the passing trees.

On the radio, a rock band played a new arrangement of an old song. Moore recognized it from his early days with the Agency, on his mandatory tour in Saigon. It was a Beatles song: "Yesterday."

Rukovoi said, "I cannot risk doing anything while Nevelsky is here. If we start now, we must allow a hiatus until he leaves."

Moore thought about it "All right," he said. "That's a possibility. But I don't like it, and I'm going to find a way around it if I can." He glanced at his passenger. "Do I take it that means you're in?"

Rukovoi did not answer.

"Yes or no?"

Another pause, then: "Yes."

Moore looked at his watch. "It's getting late. We'd better turn around." He pulled off the road and headed back toward where he had picked Rukovoi up. The Russian was again staring out the side window. Moore could not see his expression.

After a few miles Moore said, "It's going to be safest and easiest if we do everything by drop. Is there someplace you know that we can use?"

Rukovoi did not turn away from the window. "Two, perhaps three."

"Good."

There was another silence. Moore was finding it harder to go on with it than he had expected. In the past, when he had turned an agent, he had felt in control, and he had felt a kind of contempt for the man who had succumbed to his bribes or blackmail. Something about Rukovoi was different. With him, Moore could feel neither control nor contempt.

He said, "I'll have to test you from time to time. You understand that."

"Of course."

"Bear this in mind—no games, no second chances. None."

"I understand that." Rukovoi's voice was flat, yet Moore felt he had been rebuked for belaboring the obvious.

Again, he allowed a silence before he spoke. "There are some questions I have about the KGB staff at the embassy."

"I may not know the answers."

"Try."

"As you wish."

"Last count, you had twenty-three people at the *residentura*. But we're hearing rumors now that there are changes, people being added. Tell me about it."

"The rumors are correct. By the end of the month, the number in the political division will have doubled, from eight to sixteen, and there will be six new people for Department A—disinformation."

"Why all the new activity?"

There was no answer. Moore waited, then looked over at his passenger.

"Alex . . ."

"I do not know. It is only by chance that I heard about the new personnel."

"Could it have something to do with General Nevelsky's trip to Vienna?"

"I must assume that it does. . . ."

Moore tried a different approach. "When was the last time Nevelsky came out into the field?"

"He does not send me his itineraries. I can only tell you about the last time I saw him. It was almost a year ago. We were both in Rome."

"What was happening?"

"I was there for a week for an international mathematics congress. I saw him only once, and I was not involved in his operation. I think it had to do with making an accommodation between the Italian Communist Party and the terrorists."

"Nevelsky was an emissary of some kind?"

"No. I think you might call him a coordinator."

"Who was he acting for?"

"There was a rumor that he acted for the Central Committee."

"The Central Committee. That's interesting." Moore downshifted and let the engine slow the car. "We're almost there. You'd better start looking for your car."

Moments later, Rukovoi said, "There." He pointed.

Moore slowed, but he did not stop. He glimpsed a flash of red off in the trees. He drove another half mile and then made a U-turn.

"You think Nevelsky's going to be doing errands for the Central Committee here in Vienna?"

Rukovoi laughed; the sound was overlaid with tension. "Errands. That is very funny. It would make the Comrade General angry to hear you say he was doing errands. . . . But I think the answer to your question must be yes. This must be a matter of the highest priority, or he would not come to Vienna. He would oversee the operation from Moscow."

Moore pulled up near the dirt lane where Rukovoi had parked.

"Then I've got to know what it's about. It'll be your first real assignment. A trial run."

Rukovoi said nothing; his face was clamped against emotion. He pushed the car door open.

"One more thing," Moore said. "Before you go, you'd better give me the locations of your drops."

———

In the basement of the building that held the Robbins safe-house apartment, there was a long, stone-walled room. The wooden outer door was painted black, and it led to a small, empty anteroom and a second door, thick and thoroughly insulated, which opened into the room itself.

Moore locked both doors behind him. He went to a tall steel cabinet, unlocked it, and took out a large revolver, a box of ammunition, and a pair of ear protectors. He relocked the cabinet and put the gun and ammunition down on the counter of the shooting range. He put the ear protectors on; they were like large plastic earmuffs.

He did not hear the door open and close behind him. He was clipping a target to its carrier when he became aware that Robbins was standing by the counter at his side. He took the ear protectors off.

"I got an answer from the home office," Robbins told him. "They say you have to go."

"Why? What the hell can be so important?"

"Debriefing. You're overdue. So am I: I'm going, too."

"Joan isn't even back yet. You'd think they'd wait until she was here before they had us leave."

"The way I get it, they've recalled the other operations groups and most of the people at the embassy, too."

Moore turned away from him and adjusted the target. "They're up to something."

"What can they be up to?"

Moore cranked the handle of a pulley wheel, sending the target on its way down the line toward the other end of the firing range.

"You're telling me they're calling the whole station in at once," he said. "Isn't that right?"

"More or less."

"When was the last time you heard of anybody doing that?"

The target snapped to a halt. Robbins's head turned at the noise, then turned back. "Okay. So we haven't heard of it before. So what? It doesn't mean it hasn't happened. Hell, they close stations from time to time."

"Sure they close stations. For economy. Because they're not producing anything. But we haven't exactly been sitting on our asses here, Jordie. There's plenty of Soviet Bloc stuff going on. And what about the OPEC group? Or Western Europe? We're right at the crossroads here. Vienna, for Christ's sake. Not so long ago it was the hottest station in Europe."

Moore picked up the revolver. It was a .357 Magnum, heavy and awkward. He pushed the cylinder out and began to load it, one bullet at a time.

"I'm telling you, Jordie, it's crazy. Who the hell do they figure is going to watch the store while we're all back there dancing around in Virginia, waiting to be polygraphed, or whatever."

Robbins grinned. "We could put up a sign—This Station Temporarily Out of Order."

Moore snapped the revolver's cylinder back into place. "I'm not going."

Robbins put a hand on Moore's arm. "Greg . . . we've got to go back. You can't just ignore them."

"I'm not ignoring them." He put the gun down on the counter. "I told you I was in the middle of something important. I don't even know yet how big it is, but it's for sure not something I can walk out on now. Believe me, it's a lot more important than any routine debriefing at Langley."

"I mentioned that you were up to something special in my last cable to Wilson," Robbins said.

Moore looked at him sharply.

"I thought it might buy you a reprieve."

'What did he say?" Moore's tone was casual, but his eyes were fixed intently on Robbins.

"He blew his top. Wanted to know what the hell you thought you were doing, going off on your own like that, not reporting what you were up to."

"Jesus!" Moore exploded. "What am I supposed to do, raise my hand if I want to go to the potty?"

"You have to remember, Greg, you're not a singleton

anymore. We do things a little more by the book than you're used to."

"That's a crock of shit, Jordie, and you know it—I haven't worked alone in more than five years. I know all about the Mickey Mouse. I file my reports like a good boy. But some things are more sensitive than others. You let what you're doing out of the bag too soon, and you can blow the whole business. I'll make a report when I've got something useful to say."

"Okay. Okay. Take it easy, will you? I'm not saying he's right. I'm just telling you what he said."

"And I don't like it. For fifteen years, I've done my job and nobody's said boo. Now, all of a sudden, Wilson tells me when to squat and expects me to ask how much."

Ignoring the ear protectors, he snatched up the massive revolver and fired rapidly until the gun was empty. The repeated shots made a single deafening sound, echoing in the confined, hard-walled space. He put the gun back on the counter.

Robbins reeled in the target. The five bullets had torn a jagged circle in it, a fraction of an inch off center, obliterating the bull's-eye.

"Do I pass?" Moore asked, flat-voiced. He could barely hear his own words over the ringing in his ears.

"Yeah," Robbins said. "You pass."

———

Rukovoi walked slowly down a corridor in the Russian Embassy. He had a report to file, and he wrote his reports at the embassy the day he submitted them. He did not like to have them around his apartment.

He felt mocked by his own habitual care and discretion. Even if Volodya were a spy, he never would have learned anything from his father. But that did not matter. No amount of care mattered in the face of the appearances Gregory Moore could create with his photographs and his itineraries.

Rukovoi unlocked the door to the large gray office they let him use. As always, his eyes went to the bigger-than-life portrait of Lenin on the wall. He was three steps into the room before he realized he was not alone.

At an open cabinet on the far wall, a man was pouring himself a drink. He was cadaverously thin, stoop shouldered, totally hairless. His fingers were long and bony, like the legs of a huge, pale spider. He put down the bottle of vodka and turned toward Rukovoi, who managed to choke out a greeting.

"Comrade Nevelsky. You are early. What a pleasant surprise."

"Good day, Alexander Ivanovich. Come in. Sit down."

Rukovoi nodded stiffly and crossed the room to the couch.

"Would you like a drink, Comrade Rukovoi? Vodka? Scotch? . . . No? As you wish." Nevelsky carried his own drink to the old wooden desk that stood in front of the room's perpetually curtained windows.

"We have much to discuss," Nevelsky said as he sat down. "But there is one thing. . . ." He took a notebook from his jacket pocket. "Just a detail, you understand." He leafed through the notebook. "I have only this morning read your most recent reports, and I see that you have twice recently been in contact with an American . . . Gregory Moore. Formerly of the Central Intelligence Agency. Or so they say."

"Yes."

"I am sure you have a reason for this. But your

reports are unclear." Nevelsky spoke quietly. "It troubles me, because it is not your assignment here to have contact with members of the CIA."

"No. Of course. But this is not precisely part of my regular work." Rukovoi realized that he was straining toward Nevelsky. He forced himself to sit back.

"Tell me, then, about your Mr. Gregory Moore."

Rukovoi cleared his throat before he spoke. "Approximately two weeks ago, Gregory Moore approached me with a clumsy proposal that I should work for him. He said he would pay handsomely for whatever information I could provide."

"I saw nothing of this in your reports."

Rukovoi fought the impulse to sit forward again. He waved his hand dismissingly. "I saw at once that he did not seriously expect me to be interested. There had to be another reason for the approach. I wanted to wait and see before I elaborated further. I saw no sense in creating unnecessary speculation until I was sure what was happening."

"We are all grateful for your consideration, I am sure." Nevelsky was being openly sarcastic. "May I assume that by now you know what is happening?"

Rukovoi was beyond maintaining an appearance of calm. He stood up and began to pace.

"After the first approach," he said, "I came to the embassy and looked at the file on American intelligence personnel in Vienna. From what I read about Gregory Moore, he seemed to be a clever man, and a person of skill and experience. For a long time it appears he was not a part of the usual command structure. It was many years before we were certain he was an operative. Now the records say he was fired. He is employed by an electronics manufacturer."

"And you are a mathematician." Nevelsky's sarcasm was undiminished.

"Yes. But it is possible that Moore actually was fired. It would explain what he has done."

"Yes?"

"He may have decided to work for us because he is bitter at having been fired. It was not recently, but such reactions can take time to develop. He must have assumed no one would think of approaching him, so he had to come to us. But if he simply offered us his services, we would be suspicious, would we not? He would anticipate that. So instead he pretended to try to recruit me, in the hope that once contact was established, I might use the opportunity to suggest he work for us."

"How very devious of him." Nevelsky studied Rukovoi. "Do you seriously believe this story you are telling me?"

"I tell it to you now only because I am sure of it. At our second meeting, I made it clear to Moore once again that I would not help him, and I broached the idea that he might work for us."

"What did he say?"

"He did not reject it."

Nevelsky's expression clouded. Rukovoi thought he looked worried: He would see the turning of Gregory Moore as a major coup for Rukovoi.

"Perhaps you were right to deal with the situation the way you did," Nevelsky said. "But, still, I do not think we can trust this Moore. Whatever he says, he will have to be watched carefully."

3

Moore leaned against the wall, several feet from the score of others waiting along the front of the narrow, open arrivals area.

The frosted and etched glass panels opposite him slid back in their tracks. A man walked through carrying a briefcase and a hang-up clothesbag. As the panels were closing Moore glimpsed a stream of passengers on their way from Passport Control.

A group of four came through the sliding doors: a tourist couple, another businessman, and a lithe woman with compelling, wide-set eyes under smoothly arched brows. Her dark hair was cut dramatically short. She strode across the waiting area with a purposeful grace.

Moore stared at her, then moved to intercept her.

She saw him coming and stopped, put down her suitcase and the light trenchcoat she was carrying.

He took her in his arms and she pressed close to him. The heat of her body radiated through her thin cotton dress. As they kissed, his hands roamed over her back, touched the exposed nape of her neck.

He held her at arm's length and examined her head, making an exaggerated, almost comic production of it.

She laughed. "Looking for something?"

"Well," he said, "it seems to me I remember this

beautiful long-haired-type person. Joan Wheeler, I think she was called."

"Yep. I remember her. Left her in Washington."

"I don't know." He made a face. "I kind of liked her."

She patted his arm. "And she liked you. But I'm afraid you're just going to have to make do with me instead."

He pulled her close and kissed her again. "I guess you'll do fine. But it's going to take me a while to get used to that haircut."

"You can have all the time you want."

Arm in arm, they made their way through the crowd just off the plane from London. Not far behind them, though they did not notice him, was a man about six feet tall, in a dark coat; he limped slightly as he made his way toward the airport exit.

As Moore held the door for her he said, "How is every little thing in the District of Columbia?"

"You won't believe it," she told him.

"Try me."

Outside the terminal was a large maroon bus that seemed to be made mostly of windows.

"We taking the bus?" she asked.

"No. I have the Merc."

They started across the parking lot. Behind them, the man with the limp paused next to the bus, watching.

Moore headed Joan down a lane of parked cars.

"All right," he said as they walked. "Let's have it."

"Suppose I told you they were brewing another hate-the-CIA witch-hunt on Capitol Hill."

Moore glanced theatrically. "Oh, God. Not again."

"Maybe it's not 'again.' More like 'still.' But this one looks like the worst ever."

Moore caught sight of the dark green Mercedes and angled toward it. "I wonder if it has anything to do with the wholesale summonses they're issuing, calling us all back to the fold."

"Wholesale summonses?"

"Sure thing. While you were gone, they called me and Jordie back. And most of the people based at the embassy. For routine debriefing, they said."

"No kidding. What happened?"

He stopped to unlock the car's trunk. She put her suitcase and trenchcoat in and he closed the lid.

"I refused. And I gather somebody at the embassy gently pointed out that the schedule they'd proposed would leave zero people to staff the station."

"And?"

"I don't know. Stalemate, I think. At least, I haven't heard anything lately."

"That's very interesting."

They got into the car and he started the engine.

"You know," she said, "I saw a lot of familiar faces when I was at Langley, but I didn't think much of it. Now, though, it seems much more significant. I wouldn't be surprised if they were calling in people from all over Europe."

"Something's up. Jordie just pooh-poohs it. But I think he's wrong."

"Something's always up at that place. I'm glad we're out in the field, where all we have to worry about is the Russians and their friends."

He reached across for her; she leaned over to meet him. They kissed: warmly, then passionately.

He said, "I'm glad you're back. I missed you." The words came out with difficulty; they carried more emotion than he had expected.

She touched his cheek, kissed the corner of his mouth lightly, rested her head on his shoulder.

"I missed you, too."

They kissed again.

Moore put the car in gear and followed the exit signs through the parking lot to the line of cars turning onto the road to Vienna. A limousine joined the line behind them, and then a dirty gray Opel; in its passenger seat was the man in the dark coat.

On the way into town, they were silent, engrossed in each other's presence. Moore glanced at Joan; when their eyes met, she put her hand on his thigh and squeezed suggestively.

He remembered the first time he had seen her. That day, he had been the one arriving—at the Virginia training facility everyone called "The Farm." He was back from Bonn and Vienna for some refresher training, and she was a new Career Trainee with long black hair and a tomboy body, looking more like a child of the late sixties than a woman of the mid-seventies.

He smiled at her that first day, more warmly than he had intended or realized. Weary of Europe's cultivated artifice, he took pleasure in her youth and freshness, her Americanness; he had gone on smiling.

Inevitably, that had led to more, although experience had made him wary of romantic involvements within the profession. But he had just been stung by a woman almost ten years his senior, and he badly needed someone who would look up to him, who would defer, even a little, to his age and his superior worldliness.

Joan proved to be smarter and tougher than his first impression of her, and she was unshakably independent, hardly the adoring acolyte he had been looking for. But, surprisingly quickly, comparisons between her and any other woman became meaningless. What mattered was how exhilarating it was to be with her.

Their jobs had kept them apart, but the pleasure they took in each other seemed to intensify with the separations, and it grew even more when the unpredictable hand of the Agency placed them both in Vienna.

He stopped for a red light and looked over at her. She was staring out the windshield, frowning.

"Something wrong?"

She turned to him. "It really feels lousy, is all, being the brunt of all that hysteria about the evil CIA."

"As long as you know it's hysteria."

The light changed. Moore put the car in gear.

"It's not that easy for me," she said. "And I don't see how it can be easy for you either. You were some kind of idealist when you joined, weren't you? Make the world safe for American-style democracy. Time to be hard-nosed in a hard-nosed world. All that post-Kennedy patriotism."

"Well . . ."

"Don't just say 'Well.'" Her animation increased. "They talk as if we were all thugs."

"Some of us were," Moore said. "Are."

A man in an orange vest flagged them to a stop at the beginning of a construction site.

"Some. Maybe some. But that's not what they're saying."

"People have to let off steam from time to time. And the Agency is a pretty good target. We've made an awful lot of stupid mistakes over the years."

"Well, it hurts."

The flagman waved them on. Moore drove slowly past a crew digging at the side of the road.

"Damn it," she said. "When I signed up, I thought— all right, the government may be full of shitheads, but at least there are some people who know what they're doing. The President was a crook and a liar and God knows what else, but one thing he didn't get away with was subverting the CIA. It bothered me, the beating the country was taking all over the world. So I was going to do something constructive. And ever since that day, nobody has had a decent word to say about the Agency."

"I don't like it either," he said. "I've been trying to tell myself it's just a lot of isolated instances, and the Agency's still pretty solid, underneath."

"Are you sure?"

He looked over at her. "No. Not anymore."

———

When Moore checked the first of the message-drops he and Rukovoi had agreed on, he found a note asking for a meeting.

Moore rented a car and parked it a block from the busy corner Rukovoi had suggested as a starting point; he was almost an hour early.

When Rukovoi arrived, Moore kept himself out of sight, watching the patterns of movement around the Russian. Once he was satisfied that Rukovoi was clean, Moore walked out into the open, where the Russian would be sure to see him. Then he walked straight to his rented car. When he pulled out of the parking space, Rukovoi was waiting for him.

Moore drove by a roundabout route to an old

castle-hotel west of the city. It was a gray day, with a wintry chill in the air. The countryside was bleak.

Moore bribed the desk clerk for an isolated room; they were shown to one high in the building, warm and cozy, with comfortable old furniture and a view past the castle's crenelations and out over the Vienna woods.

"I presume you have some information for me," Moore said when they were alone. "Something about the new personnel at the *residentura*, and something about Nevelsky's trip to Vienna."

"There is another subject we must discuss."

"What is it?"

"Nevelsky is suspicious."

Moore was alarmed. "You're sure?"

"He confronted me."

"What did you tell him?" Moore's alarm had turned quickly to wariness; there was no way of knowing what Rukovoi was really up to with this.

"I told him that you approached me and that I refused to help you."

"Did he buy it?"

"I said that *I* had turned *you*."

Moore stared at him for a second, then burst into laughter. "Alex, you're brilliant."

His mirth faded quickly. "There's only one problem. As an ex-employee of the Central Intelligence Agency, I may be plausible as a disgruntled turncoat, but I'm a lousy source of information."

"I told Nevelsky you might work for them again."

Moore felt a stabbing of alarm. "Oh?"

"If there was something you could offer your superiors. A new source of information."

"You."

"Yes."

Moore shook his head. "You really are brilliant."

Rukovoi sat down in an overstuffed armchair. There were more lines than Moore remembered in the Russian's Mongol-warrior face.

His voice showed the same fatigue. "It has become very complicated. Nevelsky wants to have credit for suggesting that I give you information so you can bring it to the CIA. It means he will want to participate in selecting the information you are given. That way, if you are helpful to my career, you are also helpful to his."

"The information you'll be giving me will be phony, of course."

"Precisely."

"So you get good information from me, and feed me false information to take back home. Two for the price of one."

"There is a third benefit we might gain as well."

"Oh?"

"It was mentioned that your superiors would not expect to get information without paying for it. Nevelsky doesn't think I am a good candidate for ideological conversion." Rukovoi's eyes narrowed. "Or for blackmail. But he has boundless faith in my materialism."

"So he wants money, too?"

Rukovoi nodded.

"Nevelsky doesn't miss a trick, does he?"

For the first time, Rukovoi smiled. "If I must be honest, the money was my idea. You understand, I had to participate in the planning with full enthusiasm."

Moore walked to the window and looked out. A

uniform layer of clouds hung low over the bare trees on the hillside.

"It's going to take a little doing to work all this out," Moore reflected. "If you're going to be giving me real information and false information at the same time, we'll need a way to identify which is which. And we'll have to find a way to make Nevelsky believe his false information is being taken at face value. It means setting up a double-blind system for handling the information at Langley. Security at my end is the most important thing. If what we're really doing leaks back to your people, we've got big trouble."

"That is my concern as well. I am afraid it may be impossible to avoid."

Moore turned away from the window. Rukovoi's features were indistinct in the dimness of the room.

"Because . . ."

"I have reason to believe there is an agent of Directorate S in your headquarters in Virginia."

Moore still could not read anything but fatigue in the Russian's face.

"What makes you think that?"

"There are rumors. Stories."

"Sure. There are always rumors like that. The question is, why do you believe them?"

"There are two reasons. First, the stories I have heard were told by our mutual friend, Comrade General Nevelsky."

"Really? He tells stories about KGB penetrations in the CIA? It seems a little indiscreet, don't you think?"

"Yes, but he finds the idea very amusing. He calls the man 'Mordzh.' It is a kind of joke. It means 'walrus.' It is a great insult to call someone a walrus."

"So you think it's true because Nevelsky tells jokes

about it." Moore walked toward Rukovoi, stood over him. "It's not that I wouldn't be interested in evidence that there's a KGB penetration in the Agency. But there have been rumors like that for years now, and we've all lived with them. There have been some shake-ups, and some people have gotten excited about it from time to time, then it dies down again. Look at it from my point of view. It's awfully convenient for you if we have to worry about it now, because if you're giving me both real information and false information, and they have to separate one from the other back at Langley, the mole might find out about it and report back, and then Nevelsky would figure out right away you were lying to him. Which argues for us to cool it for a while, or forever. The whole story is tailor-made to get you off the hook. So if you're going to convince me it's true, you'd better come up with a better reason than Nevelsky's walrus jokes."

Rukovoi stood up, his action fueled by anger. "Sometimes it is not smart to be skeptical."

Moore recoiled at the abruptness of Rukovoi's motion; it took him a second to regain his equilibrium.

"You said there were two reasons."

"Yes. The second reason is that I think Nevelsky's Walrus is a person I know. A man who was once my friend."

"A Russian?"

"Half Russian. His mother was American. And he has almost certainly been in the United States for thirty years or more, by now. I knew him at school."

"And why do you think he's at the Agency?"

"I saw him in Washington. We were in the same restaurant."

"When was this?"

"Long ago. 1970. I was in the United States as a visiting professor, for one term. And to study. My friend's name is Arkady. When I saw him, I started to say hello, but he turned away from me. He was with some others, and he clearly did not want them to know even that I *thought* I recognized him."

"And you let him go by?"

"Yes. Of course. There are not many of us in your country, and no one is there without a reason. He saw me, and he turned away. I respected his wish not to know me."

Rukovoi paused and looked around the small room. There was already noticeably less light than when they had arrived. Moore moved toward the bedside lamp, but Rukovoi said, "No. For now, I prefer the darkness."

He went to stand by the window. Moore walked over and stood next to him.

"Arkady was a . . . peculiar boy. He did not like to play with the others, or to share his studies."

"But you said you were friends."

"Yes. . . . When I was thirteen, I won a prize in mathematics, for a demonstration I did. Arkady was fascinated with it. He came to me and told me he must learn more. And he bribed me."

"He bribed you?"

"It was during the war. Everything was in shortage. He gave me food . . . eggs, milk. Once, he gave me a chicken. I do not know where he found them."

"And so you taught him."

"He was a very good student. He asked useful questions and he listened carefully. It seemed to me then that he remembered everything."

"And you stayed friends?"

"Until he left for a special school."

"When was that?"

"Just at the end of the war." Rukovoi left the window and sat down again in the armchair. "It was a place far from us, and we knew it by rumor only. We thought is was a special school for foreign languages."

"He was good at languages?"

"He was a prodigy. It was said that he spoke English perfectly. As I said, his mother was American. And he spoke at least six other languages fluently, even at thirteen. His memory was almost perfect. He forgot nothing. And he was not stiff, or like a machine, in the way such people can be. He was clever and articulate. Even so, he had no friends but me. And we were . . . *droogy*. There is no English word . . . friends, but more than that. Very . . . close."

Moore could barely see Rukovoi; outside, the sky was darker.

"You didn't meet him again until Washington?"

"Yes. As I said."

"You're sure it was him?"

Rukovoi's anger surfaced again. "Arkady was not a person I could easily mistake for another. After twenty-five years, his face had not changed a great deal. And he was frightened to see me. I am sure of that."

"How did you find out who he was?"

"His American identity? I never learned it. I learned only who was at lunch with him."

Moore waited.

"There were three men at the table. One of the others was a man named Richard Helms. I was told his title was Director of Central Intelligence. The other man was one of his deputies."

"And the third was your friend Arkady."

"Yes."

"It's a very convincing story."

"Yes. It was a very convincing experience. I thought about it for weeks."

"Your Arkady would make a perfect agent-in-place. Articulate and sociable, but with no real need for human contact. Phenomenal memory. Fluency in languages, especially English. And an American mother. Christ!" Moore paced in the tiny area between the bed and the fireplace; he had a sudden feeling of confinement. "And they sent him to a special school. A spy school."

Rukovoi said nothing.

"How would Nevelsky know about this friend of yours?"

"From his father. Nevelsky says his father is case officer for *Mordzh*. General Nevelsky's father was a great war hero. He was involved in some way with the *Rotekappelle* in Germany. Afterward, he became an important espionage agent against the West. In many ways the general stands in his father's shadow. In his relaxed moments, he speaks freely of his father's accomplishments. You understand, he does not say 'my father did this,' or 'my father did that.' It is more vague than that. He speaks of 'we,' as if he meant the entire Committee for State Security. But the stories are always about his father. I heard about *Mordzh* for the first time in such a conversation. . . . There is this in General Nevelsky's favor: When he talks about *Mordzh*, he does not give any details. I am sure only of this: *Mordzh* is top secret and very important. *Mordzh* is a source of information about American intelligence. *Mordzh* is probably in the United States. From these things I deduce that *Mordzh* is Arkady, and he is an official in the CIA, with a position high enough for him to have had lunch with the Director in 1970."

"Or the whole thing could be just a figment of Nevelsky's imagination. Or yours."

"It would be very dangerous to assume that."

"Yes. We'll have to be careful."

Both men fell silent. Moore glanced out the window; there was nothing to be seen.

"We'd better go," he said.

4

Moore's desk at Teletronics was almost buried under schedules, requisitions, and work orders for the coming exposition and convention, and a blanket of pink telephone-message slips. Moore was gearing himself for a long day and night's work when there was a tap at his door.

"Come in."

It was Walther Krantz, a short man in his fifties with white hair and a skier's tan he cultivated at Gstaad. Krantz's title was the same as Moore's, but his job description made him Moore's boss at Teletronics.

"Gregory. Good morning."

"Good morning, Walther."

"How's it going?" Krantz had spent some time at Harvard Business School and at MIT; he was proud of his Americanisms.

"It's going fine." Moore looked down at his desk. There was no point in avoiding the obvious. "Actually, I'm a little behind."

"Yes. Mr. Walsh asked me to look in on you. He's very anxious for us to do as well as we can at the exposition. He thinks it could make a big difference."

"Tell Mr. Walsh not to worry." Walsh was president of Teletronics's European division. His base was in Frankfurt, but he had an office in Vienna; he was there for the two months preceding the convention and exposition.

Krantz backed out of the office. "Okay. Glad to hear it. Just a word to the wise, you know."

"Sure, Walther. Thanks."

Moore did his best to keep his mind on his work, but his concentration was repeatedly interrupted by thoughts of Rukovoi and Nevelsky, and of *Mordzh*. It took him until ten-thirty that night to get all his minor chores out of the way and the major ones organized into chunks that looked manageable. He called Joan and told her he was on his way.

The square outside his office was bright with yellow-orange lights, and there was a moderate flow of cars and pedestrians. St. Stephen held his sword indefatigably skyward, silhouetted against one of the massive Baroque piles that lined the square; atop the building was a bright neon sign that said MOBIL.

Moore pulled his coat closed against a sharp wind from the north and headed for the *Strassenbahn* stop. He almost collided with a giggling bunch of girls on their way out of a McDonald's. He was too preoccupied to notice the man in a dark coat behind him, limping slightly as he hurried to keep up.

There was a streetcar at the stop. Moore ran for it along with a half-dozen others crossing the square. He hopped onto the second car, fished a ticket from his pocket, and slipped it into the machine to be punched. The doors were hissing closed when someone outside pressed the button that opened them again.

The sharp bell of the ticket-punching machine brought Moore's work-fogged mind into focus. He took a quick inventory of his fellow passengers: a couple homebound from the opera, a trio of university students, a portly woman in a torn coat and a babushka. They all looked tired and jaundiced in the wan yellow light of the car.

Moore shifted in his seat, bent over to tug at a boot, then sat back. There were three people behind him: a portly man in a Tyrolean hat and a trenchcoat, a garishly made-up woman with bleached-blonde hair, a man with a round face wearing a dark overcoat. Moore guessed the round-faced man was the latecomer.

People got on and off as the streetcar progressed up the long hill. Moore kept cursory track of them. At his stop three others got off with him.

He was less than two blocks from the streetcar stop when he decided he was being followed. He turned right at the next corner and walked another two blocks, trying to draw a map of the neighborhood in his mind. He walked three more blocks, then made another right and almost immediately a left, the first of four possible turnings within fifty yards of the corner.

He backed into a doorway and watched the end of the block. Moments later, a figure came into view, walking hesitantly—a round-faced man in a dark overcoat. Moore remembered him from the *Strassenbahn:* the latecomer. He paused at the intersection and looked down the street in the direction Moore had taken. After a short while, he moved on.

Moore slipped out of the doorway and made his way quietly along the street, away from the intersection. He turned at the first corner and again at the next corner he came to, keeping up a zigzag path past the dark and quiet houses. Before making the last run, he stopped and withdrew into the shelter of a private driveway, standing motionless for five minutes, until he was sure he was alone.

He walked the final two blocks to Joan Wheeler's apartment house more calmly, but still alert. He unlocked the outer door and crossed the lobby quickly. In the mirrored, glass-doored cab of the elevator, he felt naked and exposed. The elevator rose slowly, red-carpeted hallways succeeding each other rhythmically.

He was at Joan's door when it occurred to him he might have been hasty in assuming the man in the dark coat had been sent by Nevelsky. There were others who might want to have him followed. Like Alexander Rukovoi.

Joan was in the small foyer, waiting for him.

"I heard your key in the lock."

He kissed her and held her tightly.

"Hey," she said, responding to his mood. "You all right?"

"I'm fine." He kissed her again, let go, looked at her. She was wearing a simple lavender dressing gown; it had a silky sheen where it fell softly against the curves of her lean, strong body. The gown had no buttons; her skin showed in a thin wedge down to the sash at her waist. She had put the collar up; it shrouded the nakedness of her neck.

"You look beautiful," he said. "Something new?"

"Mmm-hmm." She leaned forward and kissed him. Her mouth was almost on a level with his. When they had first become lovers she had joked about his height, claiming she had never before been as tall as a man she was going out with. But he preferred it that way—he liked a woman he could look straight in the eye.

"Buy it in Washington?" he asked, and knew at once it was the wrong question.

She stepped behind him to help him out of his coat. "You're even later than I expected," she said.

He let the evasion pass. "I'm later than I wanted to be. There ought to be a crew of us working on that convention instead of just me. I don't know what Walsh thinks he's doing. He knows I have other things to worry about besides Teletronics, Incorporated. What the hell makes him think I can take four times my normal work load for two months straight?"

"Maybe he's forgotten you have another job that's more important."

"For *now*, I have another job," Moore said, heading for the living room. "With all this nonsense—calling people back for polygraphing or debriefing or whatever —who knows how long there'll be anybody here at all."

"You're exaggerating."

"Sure I am: I'm tired and out of sorts. I could use a brandy. You?"

"Sure. If we can have it in the bedroom."

"The best place."

As he poured the cognac, he said, "If Jordie were here, I'd have him take up this Walsh business with Wilson."

"Why don't you do it yourself?"

"Two reasons: That's not how my reporting structure works. And since I refused to go back, Wilson and I aren't on the best of terms."

"Jordie said he wouldn't be at Langley more than a few days."

He gave her one of the brandy glasses. She hooked her arm in his and leaned against him as they walked down the hall. In the bedroom, she put her glass on the nighttable, went straight to the closet, slipped out of her dressing gown, and hung it up.

Moore watched. It seemed to him that she was in a hurry to be out of the lavender gown. As she crossed the room to the bed, the thought was driven from his mind. She moved smoothly, with little wasted motion. Even her breasts—fuller than they seemed when she was dressed—hardly bounced.

She lay down with her hands under her head and one leg raised. The soft light of the bedside lamp made shadows that emphasized the dips and hollows of her body.

For a long moment, Moore was motionless. Only his eyes moved, tracing her leanness, the faint hint of muscle under her smooth skin. The bent leg drew his eyes to the center of her, a small, dark pool; he could just see the soft flesh on the inside of her raised thigh, her only trace of plumpness. It had always charmed him. He moved to the bed and put his hand there.

She smiled and shifted so she could clasp his fingers between her thighs. His hand pushed higher, touched wetness. With his free hand, he unbuttoned his shirt, opened his belt, unzipped his trousers. She released his hand so he could pull off his clothes. He dropped them where he stood and threw himself onto the bed.

Lost in appreciation of her sleekness, consumed by her warmth, he managed to forget about both the man who had given her the lavender dressing gown and the round-faced man in the dark coat.

In the morning, over coffee, he asked her. "Do you know anybody in town who's about forty, six feet, broad face, dark hair and eyes, with a slight limp on the left side?"

"In the business, you mean?"

"Yes."

She took a minute. "I don't think so. Except maybe Valchek from the STB."

"No. It wasn't Valchek. Somebody I've never seen before."

"I can't think of anyone else." She finished her coffee. "Why?"

"Whoever he is, he was following me last night."

"You sure?" she asked.

"Moderately."

"Maybe he's one of the new Russians." She rinsed out their coffee cups and dried her hands on a dishtowel.

"I guess so."

"Greg . . . are you up to something?"

"Not especially."

At the foyer closet, reaching for her coat, she stopped. "I wish you'd tell me. I don't want to be caught by surprise if . . ."

"It's nothing to worry about."

She pulled her coat off the hanger. As he reached for his, she kissed him. "You're a lousy liar."

On their way out she stopped again. "I'm not asking you for the details. I know better than that. But at least don't treat me like I was some innocent little girl."

"All right, Inspector, I confess. I do have something new going."

"And it's dangerous."

He shook his head. "I don't know. I didn't think so at first, but now I'm not so sure."

———

Rukovoi sat at the small round table in the breakfast room next to Natalia's kitchen. Sun streamed in the window next to him. The view, from the top floor, was of the other three sides of the Palais von Hildebrandt—pink stucco with white trim and a profusion of windows—and the inner courtyard below.

Natalia came in from the kitchen carrying a silver coffeepot and a basket of croissants. She was wearing green, as she often did. It set off her green-and-gray eyes and her red-blonde hair. Rukovoi sometimes teased her about having a secret desire to be Irish.

She sat down and poured them coffee.

"Nevelsky was quite vocal about you," he said, picking up the thread of their conversation.

"He's jealous."

"I'm sure, but . . ."

"He's such a petty man," she said. "You shouldn't let him bother you."

"I suppose I shouldn't. But he makes me think of Siberia and insane asylums."

"He couldn't do that to you. You're too important." She was smiling. "A member of the Academy of Sciences. A Hero of the Soviet Union."

The lightness in her voice made him feel as if she were making fun of him. "Natalia!" His own anger shocked him back to reality. "Forgive me. You're right. I am being oversensitive."

He drank coffee. It was rich and full of flavor; it made him feel better. He took a croissant, still warm and soft, tore off a piece and buttered it. He looked across the table at Natalia. There was something about being with her that made him think about how good life was.

He had been surprised, after his wife's death, to find that he had no interest in the attractive girls who were suddenly available to him as a man of relatively high position and special privilege. But Natalia—*Gräfin* Natalia von Hildebrandt—was a woman, not a girl, and that was what made the difference for him. Her intelligence, her sophistication, her maturity—all of these captivated him. The awkwardness and dishonesty and pain of their beginnings together no longer mattered. All he cared about was what they had now. He doubted there was a woman in all the Soviet Union to compare with her.

"What shall we do today?" she asked. "We haven't had a free weekday like this in so very long. Could we go shopping? Or is that too capitalistic?" She smiled, and this time he smiled in response.

"I should get some new clothes for Kitzbühel," she went on, "and I want you to like them." She paused and looked at him more closely. "We *are* going to Kitzbühel?"

His smile turned rueful. "You read me so easily. . . . I am afraid you will have to go without me. I'm sorry. I cannot leave Vienna now."

"You mustn't worry about Nevelsky. He can't harm you just because you have a rich, aristocratic girl friend. . . . I'll even join the Party, if it will help. As long as you will not make me listen to the speeches."

He laughed. "Yes. The speeches would be too much." He took her hand. "You know it isn't that. People higher than Nevelsky have decided there is no harm in our sharing a bed. It is not that which interferes." He stopped. It made him uncomfortable even to allude to the tensions and the mutual deceptions of their beginning together. "It is the other matter which is keeping me here, for now."

"The American?"

Rukovoi nodded. "Perhaps I·should have stood up to him that first night. But I thought the chance was too great that if I did he would carry out his threat, if only out of spite. The risk was too high. But now I am not sure. . . ."

He broke off and studied her. She had on only the faintest makeup, and the morning sun etched clearly the lines on her face. He pressed her hand.

"I think I am tired, Natalia. Weary. I have had enough of Nevelsky and all the people like him. For them, everything must be a struggle for power and position. No day can be allowed to pass without some kind of deceit. What they do has no relation to the good of the country, no matter how often they invoke their patriotism. It is all done for its own sake, for the pure excitement of treachery, the thrill of exerting their power. Now I am caught up in the same web, more thoroughly than I ever dreamed in my worst nightmare. . . ."

"Is it too late? Is there no way you can undo it?"

"I don't know," he said. "I don't know." He looked out the window. In the courtyard, the trees and shrubs wore a pale-green dusting of buds. A little girl sat under one of the trees—a tiny figure in a red jacket, with a crown of light brown hair. Watching her, Rukovoi thought of his own daughters, and his son. He turned back to Natalia and let himself be warmed for a moment by her concern.

"Perhaps there *is* a way to undo it," he said.

———

Moore locked the door and walked straight into the apartment, past Jordan Robbins, who was typing a report.

He pressed against the wall next to the living-room window so that he could look out without being seen. Someone had followed him from Teletronics. Not the round-faced man with the limp, but someone else.

In the noontime crowds, Moore had not realized at first there was anyone behind him. Then, once he had spotted the man, Moore had tried to lose him. He thought he had succeeded, but he was not sure. It had been a long time since he'd had to watch his back with any regularity; the basic skills came back quickly enough, like driving a stick-shift car or riding a bicycle, but the subtler ones needed practice. It left him feeling uneasy. He stood by the window watching the street for several minutes, but he did not see the man he was looking for.

He went into the kitchen, took two tall, tapered glasses out of the closet, and opened two cold bottles of Gold Star. He did not particularly like the local brew, but Robbins refused to stock anything more expensive.

"I'm pouring you a beer," he called.

"Thanks," Robbins yelled back.

Moore carried the glasses into the living room. He took the wingback chair, and Robbins sat on the brocade Victorian couch.

"Hits the spot," Robbins said.

There was a newspaper on the coffee table. Robbins picked it up and waved it at Moore.

"You see this?"

Robbins flipped it to him. It opened in mid-flight and fluttered to the floor.

Moore bent over to retrieve it. It was the *International Herald Tribune*. He looked at the front page, but he did not see anything that seemed especially interesting.

"Lower right," Robbins told him.

Moore looked, saw the headline.

"Senator Demands End of Spy Group," he read aloud.

"That's the one."

Moore skimmed the article.

"What do you think?" Robbins asked.

Moore looked up. "He's a crackpot."

"From his record, he can be a pretty persuasive crackpot."

"They can't terminate the whole Agency. I don't see how they can even talk about it."

"I'm not so sure," Robbins countered. "The Congress and the President set it up in the first place. Why can't they shut it down, too?"

"For one thing, it's too big. It does too much, employs too many people. They might as well try to shut down General Motors or the Post Office. . . . Christ, you remember the fuss when Turner fired a few hundred operatives."

"That died down quick enough."

"Still . . ."

"I know what you're saying. And yesterday I would have agreed with you. Before I got Wilson's latest love letter. Today, I'm not so sure."

Moore folded the paper and put it on the floor. "What does he want now?"

"Didn't I tell you?"

"No."

"Well, it's very simple. They've cut off our water, more or less. Starting from the first of next month, our cash allocation is cut by fifty percent. We have instructions to wind up all but Level One business. And we are all to hold ourselves in readiness to report to Wilson at the home office, at a time to be specified in the future. 'No less than ninety days from the date of this communication nor more than six months,' I believe is what it says. They're sending somebody out to supervise the stuff we're winding up. Guy named Hawthorne."

"That's crazy."

Robbins shrugged. "Maybe it is, maybe it isn't. The embassy-cover people got something similar, I hear. What it sounds to me like is they're either going to shut down the station or else they're sending a whole new crew in to staff it."

Disgusted, Moore stood up and went to the window. This time he stood directly in front of it. Someone in the street below moved out of his line of sight, too quickly for him to see more than the motion.

––––––––––

That night, Moore worked late at Teletronics. When he looked up from his desk, the clock said 10:05. He reached for the phone.

Joan answered immediately.

"Sorry," he said. "The time got away from me, for a change."

"It's okay. I kind of thought it might work out this way. I'm pretty tired anyway."

"I'm going to work another hour or so, and then I think I'll go home and get some sleep."

"Good idea. I'll see you the day after tomorrow."

He hesitated, on the verge of suggesting they get together the next day instead of the day after, but he knew that would only be asking for trouble. He did not want to push her about what she was doing tomorrow night. Stifling an unaccustomed flare of jealousy, he said, "Sure. And I'll try to get finished at a reasonable hour."

"Sleep well."

"Yeah. You too."

He worked until eleven-fifteen, then straightened his desk and locked up the office.

He took the streetcar home. When he left it, he was aware of someone getting out of a car that had just pulled up at the curb.

He took a short detour on his way home, making what amounted to a full circle; the presence behind him remained there. He walked for another block, thinking about what to do, until he remembered that there was an old *palais* being renovated nearby. He was sure the street door would be open, even at this hour.

He had to loop back the way he had come, and he would have to do it without warning the man behind him. He kept on at the same pace to the end of the block, crossed the street, turned left, and crossed again. His human shadow stayed faithfully behind him.

When he turned onto the block he wanted, he found an unexpected bonus. There were no streetlights. Only the dim light of stars and the glow from a few curtained windows let him see the partly open doorway a short distance down the block. He hurried to it and ducked into the dark passageway beyond.

Moments later, he heard footsteps. They stopped, then resumed. Stopped. Started once more. Moore strained to hear. The feet crunched on chips of concrete, plaster dust, other debris of the construction. Stopped again. Moore guessed that the man was studying the doorway now, deciding what to do.

Suddenly it was not enough to shake the man off. Moore had to know who was following him, and why.

A single footstep. The man seemed about to turn away.

Moore lunged from behind the door, grabbed the man's coat, and pulled. Off balance, the man clutched at him, and together they reeled through the open door and across the passageway. They clattered into a stack of boards. Moore recovered in time to grab the man, slam him against the boards, pull him up, slam him down again. The second time, his legs grappled Moore's and they fell together.

They rolled on the dusty floor, crashing into a bucket and then a wheelbarrow. It was too dark to see more than vague shapes. They fought by feel.

They pummeled each other, grasping for a firm hold. Moore found himself on top and rammed the edge of his forearm against the man's throat. The man grunted with pain. He squirmed, reaching for something. Moore caught the groping arm with his free hand and jammed his forearm tighter against the man's throat.

"Who are you?" Moore panted.

There was no response.

"*Wer sind Sie?*" Moore tried.

Again, no response.

Moore pushed harder with his forearm. The man gagged. Moore lightened the pressure.

"*Wer sind Sie?*"

Weakly, but with defiance: "*Niemand.*"

Moore leaned forward again, pressing harder. He could feel the man's larynx under the bony edge of his forearm. The man squirmed feebly under him.

"*Keine spiele!*" Moore hissed. "*Varum folgen-sie mir?*"

The only response was a groan. Moore jumped off the man, pulled him to his feet, and propelled him backward until he was up against the wall. He was limp, beyond fighting back. Moore slapped his face repeatedly.

"*Varum!*"

For a long moment, Moore regarded the silent man he held pinned against the wall, deciding what to do next. He sensed that the man was conquering his pain, preparing to resist.

Moore hit him just below the breastbone. He doubled over.

There was a knot in Moore's stomach, and he felt cold all over. For a moment, he held his breath. His teeth were clenched and he could feel the tension in his face.

He lifted the man upright again, braced him against the wall, and forced himself to seize the man's genitals and squeeze sharply. "*Varum!*"

The man began to babble in heavily accented English. "Money. I follow you because . . . I was . . . money . . . given. *Ein Mann* . . . said to watch . . . where you went. To tell him."

"Who? Who hired you?"

"*Ich* . . . I . . . do not know."

Moore took a breath and squeezed again, harder. The man screamed and tried frantically to pull away, but he was already pressed tightly against the wall.

"*Ein Mann. Ein Russe.* All I know. That is all. *Alles! Alles!*" He was sobbing. "*Ein Russe!*"

There was the sound of a distant siren.

Moore hit the man once more; he slid unconscious to the cobblestones.

Moore ducked into the pitch-dark passageway and made his way carefully to the street. He ran three blocks before he slowed down and tried to look like a man on his way home from a long night's drinking. It was not a difficult charade. The violence had left him weak, with a tendency to shudder unpredictably.

He did not go home. Instead, he walked the three miles to the private two-car garage Robbins rented for the cars he and Moore used.

One of the spaces in the garage was empty, but the dark, boxy shape in the other space was the Mercedes. Moore got in and turned on the dashboard lights and looked at himself in the rearview mirror. His face was scratched, and his hair was a tangled mess, turned a premature gray by the same white powder that was liberally dusted over his clothes. He brushed himself off and tried to comb his hair, to little effect.

He drove through the center of the city; it was dark and deserted except for a few lone men and couples on their way to or from after-hours clubs. He headed west down an empty boulevard past block after block of shuttered shops. When he was within sight of the *Westbahnhof*, he turned left and made his way through the back streets. It was not a part of the city he knew well; at night it looked almost totally unfamiliar. Twice, he had to stop and look at one of the maps that crowded the glove compartment.

He drove past the house he wanted. There was a parking space a few blocks further down the street. He pulled into it and walked back.

The lobby of the small apartment house was dim and seedy. Moore moved across it slowly; sitting still in the car had stiffened him, and there were new places that hurt.

He started up the stairs to the first landing, counting steps as he went. On the fifteenth step, he stopped and bent over toward the stair tread. The motion made him dizzy. He lowered himself to the stairs and put his head between his knees. Then he straightened up and, still sitting, felt along the riser of the stair behind him. It gave slightly. He pushed, hoping it would not creak. It gave more.

He pushed the riser far enough to get his hand in behind it and pulled out a small metal box. Inside was a packet wrapped in cloth. He was surprised; he had not expected anything. He put it in his jacket pocket. From another pocket, he took a pen and a notebook. He scrawled a short note, put it in the box, shoved the box back under the stairs, and closed up the riser.

When he was outside again, he thought about taking the Mercedes back to the garage, but he was too tired. He drove himself home and stumbled into bed, fully clothed.

Sleep helped, and so did a shower and a shave and two mugs of coffee. A styptic pencil stanched the small cuts, and by the time he was dressed, a few minutes before noon, he was surprised at how normal he looked. He got a few strange looks at Teletronics, but nothing more.

It was not until he was at home again that night that he remembered the packet he had taken from Rukovoi's message drop. He opened it carefully. It contained only a short note.

"Current plans involve destabilization of Austrian government."

Moore reread the single sentence several times. Then he made himself a drink and turned out the lights and sat in the dark thinking about the implications of Rukovoi's message.

5

On the stage at the Vienna *Staatsoper*, an unruly crowd
of fifteenth-century Spaniards watched as the King of
Spain was challenged by his son with a drawn sword.
Behind the crowd was the summit of a massive pyre
on which the Inquisition would burn scores of heretics
before the scene was over.

Moore leaned forward with his elbows on the red-
plush railing of the box and watched as Don Carlo and
King Philip argued over the fate of Flanders; he tried
to care about the Grand Inquisitor lurking offstage,
waiting until in the name of a higher Power he could
further poison the King's relationship with his son.

The people in the box's three rear seats were out of
their chairs, standing close behind him, craning their
necks to see the stage. The sensation of people so close,
in the dark, made him sweat with anxiety.

He looked to his right, admired Joan's profile—lean,
like her body, with a straight nose and a smooth brow.
Her features seemed almost austere: Her profile, in
repose, gave no hint of her broad and generous smile.
Wisps of dark hair curled behind her ears. In the
semidarkness he could see a shadow on the nape of
her neck. He still missed the full, sleek tresses that had
hung almost to her shoulders.

She glanced at him, put her hand on his for a moment, then went back to enjoying the opera.

After the performance, Joan held his arm as they strolled along the *Kärtnerstrasse*. The shops that lined the dark pedestrian mall were closed, but there were still several kiosks open selling wurst and bread— Viennese hot dogs—and beer.

"Hungry?" he asked her.

"Not really. You?"

"No. Maybe a snack."

She squeezed his arm, pressed it against her. "Hungry for me?"

"Always."

She kissed his cheek.

In sight of the Gothic spires of St. Stephen's, they turned around and walked back toward the opera house.

"I got a call from the magazine," she said. "Harry wants me to do a story in Budapest. He needs an article and some photographs on an American movie being shot there as a dodge to get money out of Hungary. I told him I wanted to write a story for grown-ups."

Moore laughed. "What did he say?"

"He said I was right, but he didn't have any starry-eyed kids in the neighborhood at the moment. And then we got to talking about the state of the world, and he told me that things had heated up some more in Washington."

"I keep expecting to wake up and find that everybody's come back to their senses."

"Harry wasn't too explicit, but from what he said the people at the top have started calling each other names in public. Accusing each other of subverting the Agency, turning it into a private preserve, ignoring the National Security Council and even the President."

"Christ! What the hell can they have in mind? How can anybody expect to come out of that kind of thing

with a shred of effectiveness? Can you imagine trying
to recruit anybody? I don't mean agents, I mean our
own people. Scientists to analyze satellite pictures.
Anybody. . . . You'd think they'd keep their fool
mouths shut. If they've got to tear each other up, all
right, but it's just plain stupid to do it in public."

"You don't have much use for them, do you?" she
asked. "Collins and Wilson and the others."

"Not these days. Except maybe J.P."

"Briggs? Your rabbi?"

A snort of laughter. "My rabbi, indeed. Sometimes
I wish he hadn't been so good to me."

"What do you mean?"

"All those years I was his bright young man, working as a singleton on special projects instead of slogging
my way up through the ranks—all that time I was
keeping my illusions intact, in spite of what was going
on. You were right—I was an idealist when I joined,
and I'm afraid I haven't learned very much since then.
I still have illusions: I still think there's some good to
be done. Even with all this stupidity."

"Aren't you being a little hard on yourself? And on
the Company?"

"Listen to you—you have as many illusions as I do.
But at least you're entitled to them. Privilege of youth."

She punched his arm lightly. "There are plenty of
people who think I'm old enough."

"Don't remind me."

She pulled away from him. "That's not what I
meant." She stopped, pointed at a suit in a shop
window. "Would you wear that?"

He looked. "On Halloween, maybe." He pulled her
to him and kissed her.

She pressed against him briefly. "That's more like it."

There was an abrupt noise of laughter and footsteps. A pack of young people burst out of a side street. Several of them wore embroidered patches on their army-surplus jackets: large and round, white with bright orange sunbursts haloed by the legend ATOMKRAFT? NEIN, DANKE.

"Atomic power? No, thanks," Joan read. "Is there another flap about nuclear power?"

"Who knows?" Moore said. But his mind held a sharp image of Rukovoi's note. The latest twists in Austrian politics would bear some looking into. "It's all I can do to keep track of our own flaps and squabbles. And like I said, this latest one in Washington has to take the cake for stupid."

A sudden thought made him stop walking. "Unless it's a cover of some kind. For something else."

"Like what?"

"I can't imagine. But it's the only thing I can think of that would explain it."

She thought for a minute, then said, "Maybe I can find out some more about what off-the-record stuff my colleagues in the press are getting and what they think it means."

"I wish you would. I'd be happy for any information I could get at this point, whoever it comes from." He stopped. Unwittingly, he was straying back into unpleasant territory. "Could you get an assignment that would help?"

She thought about it. "I don't know. I don't think Harry would be interested in this kind of thing. It doesn't have the right European implications."

"What about *Stern*, or *Paris Match*?"

"Maybe. If I could find the right hook. But I think

I'm best for now just nosing around a little, like I'm looking for background."

"You know best," he conceded. "What do you say? Shall we go home?"

"Let's. I'm getting cold. I keep thinking it's spring, and it keeps fooling me. My place?"

"My place."

In the cab home he held himself away from her, and when they were in his apartment he led her to the living room instead of the bedroom.

"A little brandy?" he suggested. "It'll take away the chill."

"Well, all right. Sure. Why not?"

They sat and talked about the opera, trying to decide what the students in the standing-room section had against the tenor. It was a light conversation; their minds were elsewhere.

Moore lingered over his brandy, poured himself a second.

"You're stalling," she said.

"I'm enjoying just sitting here, being with you."

"Me too. You're a swell fellow and I'm a super gal, and it's nice that we like each other. But as much fun as this is, right this minute I mostly lust for your bod."

He laughed. "All right. Let's go."

In the bedroom, they undressed each other slowly. Their bodies were touching as they moved to the bed. He kissed the hollow at the base of her neck, ran his tongue along the cleft between her breasts. She shuddered with pleasure. Her hand went to his chest, then downward.

The phone rang.

"Damn!" he said.

"Let it ring."

He kissed her. "I'll be right back."

He bounded out of bed and strode quickly into the living room.

"Hello?"

"Wolfgang?" asked a gruff male voice.

"*Nein.*"

"*Ist das* 29-06-18?" It was Rukovoi.

"*Nein.*"

"*Ich bitte um Verzeihung,*" he apologized.

Moore hung up and walked slowly into the bedroom; the night air was cool on his skin.

"Wrong number?"

"What else?"

After a few minutes she said, "Your mind isn't on what you're doing."

"No . . . I guess it's not."

She sat up and wrapped her arms around her knees. "It was the phone call, wasn't it?"

"Yes," he acknowledged after a moment.

"That was why you wanted to come here instead of my place. And why you were so slow getting to bed. You were expecting it, weren't you?"

He said nothing.

"Well . . . weren't you?"

"Yes."

She sighed. "Oh, Greg . . ." She got up, walked around for a minute, stood with her back to him. "Times like this, I get sorry I quit smoking."

"Joan, I . . ."

She came back to bed. "It's all right." She put her hand on his knee. "I'm just disappointed."

"Me too."

"Do you have to go so soon?"

"Not until dawn."

"Maybe we should have a drink or something."

"I guess so. I'm a little tense and I'll need the sleep."

She leaned against him and he put his arms around her.

"Damn it, Greg, sometimes I wish we were bank tellers or something."

His arms tightened; he pressed himself to her.

"Yeah," he said. "Me too."

Moore stood waiting at the head of the long, broad boulevard that ran through the Prater park. Above him, the huge ferris wheel was only partly visible, its massive arc swathed in dawn mist.

In the distance there was the rumble of a truck; its engine strained as it started up the hill toward the Danube Canal and the center of the city.

He checked his watch. Rukovoi was late. It made him worry. The mist made him worry, too. It occurred to him that he could not know if Rukovoi's call had been an honest response to the message under the stair tread or if it was part of a setup of some kind. Staying in one place, waiting, might not be the healthiest thing to do.

A dark figure materialized in the murky distance. It was the right shape to be Rukovoi, and the uncompromising gait was right. Moore watched his approach.

"I'm sorry to be late," Rukovoi said.

"That's the least of our problems," Moore responded testily. He began to walk.

Rukovoi, taken by surprise, hurried to catch up. "There is something wrong?"

"You're goddamn right, there's something wrong." Moore was keeping his voice down, but anger seethed in his words. "I'm breaking my ass to keep people off your back the way I promised. It's no help to me to have a platoon of Russian agents following me around."

"What are you talking about?"

"Just what I said. I'm being followed. All the time."

"*Borzhemoi!* When did it start?"

"A few days ago."

"I know nothing about it." Rukovoi's voice was harsh.

"Listen to me, Alex. I stopped one of them. We had . . . a disagreement. I persuaded him to talk to me. You know what he said?"

Silence.

"He said he was hired by a Russian."

"He could have been lying."

"Maybe. But I doubt it."

"Perhaps, then, he *was* hired by a Russian. There are a great many Russians in Vienna. Not all of them work for State Security. Not all of them are even Russian."

"It's possible, I suppose."

"Gregory, why would I be involved in such a thing? It is not in my interest to have people following you. I would only increase my own peril."

"Nevelsky?"

"Perhaps. He might hope to catch me in a lie by learning more about your movements."

"It could be very dangerous. For both of us."

"Yes."

They walked through the mist in silence until Moore asked, "You've learned why Nevelsky's here?"

"In part."

"Your note said there were plans to destabilize the government."

"Yes."

"How?"

"Politically only. There will be demonstrations. Issues will be created."

"Outside pressure?"

"I doubt it. As I understand what little I have heard so far, it is important to Nevelsky—and to the Central Committee—for everything to be as quiet as possible. There will be massive financial and planning support for the local Party."

"Will that be enough to make the difference?"

"Someone must think so. It is not my field of expertise."

"There has to be something more. An incident."

Rukovoi did not answer.

"All right," Moore said. "Never mind that for now. What do they hope to gain?"

"I think it is meant to serve as an example of benign government by pro-Soviet Communists. It would be very valuable to have that here. The Party in Italy is losing control of the far left. And there is the transition in Yugoslavia to think about. Austria has borders with both countries. . . ."

"So it could be a staging ground for intervention," Moore put in.

"No. The Central Committee is too careful to do that."

"Like they were in Czechoslovakia?"

"That was more than a decade ago. Things are not the same now."

"Maybe." Moore walked in silence, then stopped. "Alex," he said. "Your people could be playing with something a lot more dangerous than they realize. This isn't Indochina or Africa. Americans feel connected to Europe, and I don't know what would happen if you got caught making a real push here. Moscow may think of Vienna as being up the road from Budapest and east of Prague, but from our side of the ocean it looks different. After all, it's only a hundred miles or so from the Vorarlberg to the French border. For us, Austria is a Western country."

"I doubt this is meant as a provocation."

"Intentions don't matter. Think of the reaction in Bonn and Paris. Washington has enough trouble with NATO as it is. We couldn't afford to sit still if it got out that Moscow was trying to topple Austria. I'm telling you, Alex, this is more than another case of the superpowers jockeying for position."

"I think you are being melodramatic. We have said before: Neither of us makes policy. I am a mathematician and a collector of anecdotes told to me by foreign scientists. And you, too, are a collector of anecdotes. And a subverter of the innocent. We should not go beyond our limitations."

For the next ten days, Moore was too busy to dwell on his conversation with Rukovoi. His time was consumed by Teletronics's preparations for the convention and exposition. Then there was the event itself to deal with.

In those two weeks spring transformed the city. The air was milder, the winds less harsh. In the parks, the trees were decked in fragile pale green leaves or transformed by blossoms into vast pastel puffballs. Music was being played again in the kiosk in front of the Kursalon, and waiters moved among the red chairs and white tables in its outdoor café. Moore noticed none of it.

On the first day of the exposition, there was an

envelope under his apartment door from Jordan Robbins. He put it on a table in the foyer, to be opened when he had time.

The morning after everything had been dismantled and packed away and the last of the suppliers and customers had gone back to where they had come from, Moore read the note.

It was short, but it was not sweet: As promised, a man named Hawthorne was on his way from Langley to begin wrapping things up in Vienna. Robbins was warning Moore to be prepared to make himself available on short notice.

He checked the calendar on his watch; Hawthorne had been due to arrive the night before. Moore saw no point in delaying the confrontation. As soon as he got to the office, he called to cancel a meeting with one of the agents in his regular network, and then he called the American Embassy.

Hawthorne had a temporary office in the embassy, one of the rooms for visiting firemen. When Moore came in, Hawthorne was sitting behind an old mahogany desk, going through a pile of papers. He stood up and came across the dull red carpet, his hand extended in greeting. He was a big man, almost a head taller than Moore, ruddy and full of heartiness; his bright blue eyes were rimmed with smile wrinkles. He made Moore think of a football player selling insurance.

"I'm Roger Hawthorne," he said as they shook hands. "It's a real pleasure to meet you."

Moore muttered something appropriate.

"Sit down," Hawthorne said, his cheerfulness undiminished. He waved an arm toward a pair of couches facing each other across a coffee table. "Make yourself comfortable."

Moore stood where he was. Hawthorne's smile faltered for a moment, but it returned almost full strength.

"Look, there's no point in making this any more unpleasant than it has to be. After all, it's kind of a victory for you, isn't it?"

Moore looked at him without comprehension.

"I mean, I don't know the whole story," Hawthorne said, "but the way I get it, they let you stay here for a good long while after you got your orders to go back. They didn't boot you out for refusing those first orders either. And let me tell you, they weren't so easy as that on everybody."

"Really," Moore said blankly.

"Nosiree. They take this reorganization very seriously back home. The way they see it, if we can't shape up, we're going to have to ship out. And anybody who looks to be making waves is just getting chopped off at the knees. Except Gregory Moore. . . . I wish I knew what you had on them."

Moore let the crack pass.

"So," Hawthorne went on, "they postponed my trip out here almost two weeks, and then they gave me special instructions. One of which is to impress on you the absolute urgency of your making a brief—and I'm supposed to underline that—a *brief* trip back."

Hawthorne paused, waiting for a response from Moore. There was none. To cover the moment, Hawthorne dug in his jacket and pulled out a pack of cigarettes. He held it out to Moore, who shook his head. Hawthorne lit a cigarette for himself and then held the pack out again. "You see these? I didn't believe it. Pack of cigarettes, and it looks just like a pocket off the ass of somebody's jeans. Marlboro ought to get into something like that." He put the cigarettes back in his pocket. "Anyway—a *brief* trip back. So that you can work out an acceptable *modus operandi* with the powers that be."

"I have the feeling I'm being handed a line."

"Oh, no. They were perfectly sincere. In fact, I can't say when I've seen Wilson so eager. He positively vibrated with it. Whatever you've got, they want it bad enough to talk nice to you."

"I'll believe it when I see it."

"You'll go back then?"

"Do I have a choice?"

"Well . . . no. . . . I guess you don't."

In the Russian Embassy, Rukovoi sat on the lumpy couch, alone in the office where he and Nevelsky had last met. Lenin glared down from the wall; Rukovoi, nervous and annoyed at having been peremptorily summoned to the embassy, glared back.

The door opened and Nevelsky came in. With him was a short, slight man, so ordinary in appearance that Rukovoi had to look twice to form an impression of him.

Rukovoi stood up.

"Comrade Rukovoi," Nevelsky said.

"Comrade Nevelsky."

Nevelsky turned to the man with him. "This is Dybenko. From Department V."

Rukovoi could not help staring. Department V was sabotage and assassination. Dybenko did not seem to notice.

"Another addition to our group in Vienna," Nevelsky commented.

"I am sure you will enjoy it here," Rukovoi said.

Dybenko turned and went to sit in one of the wooden chairs near the desk.

Nevelsky walked to the liquor cabinet and opened it. "I am having a vodka. Will you join me?"

Rukovoi hesitated. He did not want it, but there was no point in starting badly. He said, "Yes. Thank you."

Nevelsky poured the drinks and came back with them. He handed Rukovoi a small glass of vodka.

"I am still not satisfied about this American of yours," Nevelsky said.

"I don't understand."

"It's a feeling I have—that he is not to be trusted." He drained his glass. "You know, they are not above using him to give us false information."

There was a sudden emptiness in Rukovoi's chest. He drank his vodka, hoping he wouldn't gag on it. "Why would they pick him? There are better ways for them to do that."

Nevelsky ignored the question. "After all," he said, "we are using him to give *them* false information." He went back to the cabinet at the side of the room to pour himself another drink. "That would be amusing, eh? If you and he were exchanging false information." Over his shoulder, he said, "What do you think, Dybenko? Would that not be droll?"

Dybenko said nothing. He put a hand under his jacket and scratched himself.

Nevelsky came back with his fresh drink. "You know, Alexander Ivanovich, the best thing for us all might be if Dybenko just shot this American. Then we wouldn't have to think about him anymore, would we?"

Rukovoi stared at Nevelsky, terrified and trying not to show it.

Nevelsky laughed and clapped Rukovoi on the back. "You must not take me so seriously, Alexander Ivanovich. We are allies, after all."

Rukovoi forced himself to smile.

6

There was a lump in the cushion of Moore's seat in the crowded jet, and for some reason the window that should have been next to him was not there. Instead, there was a tan panel decorated with tiny gold flowers. On the other side of him, a young woman with a pleasant, open face held an infant on her lap, feeding it from a bottle. A heavyset, silver-haired man sat in the aisle seat paying little attention to his wife and child.

Trapped for eight hours in an uncomfortable prison of plastic and flesh, Moore tried to make sense out of what had been happening to him in the past few weeks.

He kept coming to the same conclusion: He needed more information. He was being carried along on the tide of events, and he could not yet make out the shore. It worried him.

He saw three aspects to his situation. Most immediately there was the question of where Rukovoi really stood. Moore was suspicious of the speed with which the Russian had acceded to his demands. Confident as he was of the strength of the trap he had sprung on Rukovoi, he had expected more resistance. Either Rukovoi had been riper than Moore had realized, or he was up to something.

Then there was the question of what the Russians were up to in Austria. The implications of a strong Russian move there were enormous, especially if the

United States was caught by surprise. But he would have to check further. Confirmation was vital before he reported to Langley, in case Rukovoi was playing games with him or Nevelsky was playing games with both of them.

And on top of everything else, there were the odd goings-on in Washington and Langley. He could make no sense of the attitude at headquarters. Why would they disrupt field operations, especially operations that were in no sense illegal, just for routine debriefing? Maybe Langley was looking for ammunition to use against its Congressional enemies, but this hardly seemed like the way to go about getting it. It felt more like preparation for a general shake-out, as if they had decided to throw some people to the wolves so the rest could escape unscathed.

He called in from the airport. A secretary told him that Wilson would see him the following afternoon.

He felt stale and sour from the plane ride. A cab took him to his hotel. He did some quick hurdlers' stretches and sit-ups, took a shower, and then went out for dinner and a movie. There were people he could have called, but he wanted to wait until he spoke to Wilson.

He went to bed at ten-thirty, early for Washington but late for Vienna, where it was almost dawn.

———

Martin Wilson took a cigar from a silver-faced humidor and snipped off the end. Sitting across the broad office, Moore watched him and waited.

Wilson was a thin man, just under six feet; his most distinctive feature was his grayness. He had gray hair and eyes, and Moore had never seen him wear anything but a gray suit. His patterned tie was gray with accents of blue-gray. His round-lensed glasses had dull silver wire rims. As far as Moore was concerned, even Wilson's manner was gray.

"It's not a business for loners," Wilson said. "You know that. It never has been, in spite of what the old-timers will tell you."

Wilson paused to puff his cigar into life. Moore said nothing.

"I'm not saying you have to file every kind of report in the regulations every time it's called for," Wilson went on. "We're more flexible than that. But there are ways of doing things."

"Sure there are," Moore retorted. "And what do they get us? How many top-level Soviet penetrations have we had lately?"

"I'm not sure that's the point."

Moore felt a surge of anger. He said, "I've been doing things the Company way for fourteen years now. Even when I was operating on my own. Operational Progress Reports, Field Project Outlines, Field Information Reports. Everything by the numbers, asking 'please' and 'may I' before I did anything. It's not like I'm some kind of rebellious kid."

Wilson studied the tip of his cigar. "No, of course not. That's what's so upsetting. We're willing to let you have a lot of leeway, more than we'd give most people. But we have to draw the line somewhere, and we expect you to understand that. We can't have you going out and setting up your own network, or even just running a single agent, unless you establish some kind of reporting procedure. We have to be able to check your man out, and there has to be someone who can step in and take over if for some reason you can't keep up with it."

Moore was tired of squinting at Wilson against the

bright Virginia sunlight flooding through the window behind Wilson's antique oak desk. He stood up and crossed the salt-and-pepper carpet to a library table against one wall; the oak slab was buried under neat rows of reports and memos.

"Look at all this," he said, waving his hand at the stacks of paper. "It's a wonder you don't choke on it." He picked up one of the reports. It was the size of a magazine, but thicker, carefully printed and bound with the pages glued to the spine like an oversized paperback book. "This can't be why we're in business." He flipped through it; pages of gray type flashed past. "Suppose somebody actually learned something, out in the field. How would you know about it? How would you ever separate it from all of this?"

"It's a big world out there, Greg. We generate a lot of intelligence."

"Intelligence? All we generate is a lot of words on paper. Worse than that—we've generated a bureaucracy that's tied our hands all over the world and frightened off most of the people who could do us any real good." He dropped the report on the table. It landed with a thud.

When he spoke again, he had banished the bitterness from his voice. "A while ago, I got to wondering what would be the best way to get a decent penetration in Moscow. There's always been talk about Soviet agents in American intelligence, but as long as I can remember the word has been that we don't have any penetration over there that's worth anything. Penkovsky, they say—he was the lone exception, and even with him it was the British who got him started, not us. So one day I began to think about why that might be. I began paying attention to what I was doing, and to what everybody else was doing, as far as I could find out about it. I mean really paying attention, not just going through the motions." He looked hard at Wilson. "That's not something we're encouraged to do."

Wilson absently picked a piece of tobacco off his tongue.

A new haze of anger clouded Moore's vision. He took a moment to steady himself before he went on. "It was easy to see what the obstacles were. Just getting to anybody in Moscow has got to be a bitch, to begin with. Security is too damn heavy over there—you can't approach a target in person, and there's no way you can trust a local intermediary. Then, once you've made contact, what can you offer? Nothing to compete with the privileges they've already got. Not if you want them to stay there."

"Even if you want them to come over here, it's not so easy," Wilson commented. "They look at some ballet dancer who defected with a big splash and made a fortune, and they decide that if you want their help, you have to make them a millionaire."

"So there's something we agree on."

"That it's not easy to turn a top-level Russian? You get no argument from me on that."

"All right. Good." Moore smiled, without humor. "The more I thought about it, the clearer it seemed. The only way to get somebody really high in the Party—a Central Committee member, say, or even somebody with a shot at the Politburo—is to start with him early, before he's inaccessible. Before he has so many privileges."

"You want a drink?" Wilson asked, on his way across the room.

"No. What I want is for you to listen. If all you're doing is humoring me, we're both wasting our time."

Wilson opened a cabinet, took out a glass and a bottle. "Go ahead. I'm listening. I'm interested." He opened the bottle.

Moore said nothing.

Poised to pour himself a drink, Wilson looked over his shoulder. "Really," he insisted. "Go ahead."

Moore said, "There's a second ingredient: they're even more paranoid than we are. One thing's for sure—no up-and-coming Soviet official, even if we could convince him to work for us, would trust the security or reliability of the normal reporting system. The Russians know all the ways there are to hang people with a chain of command. You're not going to convince them that working within a bureaucracy is anything but a trap. And a sieve. If you're going to run an agent for five years, or ten, or even maybe twenty, even if you run him very loosely, he's got to have a lot of reasons to believe in your ability to keep the relationship quiet."

Grudgingly: "I see what you mean."

Moore motioned at the table full of reports. "This kind of thing is just stupid, in that context. All this paper. And so is all the bullshit about 'tradecraft' we're always handing out. There's only one way to do it, assuming we're not going to plant someone of our own over there, which you know as well as I do we're not going to get away with."

"No. Probably not." Wilson replaced the bottle and closed the cabinet.

"All right. So we have to recruit someone, and the only way that's going to happen that has any long-range possibilities is by establishing a relationship based on something like trust."

Moore paused to give Wilson room for a response, but he said nothing.

Moore went on: "If someone could find the right Russian at the right time, and if he could convince the Russian to trust him—on a one-to-one, personal level—then we might have a shot at it. *Maybe.* You'd need some leverage, too. Something to hold over his head at the beginning, to get it off the ground. But once you get going, you have to turn it into something that seems mutual. The two of you have to be allies, sharing this dark secret that you have. It's like a special kind of friendship. Or maybe it's more like an S-and-M love affair."

"S-and-M?"

"Sadism and masochism. Where one lover beats up on the other."

"I see." Wilson sipped at his drink. It was dark amber; straight bourbon, Moore guessed.

"That's all well and good, Greg," Wilson granted. "But I don't see why it means you have to hold out on us."

"Damn it!" Moore's fists clenched. To get a rein on his frustration he turned and put his hands on the library table. His elbows were locked and the muscles of his upper back were taut. "I'm not holding out on you. I'm offering you the most important intelligence asset you've ever had."

"No, you're not," Wilson said mildly. "You're not offering us anything. All you're saying is that you'll give us some information from time to time." He shook his head. "You're not even telling us who your man is, and without knowing that, how can we check on what he gives us?" He rolled the tip of his cigar carefully in a crystal ashtray, breaking off a solid cylinder of gray ash.

"How do we know what this Russian of yours is really up to? He could end up feeding us all kinds of nonsense. And what kind of asset is he if we can't generate any questions for him to answer? . . . It's no good, Greg. You have to come aboard with this. You don't have to tell *him* about it. You can tell him anything you want. But you can't go it alone."

"Not a chance," Moore said. "It can't be done that way. Once you come into it, you're bound to start meddling here and there. You just said so yourself. You want to generate questions for him to answer." Moore was tired. "What you're saying has nothing to do with what I've been talking about. A guy like this isn't somebody you can ask questions like he was a junior researcher."

"What are you going to do, then? Wait for him to come to you? To volunteer information?" For the first time, there was an edge to Wilson's voice.

"I think you have to, up to a point."

"And what impels him to do that? You don't expect to convert him ideologically, too, do you?"

"Yes. In a way."

"By blackmailing him?"

"No, by *not* blackmailing him. That's what I'm trying to say." Moore went back to the couch and sat down. The faint hope he had harbored of making Wilson see the situation differently was ebbing.

"You can't keep on using the original blackmail," Moore went on wearily. "You have to get him so tied into working for you that he can't pull out without ruining himself. And you've got to give him room to fit what he's doing for you into his own value system. So he's doing something for his own country, too. Or world peace. Something that lets him live with himself."

Wilson nodded. "If you can. It sounds like a tall order to me." He took the ashtray from his desk and walked over to sit facing Moore. "But then, why not let us come up with some questions for him to answer? Within that context."

"Because it won't work. Even if there's no leak on this end, he's sure to sense what's happening. And there goes your trust."

"Not necessarily. Not if we're careful. I think we can have it both ways."

Moore's anger was back. Without willing it, he was on his feet again, glaring at Wilson. "That's really how you see the world, isn't it? You want to have everything both ways. Lie and cheat and double-cross and come out of it all with clean hands. . . . Well, I can't operate that way."

Wilson stood up. He was two inches taller than Moore, but it seemed like more. His gray eyes locked on Moore's. "There's no point in name-calling. It's not going to help."

"I'm not sure anything's going to help," Moore said. He turned away. "I'm going to stop trying, in fact." Turned back. "It's very simple. Take it on my terms or I'm going to let him go."

"You'll drop the whole thing?"

"That's right."

"What's the point? You claim that if you do this my way, you're likely to lose your man. Isn't it better to take that risk than just to drop him before he's given us anything at all?"

"No."

"No? What do you mean, 'no'?"

"I'm turning the man's life inside out. If I keep him working for me, on some level he's going to hate him-

self and resent his family and mistrust everyone in his
life. And no matter how he rationalizes it all in the end,
those feelings will never really go away."

Wilson shrugged. "It's that kind of business. Do you
suppose it's any different for the others you've turned
in the course of your career?"

"No. No different."

"I can't believe you're getting squeamish. Or senti-
mental. Not Gregory Moore."

"No, I'm as hard-nosed as ever. I do what it takes to
get the job done. But I have to believe there's some
benefit in it. The point is, this particular guy could
turn into a source high enough in the Kremlin to really
matter. That buys a lot of personal grief, for him and
for whoever else I have to pervert or ruin along the way.
But this is a good man, and I stop short of destroying
him just so some chair-warmers back here can ask him
a lot of pointless questions they could just as easily ask
half a dozen other people."

Wilson took his cigar from the ashtray and puffed on
it. It was dead. He went back to sit at his desk and
used a large brass lighter to get the cigar going again.
He looked up, his eyes shining with earnestness. Moore
was surprised to see him counterfeit something so close
to real emotion.

"I didn't want to bring this up," he said. "I thought
I could make you see it from a professional point of
view, and there was no point in getting involved in
everything else that's going on."

"Like what?"

"There are some people in Congress right now who
are trying to shut us down. All the way. There's a
proposal floating around the cloakrooms in the House
and the Senate that calls for the whole Agency to be

eliminated, and it's being taken quite seriously. If it comes to a final battle, we're going to need all the ammunition we can get. This Soviet penetration of yours could be a big gun for us."

Moore shook his head. "That's pretty farfetched."

"I wish it was, Greg. I wish it was."

"Just like that, they think they're going to close us down?"

"That's right. They'll keep some of the overt analytic functions—satellite photography and things like that—but they'll spread the work around town, give it to other people to do."

"Jesus."

"Yes. Exactly. And think of what it means to you. If they do shut us down completely, that's the end of all our assets. Everything. You'll lose your man for sure, and it will be just the kind of waste you say you want to avoid. But if you'll be sensible about it, you may have a chance to keep him, and even if you don't, at least you'll have done some good helping us stay in business. That ought to be enough reason by itself to risk one Russian's peace of mind."

"Sure. Assuming I buy that premise, which I don't."

"Meaning?" Wilson was watching him closely.

"There's no way they could close the Company down completely."

"Why do you say that?"

"Because it's true." Moore felt suddenly calm. Wilson was pushing too hard. Whatever was on his mind, bending Moore to his will was only a part of it. "The most they can do is change the names and shuffle the titles. Fire some people, for show. But the Company will survive, by this name or some other. It has to. It has too much power for it not to survive."

There was a long silence.

Abruptly, Wilson stood up. "Look, Greg, we've got to set up some kind of regular structure on this Russian of yours. What if you get hit by lightning?"

"I've made provisions for that. Somebody will take over for me."

"It's not enough. You simply cannot continue to run him yourself."

"I can. And I will."

Wilson's jaw clenched for a moment. "You're being rash and willful, Greg. I understand it, but that doesn't make it right. Give it some more thought before you make up your mind."

Natalia and Rukovoi followed the *maître d'hôtel* through the Hotel Sacher's dining room. He stopped at a table next to the polished wood wall.

Rukovoi watched while the *maître d'* held the chair for Natalia. She took her seat with the perfect ease of someone for whom men had always held chairs and opened doors.

Rukovoi thought she looked particularly beautiful. Her red hair gleamed in the light from the brass sconces on the wall; her eyes shone with pleasure. The chiffon evening dress she wore was a medley of blues and greens; it deepened the color of her eyes and made her skin look even fairer than usual.

As he sat down, Rukovoi glanced around the room. A few tables were occupied: an elegant family of three, speaking French; a table of men—German, he thought, or Scandinavian—all in their forties, healthy and vigorous looking, in impeccably tailored clothes. Briefly he looked down at himself. Even in his best suit, he looked drab and stodgy. Russian.

The *maître d'* hovered nearby. Rukovoi ordered champagne. When it came, he lifted his glass.

"Happy Birthday."

She smiled. "Thank you. And many more, I hope, all of them with you."

They drank. She said, "You look so . . . gloomy."

"Not tonight. Tonight I cannot be gloomy. We are celebrating."

She smiled again, briefly, with affection and understanding. "Yes, my dear Alexander. Even tonight, I am afraid, you can be gloomy."

He sighed. "I thought I would feel better when Nevelsky left."

"Do you think you convinced him?"

"For now. He did not want to believe I had beaten him another time, but he accepted it, in the end."

"Then why are you worried?"

"He will change his mind. The suspicions will always be there. When I begin sending information, he will learn what he can about it and carefully scrutinize what he learns. And his suspicions will come to the surface again as soon as he receives a report which for some reason he thinks is odd. It could be anything. And I will not know about it until it is too late."

She stared into her champagne glass. "If only the American had left you alone. . . ."

"He was doing his job." Rukovoi pulled the bottle from the ice bucket and wrapped the towel around it. Water dripped from its base onto the tablecloth as he poured them more champagne.

Natalia did not look up. "All those filthy lies? Is that his job?"

He put the bottle back in the ice bucket and touched her hand. She lifted her head.

"It's true that he could have been more subtle in what he did," Rukovoi acknowledged.

Now she was indignant. "He turned a simple matter of personal shame—not even that, perhaps—into an appearance that you and Volodya might be traitors. And you say 'He could have been more subtle'? Alexander!"

He sipped champagne. "If I must admit it, Gregory Moore is interesting to me," he said. "Since we are to be so closely tied to each other, I must understand him."

"And do you?"

"No. Not well. It has been too short a time that we are acquainted. There are some things about him which seem clear, however. The way he began with me, for instance. The very thing which disturbs you. It is because he wishes to think of himself as ruthless."

"He has convinced me."

Rukovoi was amused. "And me. He acts the part so well that the effects are the same as if it were real. But there is something else behind what he does. Something more. I suspect it is that Mr. Gregory Moore is a romantic. He still believes that the world is made better by dedication to a cause, and by hard work."

He watched a thin line of bubbles rise through the pale gold wine. He lifted his glass. "But we do not have to think of him now. Until he returns, he will not bother us."

7

Moore got off the bus with a small crowd of people headed for the buildings at the top of Capitol Hill. Several of them walked the same route as Moore— along the sunny streets and up the broad white steps of the Library of Congress. Among them was an athletic young black man in a white shirt and jeans.

At the entrance to the dome-ceilinged reading room, Moore paused to get his bearings. He skirted the circulation desk, round like the room itself and its concentric rings of reading tables; he walked down the center aisle toward the hallway to the catalog room. There were two small librarians' offices off the hallway. One of the librarians was free to help him.

While Moore was getting instructions on how to use the microfilm readers, the young black man who had followed him from the bus took a seat and tried to look busy.

It took time for Moore to reaccustom himself to the odd sensation of reading a newspaper he could not touch. At first his hands were clumsy on the controls, but gradually the old skills returned and he was operating the machine almost without thought, sunk deep into the limbo world he always entered when he was doing this kind of research.

Watching the endless stream of glowing print roll by, Moore had the sensation that words on paper were no longer just symbols of his work: they had instead become the very substance of it.

He read article after article. Much of it was repetitious, but there was at least one new nugget of information in each piece. The headlines made a familiar progression: NEW CIA ABUSES REVEALED; CIA DIRECTOR CALLS CHARGES EXAGGERATED; SENATOR DEMANDS INQUIRY.

The Director had gone up to Congress for a show-and-tell session. Moore was amused to see that they had brought out the old electric dart gun again, and it had successfully weathered its third use in ten years as a CIA secret reluctantly revealed, complete with breast-beating and self-justification and more than a little sly pride. It was the only thing he read that amused him. The operations described in this round of revelations were even gamier than the things which had come out in the earlier fits of disclosure the Agency had endured. And this time there was nothing that was merely laughable, like the depilatories and itching powder so prominent in the Cuban horrors revealed half a decade earlier.

The Congressional uproar was especially loud this time because the abuses had continued in spite of repeated assurances of reform. Editorial after editorial struck the same note: With all that's happened, with all the talk of legality and accountability, how can they still be doing these things? Having agreed to avoid covert action except in cases of dire national emergency, how can the CIA still be out meddling in the internal politics of countries all over the world, as if it were accountable to no one?

Twenty minutes into his fourth hour of reading, he stopped. He felt as if he had fallen down Alice's rabbit hole. His former picture of reality had finally and ir-

revocably been stood on its head. Whatever illusions
he had once harbored, he could no longer maintain
them.

It was as if there were two mentalities that simul-
taneously pervaded the Agency: one for which there
was no reality but words on paper and which measured
its success by the volume of material it produced, and
a second whose attitudes ranged from a childish pleasure
in make-believe and subterfuge to outright bloodthirsti-
ness and whose primary goal seemed to be gaining and
keeping control of political events wherever it could.
And this bureaucratic homicidal schizophrenic was
blundering through the world, ignoring what should
have been its primary objective: the gathering, analysis,
and dissemination of strategically and tactically valuable information, in a form that would allow it to be
used to best advantage.

He left the library and was dazzled by the brightness
of the afternoon. He stood for a moment staring
blankly through the trees at the Capitol Building,
deciding what to do next. And thought of Bill Grogan,
All-America soccer player, Rhodes Scholar, Marine
Corps officer, and now congressman. The last time
they had seen each other—lunch at Sans Souci almost
two years before—Grogan had talked about trying to
get a seat on the Intelligence Oversight Committee of
the House. Whether he had made it or not, he seemed
like a good person to see.

Once Moore talked his way past the first two levels
of secretaries and assistants, he reached an aide who
remembered his name, and things became easier.
Grogan had made the Intelligence Oversight Committee, and he would be delighted to talk to Moore, if
he could come by at about five.

Moore walked the Capitol Hill streets of northwest Washington, trying to put out of his mind the CIA exposés, and Wilson, and Rukovoi, and the interlocking problems they presented. He found a luncheonette where he could get a cup of coffee and a magazine. He bought *Road & Track* and read about rotary engines and independent suspensions and Grand Prix racing. With his second cup of coffee, he ordered a homemade tea biscuit; it turned out to be dry and heavy and bitterly astringent. He left most of it on the plate, dropped a dollar bill and some coins next to his coffee cup, and went outside. He was not aware of the young black man in the booth behind him who folded his newspaper and followed him into the street.

Grogan came to the door of his office, smiling, his hand extended. He was a few inches taller than Moore and at least twice the CIA man's bulk. An injury on a Marine Corps soccerfield had sidelined him permanently, and he had consoled himself with beer, steak, and potatoes. But he was still full of energy. Politics was the right game for him—he was the best smiler and handshaker Moore knew.

Later, sitting on a bench on the Mall, breathing the rush-hour fumes, Grogan was more subdued.

"I think the committee's going to vote to dismantle the Agency." The quiet comment carried mingled tones of resignation and disbelief.

"But they'll have to keep the Company people around anyway, won't they?" Moore protested. "Who else could do the work?"

"That's what I keep asking, but I'm kind of a lone voice, even on the staff. As far as the committee members are concerned, they're very leery of bringing back the old evils under a new name. Or so they say. In the end, of course, an awful lot of people will have to be rehired. But they're going to be spread out all over the map."

"What do you mean?"

"The bill we're drafting is going to replace the Agency with maybe seven or eight separate intelligence-gathering outfits."

"That's ridiculous. How are they going to coordinate it all?"

"There'll be one outfit just for that. With no power except to ask the others for more information."

"No clandestine service?" Moore asked.

A diesel truck passed on Constitution Avenue, belching black fumes which a fitful wind carried to where they were sitting. Moore stopped breathing for a moment. It seemed to him he could feel the soot settling on his skin.

Grogan coughed and stood up. "That's what they say. No clandestine service and no covert action at all." He paused. "Look," he said, with some of his former heartiness. "Here's what you do. Come to the French Embassy with me tonight. There's a reception for the outgoing ambassador. Half the committee will be there. Maybe you can learn more from them."

Moore walked the length of the Mall, past the Washington Monument, and turned off at the Lincoln Memorial's reflecting pool. There were throngs of tourists everywhere. In a month it would be impossible not only to drive but to walk in this part of Washington.

It was hot in the sun, and he felt sticky and grimy, but he kept walking, pondering what he had learned that day. It all seemed peculiarly interlocking to him, as if the revelations had been tailored to produce the dismantling of the Agency. But that impression might be a function of his perspective—coming in after the fact and seeing it all as a whole instead of as a process that had taken months to develop.

When he got back to his hotel room he stripped and did a set of twists and stretches to work out the kinks that remained from his hours in the library. Then he took a long shower. By the time he was dry, it was late enough for him to leave for the French Embassy.

The reception was being held in the embassy's largest room, but by the time Moore arrived it was crowded with chic Washingtonians, drinking, talking, and letting themselves be admired.

He circulated. It was something he had not done recently and had not enjoyed when it had been part of his job—keeping up with the chatter, trying to use everyone's constant maneuvering in a way that could give him an advantage over whomever he was targeted on that week or that month.

This time it was easier than he had expected. In spite of the official purpose of the party, the most common topic was the CIA scandal; the question that pervaded the room was not whether the Agency would be dismantled but when and into how many pieces. And Grogan had been right: A significant fraction of the Intelligence Oversight Committee was crammed into the long, thin room, along with embassy people, a contingent from the State Department, and assorted members of the White House inner circle.

He commented to Grogan on how many people were there from the oversight committee.

"Sure thing," the congressman said, grinning. "We've become real social lions lately. Every party has to have at least one of us on the guest list."

"But—seven?"

"They must have overinvited to be sure they got somebody. But they have a reputation for throwing good parties—this year, anyway. So almost everybody who got an invitation came."

Moore laughed.

"The old ambassador is kind of an intelligence freak, too," Grogan added.

Moore nodded. They all knew people who collected intelligence agents and officials the way others cultivated movie stars or artists.

Grogan jiggled the ice cubes in his glass. "Need some more anesthesia, myself. Come on over to the bar."

"I thought I'd mix a little more."

"Yeah. Sure." Grogan turned away, then back. "Hey. There's somebody over there you ought to meet."

She was the kind of woman who would once have been called statuesque. She was wearing a bright red dress that discreetly emphasized the lines of her body; her stance and the set of her head spoke of pride and self-confidence. She dominated the group of people around her.

"Carolyn!" Grogan shouted, interrupting a small man in a dinner jacket who was holding forth with great energy, waving his hands for emphasis.

She turned and Moore got a better look at her. Strong features; dark hair framing a slightly tanned face. She looked as though she might be in her early forties, but allowing for the distance and the subdued light, Moore thought she could be as much as ten years older than that.

Grogan bulled through the field of people that

separated them. "Carolyn, there's somebody here I want you to meet. Just your type."

She smiled and excused herself from the group that surrounded her.

"Congressman Grogan, you're absolutely impossible," she said. "You must be the rudest man in all of Washington."

"Maybe so, my little flower, but I get things done. And I don't have your charm and beauty to fall back on. As it were."

She laughed, glanced at Moore. "William, are you going to introduce me to your friend or are you just going to stand there and insult me?"

"No, no. I can insult you any day of the week. . . . This is Gregory Moore. A very very old, very very dear, as they say. Veritable prince of a fellow. And in this corner, wearing the red dress, Carolyn Carlson. The Right Honorable Congresswoman Carlson, Representative of the Fourth District of the Commonwealth of Pennsylvania." In a stage whisper: "A Democrat." He looked from one to the other. "And now, if you two wonderful people don't mind too much, I'm going to get myself another drink." He pushed his way in the direction of the bar.

"He's something, isn't he?"

Moore smiled. "Quite a guy."

"How do you know him?" she asked.

"Goes back a while. We were in the Marines together."

"Vietnam?"

He nodded.

"That's not so long ago."

"Longer than you think. Sixty-five."

"You're right. I forget how fast time passes."

"It's easy enough to do." Moore was struck by how intensely aware of her he was. Her presence seemed to fill up the space around her.

"What do you do now?" she asked.

"I'm in marketing."

"Oh?" She seemed suddenly less interested.

"In Europe. It's a pretty big outfit, actually. I work out of Vienna."

"Really?" Her interest was back. "That must be intriguing."

"I enjoy it." He checked her glass. "Would you like another drink?"

"Yes, I would. Thank you. Vodka tonic."

He took the glass. "Coming right up. Don't go away."

"I won't. I want to hear more about Vienna."

When he came back with the drinks, she was again the center of a small crowd. She extricated herself gracefully and came to join him.

"Thanks," she said. She took a long drink. For the first time, Moore was aware that he was looking up at her.

They talked about Vienna for a while, and then about other European cities. More than once, Moore referred to the special position he was in as an American businessman abroad—the advantages and the problems.

"There are a lot of things they just don't understand about us," he said. "Like what's happening with the CIA these days. I was telling Bill about it. They think we're crazy, exposing everything the way we do."

The smile left her face. "Their traditions are different from ours."

Moore was glad to have an opening that would let

them pursue the subject without his asking pointed questions. He picked up on the notion of political traditions, using intelligence as a running example. She joined in with real gusto; as Moore had hoped, her side of the conversation was sprinkled with references to the current controversy over dismantling the CIA.

When he thought the groundwork had been laid, he asked her a direct question about the real motivation behind the move to break up the Agency.

The silence that followed was brief but unmistakable. The legislator's eyes took on a distance, her smile lost its spontaneity. She said, "It's unusual for a business-man to be so knowledgeable about these things."

"Sure." Moore replied with carefully measured sar-casm. "All we ever think about is the widgets we make or sell."

"Forgive me," she said icily. "It's just that finding someone at a Washington reception who asks intelligent questions is a bit of a surprise."

Moore's thin lips stretched into a smile. "You really are a politician. You compliment me on my questions, but you don't answer them."

He thought she was going to be angry, but then she, too, smiled. *"Touché."* The distance in her eyes was replaced by a penetrating scrutiny. "Tell me, Mr. Moore—you wouldn't happen to be a CIA man your-self, would you?"

"Coming from you, that's hardly a compliment."

"No, I suppose not. But the question stands."

He shook his head. "I'm just an executive in a widget company, Ms. Carlson. Sorry to disappoint you." It was a lie he had told a thousand times, yet now he was not sure that he was being convincing.

She kept her eyes on his for a moment longer, then

glanced over his shoulder. "I'm sorry. Some people just came in I'd rather not fight with tonight. I'm afraid I'll have to answer your questions another time."

"Why not tonight? I don't get to have conversations like this too often, and I'm on my way back to Vienna. We could both get out of here and go have a nice dinner somewhere we can talk."

"Well . . ."

"Come on. There's got to be someplace you'd like to go."

"As a matter of fact, there is a place I'd enjoy. But you'll have to call me Carolyn if we go. I get Ms. Carlsoned to death all day long on the Hill."

Once again, he felt the warmth and force of her personality.

"I came on foot," he said. "You?"

"We just have to walk to the door and my car will appear. A little bit of diplomatic conjuring."

She took his arm and they made their way through the crowd.

The night was clear, with a touch of spring coolness; it would be another few weeks before the onset of the oppressive humidity that would ruin the summer. An attendant drove up to the embassy entrance in a silver Cadillac.

"It's too lovely to stay in town," she said as she drove out into the light traffic. "If you don't mind the trip, I know an interesting place out in the sticks. The staff lacks polish, to be charitable about it, but the chef is definitely a magician."

"Sounds fine."

Almost an hour after they had left the embassy, she pulled off a two-lane Maryland road into the parking lot of what looked to Moore like an old inn. It was a large, three-story shingle house set back from the road among towering evergreens. The glow from the ground-floor windows spilled onto a path that ran around the building, but the broad parking lot was dark. And crowded. Carolyn had to drive to the end of the lot, near the road that led to the exit, before she found a space.

Moore went around the car to open the door for her. They walked along the parking lot roadway toward the restaurant.

A dark sedan took the turn from the highway into the lot; its tires squealed on the pavement.

Moore and Carolyn were caught in the beam of its headlights. They stopped, transfixed by the sudden glare, as the car sped toward them.

There was the shriek of rubber on asphalt and the sedan slammed to a halt. Its lights went out.

Still dazzled by the headlight glare, Moore launched himself to the side, collided with Carolyn, and bore her to the ground, then in the same motion rolled over toward the car.

The night was filled with noise: rapid gunshots, bullets ricocheting from the road, shattering glass.

Moore came to his feet at the sedan's rear bumper. He could make out a man standing in the shelter of the car, his arms extended rigidly, braced against the car roof. Both hands were clamped around the butt of a large revolver, aimed at the spot where Moore and Carolyn had been standing.

Moore kept moving, rounding the rear of the car. The man turned. Moore had a fleeting impression of darkness against the dark night. Black clothes, black skin. The gun was the blackest of all, with a faint highlight along the barrel.

He lunged. Flame spurted from the gun's muzzle.

The shot was rushed, and the bullet went off into the night.

The report of the gun going off almost in his ear turned Moore's skull into a vast, reverberating echo chamber, but his momentum carried him forward. He plowed into the gunman and grappled for his arm. The gun went off again, compounding the disorienting cacophony in his head. His hands closed on the gunman's wrist.

Moore found his footing and bent sharply, turning, holding tightly to the unseen wrist, bringing it down forcefully across his chest. The gunman went over Moore's shoulder and slammed down, back first, on the trunk of the car. The gun made a metallic thump as it hit the pavement.

Panting, his head ringing, Moore blinked his vision clear. The gunman slid off the car and got to his feet. Lurched to the side, away from the car.

Moore watched him. His hand disappeared under his jacket, darted out again with a sharp click. Something glinted in the darkness. A knife.

Moore backed off. His attacker advanced in a rapid, shuffling crouch. The knife was extended in his hand, its cutting edge up, its point driving for Moore's midsection.

Moore stepped back and to the side. He felt oddly lightheaded. His hands followed a pattern that had been drummed into him long ago, so thoroughly that even now they moved without conscious direction—the left swept down across his chest to deflect the knife, continuing its circle to lift the attacking arm high and wide of its target. Moore's right hand pumped in and out twice. The first blow was delivered with the finger-tips, a spear-hand jab under the breastbone. Then, with his wrist bent back sharply, the heel of his hand smashed into the base of the black man's nose: a short, rising, killing blow.

The man went over backward. He twitched once after he hit the blacktop, then lay still.

Moore stood over the body. Perception of what had happened came to him slowly. He began to shake.

He wrapped his arms around his chest, grit his teeth, and squeezed his eyes shut. He could not allow himself to react.

He looked around for the gun, saw it, scooped it up.

Carolyn Carlson was not far away, leaning against a car. He went over to her and saw that she was holding her elbow. Her face was pale, stark against the black frame of her hair.

"You all right?"

"I think so," she said. Her voice wavered, then grew stronger. "Just frightened. And I have some bruises. What was it all about?"

"It was a murder attempt."

She stared at him, then looked nervously in the direction of the black man's prostrate form. "Shouldn't you be watching him? So that he doesn't escape."

"He's dead."

Again, she stared at him.

"You say that so matter-of-factly. Are you sure?"

"Yes."

She moved away from him.

He took her arm firmly. "We'd better go and make some phone calls."

She resisted, looking toward the restaurant.

"What?" He turned and saw a uniformed figure hurrying toward them.

Moore let go of Carolyn and put himself between her and the approaching doorman.

"Go back and get the manager," Moore told him. "And make sure nobody else comes out here before the police arrive."

"Wait a minute, buddy. . . ."

"Go get the manager. Right now."

The man hesitated, then turned and went back to the restaurant. At the door, he paused to look over his shoulder at Moore, then he hurried inside.

Moore turned to Carolyn. "I don't want you any more involved in this than you have to be."

"*You* don't want me involved! And what gives you the right . . ." She stopped. "I suppose you're right. I shouldn't let myself get pushed into the spotlight without thinking about it first. But . . . you're awfully good at this for a widget salesman or whatever it is you said you do." She shuddered, as if from a cold breeze, although the night air was still. "You're not, are you?"

"What?"

"A widget salesman."

He was saved from having to answer her by a commotion in the restaurant doorway. A group of men strode toward them like a small posse. Three of them wore waiter's uniforms; they were led by a portly man in a black dinner jacket. His scalp reflected the light of the restaurant's windows.

"What happened out here?" he demanded. His face had an unhealthy pallor, even in the dark.

"Keep your voice down," Moore said quietly.

"What? Who are you?"

"I'm only trying to make things easier for you," Moore said. "To save bad publicity."

"What?" The stout man craned his neck, trying to make out the figure standing in the darkness behind Moore.

"There's a dead man in your parking lot."

"Now, look you, whoever you are . . ."

"The police should be here soon."

"What police? Nobody called any police. My doorman comes running in with some story about a crazy man out here giving orders how we should keep people locked in the restaurant. For that, I don't need any cops."

"There's a dead man over there on the blacktop who just tried to kill a member of Congress." The words were out of Moore's mouth before he realized what he was saying. He wondered what instinct had made him turn the incident into an attack on Carolyn.

The manager's reaction was immediate: "Congress! What member of Congress? What are you talking about?"

"I told you—keep your voice down. And tell one of your clowns to go inside and call the FBI."

"Now you want the FBI?"

"Tell them they'll need the public relations squad. And call Washington headquarters, not the local office."

"Jesus Christ on a crutch!"

"Do it!"

Trailed by his three waiters, the manager went back to the restaurant, moving with surprising speed.

8

Moore was slumped on the couch at the end of Wilson's office; he was still wearing his dinner jacket, but his bowtie was open: a pair of black, dangling butterflies on either side of his unbuttoned shirt collar. Wilson was at his desk.

"The story we're giving out is that it was an attempt on her life," he said.

"It's funny," Moore commented. "I talked about it that way myself. I don't even know why. I certainly didn't expect it to stick."

"There's no reason why it shouldn't. The man you had the foresight to kill was a drifter with a long police record. We've placed him in the congresswoman's district last autumn. He's been associated with a wide variety of radical fringe groups all over the country." Wilson transferred his attention to the tip of a cigar, which he trimmed off neatly. "It seems our Mrs. Carlson beat a left-wing black lawyer in her primary. It all fits beautifully."

"Sure it does, if you don't know the truth. I'm surprised she'll sit still for it, the way you've put it together. She's not exactly one of our biggest fans."

"No, she isn't, is she? But it seems she's not going to give us any difficulty on this score. She did say that your having saved her life would not make her go easy on us, but even there I think we'll come out ahead."

Moore sat up. "You mean she actually believes it? That he was trying for her?"

"Of course. She sees herself as an important person. She has no difficulty believing she might be the target of an assassin. And why should anyone—especially a domestic radical—want to shoot at you here in Washington? As far as Ms. Carlson knows, you're nothing more than a minor spook." Wilson's mouth approximated a smile. "It isn't a bad description, in fact."

"So we lucked out," Moore said.

"You could put it that way. I prefer to think that we handled it well given the circumstances."

"You know," Moore reflected, "once or twice in the past couple of days I've had the feeling I was being followed, but I didn't do much about it. I was pretty sure they wouldn't bother me here. . . . I wonder why they did."

"Maybe they just decided to do it on the spur of the moment, and they were in a hurry. Washington's as good a place as any to kill you." Wilson lit his cigar, taking his time about it. "I wonder who was behind that poor bastard they hired. Five'll get you ten it was your super-asset from Vienna."

Moore let it go by.

"After this," Wilson said, "I'd think you'd be happy to tell us all about your Russian. It might give us a chance to keep him from killing you."

Moore rubbed his face and stood up. He was too tired to let Wilson draw him into an argument about Rukovoi.

Wilson watched him a moment speculatively, then said, "You'd better get back to Vienna and wrap it all up." There was a brusque finality in his voice. "We can't keep playing these games forever."

Moore walked to the door. "It's been a hard night," he said on his way out. "I think I'll get some sleep."

Carolyn Carlson was waiting for him when he came out of Wilson's office. She saw him walking down the dim hallway and stood up from a chair in the reception area as he stopped at the guard's desk to sign out.

They walked down the hall to the elevators.

"I thought I'd wait in case you needed a lift," she said. "They told me you wouldn't be long."

"Thanks."

"Thank *you*. You saved my life."

He shrugged off her gratitude and touched the silver DOWN arrow. Its clear-plastic frame glowed orange.

She said, "It's a little frightening, you know, how casually you take it."

"It's not the kind of thing I like to talk about."

A bell rang, and the elevator doors slid open. They were on their way down to the lobby when she spoke again.

"I wanted you to know that I was grateful. People don't save my life every day. But you should understand that it doesn't mean I'll change my mind about closing the place down." She glanced at him, then watched the numbers change over the stainless steel door. "In a way, I think tonight has made my feelings on that subject even stronger. We have to stop encouraging violence as a way to solve political problems."

"I couldn't agree with you more." He heard the anger in his voice, but he was past caring whether he antagonized her. His hand ached where he had delivered the final blow. He was bewildered by what had happened and too weary to sort out the elements of his confusion.

The elevator door slid open and they walked out into the garage, stopping to identify themselves to the guard on duty. Neither of them spoke until she let him off at his hotel and he thanked her for the ride.

He could not sleep. He tried without success to close his mind to the doubt and anxiety called up by the murder attempt. He called room service and asked for two double brandies. He drank the first one quickly; it had no noticeable effect. He poured the second one down the bathroom sink.

He lay in bed awake. Fitfully, he dozed.

At four in the morning, he sat down at the room's small plastic-topped desk and tried to get something down on paper that would help him understand what had happened and what it might mean. He could not keep his mind focused well enough for the exercise to be of any value.

At six, he finally fell asleep. It was ten-thirty when he woke up, groggy and disoriented, certain only that he had to go back to Vienna as soon as possible.

Room service brought a pot of coffee. He had the first cup as he shaved, wiping the rim of the cup with a towel between sips to keep from drinking shaving cream. Dressing, he realized there was one more person he had to see before he left Washington: J.P. Briggs, the man who had been his first mentor and sponsor at the Agency.

He made the call and was told that Mr. Briggs had no appointments available for the next two days. Moore's insistence that he was only in Washington for a limited time was politely ignored.

He finished his coffee. It left him with a sour, bloated feeling in his stomach, but it did not clear his head. He was about to go out for a walk, when the phone rang.

It was Briggs's secretary. Moore was to be at the corner of 17th and N, Southwest, at 4:33. A limousine would pick him up.

The long, black car was empty. The white-haired chauffeur drove slowly, with the radio playing. He complained about the traffic all the way to Arlington.

At the cemetery gate, he held the door for Moore and handed him a sealed envelope, then said a brusque "good day, sir," got back into the limousine, and drove off.

Moore opened the envelope. It held a piece of stiff bond paper with a single, short code number typed on it—a gravesite designation.

Briggs was waiting for him at the grave. The day was overcast, with layers of dark clouds boiling across the gray sky. They walked a long path among the enlisted men's graves.

Moore said, "I can't understand why the Company hasn't closed ranks against all this—the papers, the Congress, the whole mess."

"We were caught with our pants down," Briggs told him. "At first, everybody thought it would blow over. It's happened before, after all."

"But this time it's not blowing over."

"It looked for a while like it was going to. Then it flared up again. . . . Now it's too late to do anything. It's every man for himself." He walked in silence for a moment. "No, it's worse than that. Everybody's trying to blame the next guy, even if it means burying the Company along with the competition."

"How do you think it's going to come out?"

"The smart money's on Russell Collins. He's always

been a survivor. And he's still got Wilson doing his dirty work."

Moore looked at him. Briggs's face, which Moore remembered as being strong and hawklike, was much tireder now. There were deep creases in his cheeks and heavy pouches under his eyes.

"Where does that leave you?" Moore asked.

"Retired."

It was a shock. Thinking about it, Moore realized it was something he should have expected, but it drove home the folly and futility of what was happening. Briggs had one of the best minds in the Agency, and unlike a lot of others he had not let his years of experience harden him against change. For Collins, or anyone, to use an attack from the outside as a way to beat Briggs in a bureaucratic competition was disastrously shortsighted.

"Do you know who was responsible for the leaks in the first place?" Moore wanted to know.

"Oddly enough, there hasn't been much effort made to find that out."

"You think it might be the Russians?" Moore asked. He was not sure where the question had come from. He had not formulated the thought consciously before.

"It might have been the Russians, I suppose. I had assumed it was some clever reporters with a line to an unhappy former employee, but I suppose most of them write their own exposés, these days. Now that you say it, though, it could have been the KGB. It's more than they've ever done along these lines, but times change."

Again, they walked in silence.

Briggs stopped. They were just within sight of the line of people waiting to file past John Kennedy's grave.

"You going back to Vienna, or have they phased you out, too?"

"I'm going back. And I'm damned if I'm going to let them phase me out. Not without a fight."

Briggs put his hand on Moore's shoulder. "Well . . . you've got my best wishes, Gregory. But take care of yourself: they've got the long knives out. Remember to watch your back."

———

Natalia watched Rukovoi move from closet to dresser to bed, slowly filling the suitcase that lay open on the bedspread. She stood in the doorway, leaning against the jamb; Rukovoi's bedroom was not big enough for her to stay in the room while he packed.

He stopped for a moment. "You are so pale today. Are you sure there is nothing I can get for you?"

She hugged herself. "I am frightened, Alexander. I have told you."

"Yes. Yes, you have. And I have explained to you that there is nothing to worry about."

"In Moscow there is always something to worry about."

He went to her and put his hands on her shoulders. "You must stop talking this way. I am going to Moscow on a short business trip. It is my homeland. The place where my children live. If not that you are here in Vienna, it would be like going home."

"Are you sure?"

"Natalia!" He was angry, but he put his arms around her and drew her to him.

"Alexander, how can I make you understand? It is for you that I am afraid."

She pulled away from him. He let her go.

"If it were not for . . . that American . . ." she said, looking at the floor. The words were barely audible.

"I know what you are thinking. You are afraid Nevelsky has seen through the lies I have told him about Gregory Moore, and so he is laying a trap for me in Moscow." Rukovoi kissed the top of her head. "I tell you it is all right. There is no cause for you to worry." He spoke firmly, but he was far from sure he was right.

Joan Wheeler was at the airport when Moore got back from Washington. He crushed her to him.

"I'm so glad to see you," he said when he finally let her go.

"So I gathered." She was grinning. "Come on. I've got the Merc, but Jordie said to have it back in an hour."

On the way to the car, she asked him how things had gone in Washington.

"Badly."

"Tell me."

"There's not much to tell. The whole trip was a disaster, as far as I'm concerned."

The trip to Vienna was slow; the road was clogged with construction equipment. A faint haze of tan dust hung in the air.

"They're closing down the Vienna station," Joan said as they sat opposite a construction site, waiting for a bulldozer to cross the road.

"What?"

"The orders came while you were gone."

"They're just going to close the whole station?"

"Well, maybe I'm being overdramatic. It could be

that they're just going to put in all new people. But everybody who's on the embassy-based staff now is being rotated out. At least, that's what Jordie said. And he thinks all the commercial-cover people are going, too."

Moore slammed his fist on the padded top of the dashboard. "Goddamnit! That bastard Wilson never said a word."

The traffic crawled forward. Joan steered the car past a line of men digging a trench in the pavement.

"Did Jordie tell you if there was a time limit?" Moore asked her when they had reached a clear stretch of road.

"I think Hawthorne has some leeway, but he's already had us close down all our routine business. That didn't take him more than a couple of hours, once he had the final orders."

"And the rest?"

"We've been given notice to roll up our networks and get to work on our final reports. Hawthorne claims he's giving the three of us the most time he can. Two weeks. He says everybody else from the station will be back in Langley by then."

Moore dropped his overnight bag on the living-room floor, next to the white, Italian-modern couch. His apartment was in a new building, with plain white walls and a compact, efficient layout. Moore had furnished it simply, as an antidote to the Baroque architecture and antiques that so dominated most of the city. In spite of the apartment's size, the parklike views from the living-room and bedroom windows gave it a feeling of openness.

"If they think I'm just going to take this lying down," he said, "they're crazy."

"I don't see what you can do," Joan objected.

He hugged her, then let her go, shaking his head. "I don't either, damn it, but you don't have to be such a smartass about it." He hugged her again, kissed her thoroughly.

"Hey!" she said, laughing. "You ought to go to Washington more often. I like how you are when you come back."

Only after I just miss getting killed, he thought sourly. It brought him back to earth.

"Damn it," he said. "I won't watch my work go down the drain because those assholes in Washington are having a power struggle."

"I guess everybody feels that way."

"They must know how much they're going to lose by shutting us down."

She put an arm around his waist and leaned her head on his shoulder.

"Let's talk about it later."

"Yeah. You're right. I'm about to turn this into some hell of a homecoming."

He kissed her again, relishing the firmness of her body against him.

In the morning he made a circuit of all Rukovoi's drops, leaving the same message in each one: He wanted to talk with the Russian as soon as it could be arranged. He even thought of calling the Foundation, but it seemed unnecessarily dangerous.

He got to Teletronics late, had trouble keeping his mind on his work, and left promptly at five to go to see Hawthorne. The man from Langley was in the same office in the embassy, but he had rearranged the furniture and there was a scattering of books and papers that had not been there on Moore's last visit. Hawthorne himself looked less like a man just passing through. He greeted Moore coldly, his insurance-salesman heartiness gone.

"I assume you've heard the news," he said.

"That you're rotating out the whole Vienna station? I've heard it. I'm damned if I understand it, and I don't like it. But I've heard it."

"Let's not start off on the wrong foot, Greg, all right?"

"What else do you propose?"

Hawthorne looked at him as if he were missing his cues. "I'd like to keep this calm and businesslike. What we want to do is get everyone out of here in the next few weeks."

"And who are you going to replace them with?"

"That's none of your business, and you know it. What's important to you is that you're going to have to prepare your man to have someone new running him, starting as soon as possible."

"I can't do it." There was no emotion in the statement. It was a simple matter of fact.

"I thought all this was straightened out when you went back to Washington." Hawthorne was plainly confused. "They sent me a cable about it."

He walked over to his desk and picked up a cable flimsy. "It says I should make arrangements with you to absorb your asset." He held it out.

Moore took the cable and skimmed it. It was from Wilson, short and pungent. He said, "I never agreed to this. It's not possible."

"Of course it's possible. People transfer control of their agents every day. And they don't usually make a big fuss about demanding justification, either."

"Not this time. I don't know how many ways I have to say it before somebody starts believing me. Either I run this guy myself with no interference, or he's going to bolt. He's too smart to stand still for my bringing in somebody else. If I'm out, that's it."

He went to the door, stopped with his hand on the knob. "I don't want any part of your bureaucratic games. If you want to spend your time kicking perfectly good people out of jobs they belong in so you can have a little more power, that's your business. But I'm telling you—leave this alone. It's not something we can afford to squander."

He left the door open. Slamming it would have seemed childish to him.

When he checked the drops, they were undisturbed. Rukovoi had not been to any of them.

He left the last one and headed for the nearest *Strassenbahn* stop, wondering what to do. He thought of looking for Rukovoi at Natalia von Hildebrandt's palace apartment, or at Rukovoi's own place, but that was likely to turn into a waste of time. In the end, the best thing seemed to be to call Rukovoi at the Foundation.

The secretary he spoke to the next morning said that Dr. Rukovoi had gone back to Moscow for a few days. She expected him back in a day or two.

Moore hung up, fuming. Rukovoi should never have left Vienna without letting him know.

On his lunch hour, Moore serviced the drops again, replacing the messages he had left with new ones demanding a face-to-face meeting as soon as Rukovoi returned. He noticed on his rounds that there were pickets marching in front of the Parlament again. Before he went back to his office, he stopped at a phone booth and made a brief phone call.

At a little after nine, Moore took a train into the center of the city and then another one back out to the northern districts. He switched to a *Strassenbahn* and rode to the end of the line on a hillside in Grinzing. He checked the schedule for return trips and then walked up the winding hill of Coblenzgasse.

It was a warm night, with just a hint of dampness in the air. The street was crowded with people— couples walking arm in arm, smiling, and small groups of tourists—all of them moving with a loose-limbed ease born of drinking new wine in quarter-liter mugs.

Moore let himself be caught up in the flow. He attached himself to a group of men, all of them dressed in dull shades of blue and gray, looking vaguely sinister, like a parody version of Russian secret policemen. The snatches of their conversation that he heard had a heavy Slavic roundness to them, though he guessed that their language was Polish and not Russian.

He followed them into the courtyard of one of the wine bars that lined both sides of the street and waited while they decided to go in. He lagged behind them, going into a long, thin room, wood paneled, with a wood floor and bare wooden tables. Two of the tables, side by side near the door, were empty. The contingent of Poles bunched near one of them, making up their minds who should sit where. Moore took a seat at the other one.

A blonde waitress wearing a colorful Austrian farm-girl's dress brought him a mug of pale greenish-yellow *heuriger*—this year's wine—and told him he would find a hot table in the next room. He got a plate of *schinken* and salad and a piece of thick-crusted rye bread. He carried the plate back to his table and sat eating his ham and eavesdropping on the conversation at the table next to him. It was mostly about women; the six men seemed especially interested in the table on the other side of them from Moore. Its main attraction was two striking young women—sisters, from the similarity of their features.

When the waitress came by again, Moore ordered a pitcher of wine for the six men.

"All this flirting is hard work," he said. "You need something for your strength."

One of them translated this for the others; it evoked hearty laughter. Moore had made six new friends. They claimed to be businessmen from Warsaw, automobile-racing mechanics and drivers by hobby, in Vienna as part of an unofficial Polish entry in an international automobile rally.

They were just the kind of protective coloration he had been hoping to find. He stayed with them for almost two hours, moving to a second wine bar with them, and then a third, keeping track of the shifting crowds around them, doing his best to be sure he was not being followed or observed.

After the first hour, he felt a constant edge of anxiety that was keeping him more sober than he might otherwise have been. There was only one thing that could explain it: he was waiting for someone to take another shot at him.

It was after eleven when the Polish rally team left to make their way unsteadily to their cars. Moore wished them luck and wandered slowly down the hill toward the streetcar terminus, weaving slightly as he walked. He stopped at the entrance of a wine bar housed in a two-hundred-year-old inn and scrutinized the menu. He walked back up the block and read another menu, then returned.

While he stood there, another man stopped to read the menu. He was in his mid-fifties, with thinning silver hair. There was a red carnation in the lapel of his dark suit.

"Have you ever tried this place?" he asked Moore in German.

"No. Never."

"They have good *schinken*. If you like *schinken*, this is the best place in Grinzing."

"Really? I have had excellent *schinken* just up the street."

"Here, it is better. I am about to go in, myself."

"May I join you?"

"I would be pleased to have your company. My name is Hans Kraus." He held out his hand.

"Walter Mautner," Moore said, shaking hands.

The room had stucco walls and heavy dark beams in the ceiling, but it was much smaller than the others Moore had been in that night, and it was dense with people. A wandering trio—violin, zither, and accordion —competed with the din of a hundred drunken tourists.

A hostess emerged from the haze of cigarette and cigar smoke to greet them. Moore handed her a hundred-schilling note and asked if she could find them a table where they could sit alone. She disappeared into the crowd; when she returned, she led them to a table for four in the back corner of the room.

They ordered *heuriger* and *schinken*; when they were

served, they continued their charade by comparing the ham with other versions served in other places. They were two single men out for a night of drinking, and their conversation might easily turn from food to women or sports or even politics.

With the exception of Rukovoi, Moore had no more personal contact with his agents than was necessary; he had no patience for playing father confessor, the way so many case officers did. But Kraus was the most politically aware of the agents in Moore's regular network, the one most likely to have the information Moore wanted. He had to talk with him.

The wine bar's door opened and a flock of tourists crowded into the already packed room. The hostess rushed to intercept them. She led them to a section of wood paneling mounted on a track in the floor. Pushed to one side, it revealed a second room. The eager busload of foreigners jammed themselves into it with a maximum of noise and confusion.

Kraus fidgeted. This close, even in the dim light, Moore could see the flaws in his assumed elegance. The cuffs of his shirt were grimy; one sleeve of his jacket was frayed; his fingernails were bitten to the quick.

The waitress put a pitcher of wine on the table.

"What did they say at the meeting?" Moore asked when she was gone.

Kraus poured himself a mug of wine and drank it as if it were beer.

"There are many demonstrations planned. The Communists are working with the less radical students and some of the other left-wing parties. They say it is the time to show they are the people best able to govern Austria properly. They say they will denounce terrorism, and they will show the way to prosperity and cooperation for this part of Europe and freedom from exploitation by the warmongers of the capitalist West."

"There's not much new in that, is there?"

"I think there is. That they are denouncing terrorism is important. So also is the connection with intellectual socialist students. The language they are using has become different. And I have heard many rumors that they have become wealthy." He ran a hand through his silver hair. "They can pay me more than you do."

"Then why don't you work for them?" Moore challenged.

"I have offered to."

"What did they tell you?"

"They will give me five hundred a week if I tell them what questions you ask me."

Moore refilled Kraus's mug. "I think you should take it."

"No, no," Kraus said, reversing his ground with an attempt at joviality. "I was making a joke." He drank more wine.

"How rich are they?" Moore prodded.

"They did not give me a tour of their treasury." Kraus picked at imaginary crumbs on the table.

"You can do better than that, Hans." Moore recognized the symptoms: Once Kraus began to sulk, he was not far from alcoholic despondency.

"Yes, you are right. I can do better," Kraus admitted. "May I have more wine, please?"

"In a moment. Tell me more, first."

"I can only make guesses. They were speaking of a major propaganda effort. They told jokes about hiring an advertising agency. I have told you they spoke of demonstrations this spring, and many more in the summer. Much literature will be written and published.

For the first time in the Viennese Party, all this activity will be closely watched and coordinated. Committees are already being formed. If they are to do everything they spoke of, I am sure it will cost them millions. And money is not the only thing they have that is new. They are well organized. It is as if someone with much experience has drawn up a master plan to guide them."

"A master plan for what?"

"I do not know."

"Guess. Based on what you've seen. What could their real goal be?"

The agent looked gloomily at the empty pitcher and then at Moore. "I think that they may hope seriously to win the next elections. They could form a coalition that will have a strong majority in the Parliament. They may even hope to elect a president."

"Do they have a chance?"

Kraus shook his head. "No. The country is not ready for it, yet. No matter how respectable and persuasive they become, there are too many who are afraid of them to be swayed by propaganda alone. It will take something more; people in Austria have become comfortable and complacent. If they were frightened, if there were an incident of some kind, then perhaps the Communists might get what they want." He drained his almost-empty mug. "Now may we have another liter?"

Moore waved for the waitress.

9

At lunchtime, Moore met Rukovoi on the promenade along the Danube Canal. Rukovoi's wolfhound stepped gracefully at his master's side, head high, savoring the bright spring air.

After a time, Moore said, "Someone tried to kill me in Washington."

"*Borzhemoi!*" Rukovoi came to an abrupt halt.

"It's been a lot of years since anybody tried to kill me. It's got to be connected with you."

"It would be insane for me . . ."

"Unless you thought there was some angle you could work."

The wolfhound ran off, came back, ran off again, responding nervously to the tension between the two men. When it returned, Rukovoi petted it with rough affection. They started to walk again.

"What about Nevelsky?" Moore asked.

"It could be. He . . . he joked about it once."

"Joked about it. Think of that! . . . You'd better find out if it's one of Nevelsky's jokes, and if it is, you'd better stop him, for your own sake."

They walked in silence. The dog dashed ahead again.

"I do not understand what would make Nevelsky want to have you killed now," Rukovoi mused. "Of course . . . if he knew you were preparing false information for me . . ."

"If that were it, wouldn't he be better off letting you dig yourself a real hole, and then burying you in it?"

"Yes. Perhaps," Rukovoi conceded.

"Would he kill me to keep you from having me as an agent?"

"If he was sure he would not be suspected. But I think it is more likely that he would have you killed for fooling me. He could still expose my folly, in the end."

They were approaching a playground. There was a shout. A boy of about six stood with his back pressed against the bars of the jungle gym; he was staring wide-eyed at Rukovoi's wolfhound, which was sniffing him, rapt with curiosity.

"Alpha!" Rukovoi called. The wolfhound left the boy reluctantly. Rukovoi clipped a leash to the dog's choke collar and spoke soothingly, his head bent close to the dog's long, shaggy ear.

"How could Nevelsky know I was going to give you anything but the truth?"

Rukovoi straightened up. "There is always the Walrus to think about. If he knows, Nevelsky could have found out."

"Langley doesn't know who my source is. So your mole couldn't know . . ."

"Could not know me by name. True. But for Nevelsky it would be enough to have *your* name and a description of what we are doing. From that much information, he would be able to know I was the one you were using."

"Okay," Moore acknowledged. "I can see how that would do it, for Nevelsky. But your mole—assuming he exists—is there any reason to think he's had contact with an operation like ours? I mean, so far it doesn't amount to a hell of a lot. I haven't made any official reports. There's only the rumor that I have a high-level source. It would get lost pretty easily. CIA may not be as big and compartmented as the KGB, but even so not everybody knows everything."

"Of course not. But would not operations involving the Soviet Union be of special interest to *Mordzh*? And would it not be naïve of us to assume he works without assistance, if he is as highly placed as I think he is? If, as you say, he exists at all."

"Yeah. If . . ." Once again, Moore thought, wheels within wheels. On the one hand, it would suit Rukovoi to invent a Walrus if there was none. On the other hand, if there was a Walrus, Rukovoi was right about how dangerous it could be to ignore him.

He looked sharply at Rukovoi. "Tell me some more about your friend Arkady."

"What more can I tell you?"

"What does he look like?"

Rukovoi hesitated, clearly uncomfortable. "He is . . . He is taller than you or I, but not so tall that he would stand out. His hair had some gray when I saw him. Here." He touched his temple. "By now he must have more. He has light eyes, I think. I am not sure what color they are."

"That's all you can tell me?" Moore asked, unbelieving.

"Yes."

"You've just described everybody in the Agency over forty-five."

The Russian shrugged. "Perhaps."

"But when you saw him in Washington, you recognized him after—what?—twenty-five years?"

"Yes."

"So you can give me a better description."

"No. I will not expose him to you."

Moore was furious. "Somebody's trying to kill me, remember? And Arkady may be behind it. My guess is: if he is, you're next."

Again, Rukovoi shrugged.

"It won't do, Alex."

"It will have to do. I have agreed to work for you. I have given you important information about plans here in Austria. But I am not so foolish as to betray my country's most important agent. There are many reasons. Loyalty, though the idea may seem laughable to you; there are some things I will not do to protect my reputation. And if I told you what you want to know about Arkady, I would be completely in your power, because that is certainly an act of treason, one which would insure my death if anyone learned of it, or even suspected it."

Moore said nothing. Rukovoi was right. It meant taking the Russian's word about *Mordzh*, at least for the time being. But he had to be careful about letting Rukovoi use the mole as an excuse too often.

As Moore pondered how he might draw more information out of Rukovoi, he let his eyes be drawn to the happy noises of playing children. At one end of the playground was a massive free-form shape, roughly cylindrical, riddled with tunnels. The side Moore could see had been painted as a garish abstract clown's face. Children were crawling up a lolling red tongue and into the clown's mouth. A small blonde head popped out of one empty eye socket, giggled, then withdrew.

"All right," Moore said. "Let's drop it for now. I need more details about the Austrian political operation. Things seem to be heating up here."

Rukovoi looked at his watch. "I cannot spend the time talking about it now. There is a meeting at the Foundation. I have already missed too many meetings because of my trip to Moscow. I cannot be late."

"Not good enough, Alex. You're not just walking away from it like that."

The wolfhound growled.

"*Teesha*," Rukovoi said in a soft voice. "Quiet." To Moore, he said, "I must go. I am not playing games with you."

"I'm not letting you go, Alex." Moore's voice was soft, but there was no mistaking his firmness.

"It is as I told you. Considerable financial and organizational support is being given to the Austrian Communist Party. The operation is being conducted with the aid of people who have greater contact with the local population than a State Security political officer or propagandist. This is the reason for my own trip to Moscow. Not the only reason. One reason."

"You're involved in it, then?"

Rukovoi hesitated. "They wished to hear my opinion of certain things."

"What things?"

"The political climate among certain scientists and intellectuals."

"What did you tell them?"

"That it was favorable to what they wanted to do. You see, Gregory, I think you have mistaken what we intend here. We are merely supporting a popular movement away from extremism. We hope to convince the people that the Party is respectable and does not present any threat to the petty bourgeois."

"You make it sound like student elections in a civics class."

Rukovoi did not respond.

"There's got to be more than that, Alex," Moore prodded. "You don't overthrow a government, even at the ballot box, with that kind of program. It needs something to get it off the ground. What you described so far isn't sexy enough to make anybody want to change regimes."

There was a silence. "Yes." Then, reluctantly: "There will be an incident."

Moore glanced again at Rukovoi. "Do you know what the incident is going to be?"

"I am not sure. There will be a demonstration. At the demonstration, there will be trouble."

"Violence."

"Yes . . ."

"Shooting?"

"Yes . . ."

"Who?"

"The police . . . The police will shoot at the demonstrators. I think it will be the atomic power group. The following day, there will be a call for a general strike. There will be more violence."

"You've got agents in the police, to do something for you?"

"Perhaps we do. If that is the case, our people will be first to shoot. But Western police are easy to incite. They will do much on their own."

"This is no time for a commercial, Alex."

"It was not . . . Yes, I suppose it was. That is all,

then. The demonstrations will escalate and the government will prove itself unable to handle them. Excesses of reaction will continue. In the end, the case against the government will be made by the government's own stupidity and clumsiness and its lack of concern for its citizens."

"Very neat," Moore commented. "A little bloody, though."

"Yes," Rukovoi said unhappily. "It is that which bothers me."

"When?"

"I have not been told."

"Find out."

The dog pulled at his leash. Rukovoi reached to pat its head. "I must go now, Gregory."

"Just remember one thing," Moore said.

"What?"

"You'd better find out some more about who's trying to kill me. No matter how many jokes General Nevelsky makes, it's not funny. For either of us."

———

It was after dark when Moore rang the bell of Robbins's safe-house apartment. Robbins opened the door.

"You're late."

"An emergency at Teletronics. Sorry."

Robbins locked the door and led the way into the living room, skirting several stacks of large cardboard boxes sealed with heavy tape.

Joan Wheeler was in the living room, sitting on the couch. She smiled when she saw Moore.

"Hello, stranger."

"Hello." He kissed the air in her direction. His

glance took in the disarray of half-filled packing boxes scattered around the room.

"Excuse the mess," Robbins said sarcastically.

"I still don't believe they can close us down just like that."

"Looks to me like they already have," Robbins countered.

"And you think they're going to throw away all our networks, and the information they produce?"

"They could be figuring on setting up new networks."

"How?" Moore was incredulous. "We had enough trouble finding the people we've got now and keeping them going. Where are they going to find new people? And what happens to the individual assets, the really important ones? You can't just hand them over, like so many folders from a file cabinet."

"Like this Russian of yours? The one you're so excited about."

"Yeah. Exactly."

Robbins tried on a thoughtful expression and a Dutch-uncle tone of voice. They went oddly with his tousled blond movie-star looks. "You know, Greg, things'd be a lot easier if you'd say who he is. Maybe that way you could drum up some support, if people knew who he was and what to expect."

"Sure. They'd screw the whole thing up in ten minutes."

In the silence that followed his comment, Moore crossed the room to the couch. There was a pile of folders next to Joan. He picked them up.

"Where do you want these, Jordie?"

"The floor is fine."

Moore put the folders on the floor and sat down.

"It would be a big help if we had a little money of

our own," he observed. "There must be a proprietary we can tap for enough to keep this one asset going. What about Robbins and Company? You have any spare cash floating around the showroom?"

"Robbins and Company's spare cash goes into an Agency account in Switzerland," Robbins replied testily.

"Sure. But if it's cash . . ."

"What do you want me to do? Steal from the Agency?"

"That's a hell of a way to look at it. I'm about to lose an asset that's really important to the country. Potentially the most important we've ever had. You know me, Jordie—I don't exaggerate. So I'm asking to use money generated by cover activities to support a genuine intelligence objective. Only this one time I want to do it directly instead of sending the money to headquarters and then making out a requisition so they'll send it back."

"It doesn't work that way," Robbins snapped. "And you know it. They'll never approve your requisition."

"Because they've gone temporarily shortsighted."

Joan was growing increasingly uncomfortable. "Come on, guys. We're all on the same team, aren't we?"

Moore shifted on the couch to face her. "Right now I'm not so sure."

"Oh, for Christ's sake!" Robbins exploded.

"All right, Jordie. I'm sorry. But I think you're making a mistake."

Robbins picked up a book and threw it forcefully into a carton. "You supercilious son of a bitch. Don't tell me who's making a mistake."

"All right, Jordie, all right," Moore said placatingly. "But the fact remains that I have to find some money.

I can stay alive all right on my cover job salary, but then I'm going to have to meet my commitments to my Russian."

"Greg . . ." Joan said.

He turned to her.

"If they're closing us down," she said, "you're not going to have a cover job here. Not if they don't want you to."

He took a moment to absorb it. She was right, of course. He had simply not thought that far.

Across the room, Robbins was putting folders into a box.

Moore said, "Suppose I told you the Russians might be behind all this."

"What do you mean?" Joan asked.

Robbins stopped what he was doing. "Yeah. What *do* you mean?"

"All those revelations had to come from somewhere. Somebody had to make the information available to the press. Suppose it was our friends at the KGB. Think of how much fun they'd have, pulling the plug on everything they know about us and standing back while the politicians used it to tear the Agency to shreds."

"That's a very interesting thought," Robbins said.

"It seems to me that if we knew exactly what information came out—what operations were involved, what details were described—it would go a long way toward telling us who the source was."

"Look, Greg," Robbins interjected, "don't you think they've figured all this out back at Langley?"

"Maybe they don't want to know."

"That's an odd thing to say."

Moore waved a hand. "Don't mind me. I've been

saying a lot of odd things lately. I'm not exactly Mr. Calm-and-Detached these days. The point is, it's not enough just to read the papers the way I did in Washington. We need to find out what went on before the first news stories were printed."

"Sure. Somebody does. But . . ."

"And if it *was* the Russians," Moore went on, "maybe that would slow Congress down a little. Make them wonder if they weren't playing right into the hands of the KGB by using the revelations as an excuse to dismantle the Agency."

"Now wait a minute," Robbins began.

Moore cut him off again. "And with a little luck, that might mean that we could get a reprieve, out here on the edge of things, while they made up their minds what to do in Washington."

He looked from Robbins to Joan. "The question is— how do we get the information we need?"

"Peter Harris could help us with that," Joan ventured. "He's been doing a lot of reporting on the Agency lately."

"What about your Russian?" Robbins asked Moore. "Can he get us anything from his end?"

"I don't think he's likely to know much about this," Moore hedged. "But I'll see what I can get from him." He turned to Joan. "I think your friend Peter is our best bet." It was not an easy thing for him to say, and he could not keep the strain from showing.

"Can you get that information here?" Robbins asked her.

"I'm not going to talk to him about it on the phone. I'll have to track him down. He's probably in London, or maybe Berlin." She glanced at Moore, worried by what she had heard in his voice. To Robbins, she said,

"I'll need a couple of hundred dollars, at least. Can you give me a travel authorization?"

"Look, we're supposed to be closing down," he said. "I can't really . . ."

"We've still got a couple of weeks left," Moore reminded him. "You can squeeze it in some way."

"I don't know. Hawthorne is watching me pretty closely."

"It could be very important," Joan said.

"Well . . ."

"Cut the shit, Jordie," Moore snapped. "You can do it, and you know you can."

Robbins spread his hands in capitulation. "All right. But for God's sake, Joan, make it quick, will you?"

"A couple of days. As soon as you can get me plane tickets."

"I'll try to arrange it for tomorrow or the next day."

"Good." She took Moore's hand, squeezed it, and smiled at him tentatively, silently asking for permission, or understanding.

He nodded, patted her hand with his free one. "It's okay."

"I'd better make some phone calls," she said. She got up abruptly and left the room.

Moore watched her go. Robbins went back to packing file folders.

Without looking up from his work, Robbins said, "She sleeps with that reporter in London, doesn't she?"

"Jesus, Jordie! What kind of question is that?"

"But she does, doesn't she?"

"Yeah. I guess she does."

"I'm damned if I see how you put up with it." Robbins put a folder into one of the cardboard boxes.

"Well, why don't you stop thinking about it?" Moore

was on his feet now. "I never noticed you worrying about it before."

Robbins looked up. "I'm sorry, Greg. I didn't mean to . . ."

"It so happens we're happy the way we are. When we're together, we're together. When we're apart, we lead our own lives. It saves a lot of lying."

"Yeah, I guess I can see how that would work."

"You still should mind your own damn business."

"I said I was sorry." Robbins was annoyed.

Moore said nothing for a moment, looking at the man he had once thought might become his friend as well as his colleague. Then he said, "You know, Jordie, you've been awfully contrary today."

"You think so?"

"I do. And a little defensive, too. As if you were being accused of something."

Robbins rubbed his face, shook his head wearily. "I don't know. It must be this business of closing down. I've been trying to think of it as just another reassignment. Wilson isn't mad at *me*, after all. But I guess it got to me more than I realized."

"Yeah. I guess it got to all of us."

Leaving the apartment, Moore's mind was on Joan Wheeler and Peter Harris. He wondered sourly if Harris would give her another lavender dressing gown when she was in London this time.

When he and Joan had been on opposite sides of the world for months at a time, Moore had not thought much about her other men, and he had reason to believe that he had more than matched her in outside involvements, at least at the beginning. Now, as far as he knew, Peter Harris was the only holdover from the old days; Joan had met him when she first started to do magazine work, before she joined the Company, before she met Moore. So he supposed that in a sense Harris had more reason to complain about him than he had to complain about Harris.

He told himself from time to time that Joan only slept with the British reporter out of friendship and some echo of their old passion, but he knew it was a rationalization. And now he had not slept with anyone but Joan for more than three months. She was all that he needed. Increasingly, it bothered him that she did not feel the same pull toward exclusivity that he did.

He took the escalator down to the plaza and mall beneath the *Kärtnerplatz*. There was a clog in the traffic streams flowing around the glass-walled café at the plaza's hub. University students, their placards and T-shirts emblazoned ATOMKRAFT? NEIN, DANKE, were accosting people, offering them literature opposing atomic power, and asking for contributions.

Moore watched for a moment and then pushed into the crowd and made his way to a second escalator that plunged deep under the city to the new subway lines. He trotted down the moving steps.

The platform was moderately crowded. Waiting for the train, his mind was again on Joan. He could not let things go on the way they were—couldn't take the pain and the uncertainty. Especially with the Agency in turmoil and their futures so uncertain, he had to convince her that they belonged with each other, and no one else.

The decision straightened him up; the slouch went out of his stance and his muscles tightened. He glanced down the track toward the bright light of an approaching train.

And felt hands on his back, a sharp push forward.

He stumbled toward the edge of the platform. Twisted his body, trying to change the direction of his fall. He collided with someone who instinctively shoved him away, back in the direction of the oncoming train. He could hear it with unnatural clarity, bearing down on him, as he fell backward. One foot slipped from the platform. He thrust with the other, threw his arms and body away from the edge, clutched desperately at the jacket of a bewildered man who at the last instant dropped his briefcase, grabbed Moore's arms, and staggered back with him. They fell to the platform together as the steel-clad train hissed by them into the station.

For a few minutes they were the center of attention. Then a musical chime sounded and there was a rush to board the orange-walled cars before their doors slid closed. Almost without sound, the train slipped from the station.

Through the chill of fear that still gripped him, Moore realized that whoever had pushed him was now out of reach. He stood up uncertainly. The platform was already filling up again. Moore thanked the man who had helped him. Another train came and they got on, strangers once more.

————

Bright sunlight cast shadows along the street and sharpened the contours of the carved lions' heads on the palace doors. A rectangle under one of the lions opened and Natalia von Hildebrandt stepped out of the darkness. She locked the door and started along the street. Moore fell into step behind her.

"*Gräfin* von Hildebrandt. Countess."

She stopped. He thought he could see her back stiffen. She turned slowly and for a heartbeat said nothing. Then, levelly, she asked, "What do you want?"

He had trouble finding his voice. "I'd like to talk to you for a minute."

Her green eyes rested on him with a combination of emotions he could not quite read: disbelief, aversion, bewilderment. He was not sure. He was not used to being so off balance.

She turned away and began walking again. He walked beside her.

"I have nothing to say to you." She did not look at him when she spoke.

"I want to talk to you about Alex."

Even in profile, contempt was clear in her face. "Isn't this foolish of you?" she asked him. "And dangerous?"

She was walking more quickly, as if she hoped to outdistance him.

"I could talk to you about Gustav Biener, instead," he said pointedly. "I understand he's been promoted to number-two man in the Austrian intelligence service."

She whirled, her copper hair swinging with the motion, framing a face suddenly gone pale. "What do you want?"

"I need some information about Alex."

"No. I won't betray Alex to you, no matter what you do."

"I know you wouldn't." There was a knot in Moore's stomach. His throat was dry. "Not anymore. Not since you stopped reporting to Gustav Biener about him."

"You twist everything, don't you? Make everything worse than it is?" For the moment, hatred had banished her other feelings. "You have always done that, as long as it serves your purpose. No one is safe with you. Sooner or later, you use everyone."

"Somebody's trying to kill me," he said. "It makes me persistent."

"I hope they succeed." She whirled again and stormed down the street.

He followed.

She stopped. "I apologize," she said stiffly. "That was an awful thing for me to say. Even you deserve better. But there is no excuse for what you did to Alex. To use a man's children as a weapon against him." She shuddered. "It makes me feel unclean to talk of it."

"Oh, yes. I forget, you are a countess. Almost a princess, isn't it?" Moore was seething. "You're too pure for human failings. Like seducing a well-informed foreigner so you can report on him to your lover, the spymaster."

"That's filthy," she spat. "I never did that. You know better."

He sighed. "Yes, I suppose I do." A familiar leaden cloak of exhaustion settled on his shoulders. "I don't like this, Natalia. It's not how I want to be talking to you."

"Then stop."

"It's not that easy. There's too much at stake. The issues are too big."

"I do not understand."

"Just as well. Does Alex know about me?"

"What?"

"I was just wondering if you'd told him about your penchant for younger men. Or was I the only one?"

Her eyes narrowed and cords stood out in her neck; her lip curled. Then, abruptly, her face relaxed, her whole body. A faint, sad smile touched the corners of her mouth. "Gregory, you are impossible. I had good memories of our time together, brief as it was. Once, I even thought there was something admirable about you. It seemed to me then that you might be one of the last *chevaliers*. A bold knight on horseback, with armor that shone in the sun. I still think you could have been. But instead you have turned into what you are now. I do not understand it. How did it happen?"

"How did what happen, Natalia? I do my job. I don't kill flies with sledgehammers. I try to keep my word. What else can I do?"

Sadly: "Then why do you threaten to destroy what is between me and Alex—the only good thing that you have so far let him keep? And to destroy my happiness, as well."

"Damn it, Natalia, I don't want to destroy anybody's happiness. Right now, all I want is to stay alive." He took a breath and went on, "I need information about Alex because I have to know if he's telling the truth. If he is, then there's no harm in your talking to me. If he isn't, if he's lying, then he's setting me up for murder, and in the end he's going to do himself a lot more harm than he'd ever suffer at my hands. He may not believe that, but it's true."

"Is it?"

"Yes, damn it, it is. Most of the people I work with are a damn sight less humane than I am. I may be using Alex, and I may have threatened to mess up his life, but I've also been trying to protect him. So far. The thing is, if I can't find out what I need to know, I'm going to have to assume it's Alex who's gunning for me. And I'm not going to sit back and wait for it to happen."

He could see the confusion in her eyes. "Think about it for a while," he told her. "I'll be back to talk to you."

He walked off, leaving her staring after him.

––––––––

Rukovoi came to her apartment for dinner that night. He saw at once that she was under strain, but he did not comment on it until they were sitting in her living room drinking brandy by the light of a half-dozen tall, white tapers. It was a ritual she had initiated with the first dinner she cooked for him. It had taken him many dinners to realize that candlelight and cognac after dinner had always been a part of her life.

He sipped his brandy reflectively, then put the snifter on an end table. "Something is wrong, Natalia."

He heard her stop breathing.

"Yes," she said after a moment. "I wish it were not true, but there is something."

"What is it?"

"I spoke with Gregory Moore today."

"What! You what?"

"Excuse me. What I said was not correct. He spoke to me."

Rukovoi unleashed a stream of Russian curses.

"How dare he! The filth! It is bad enough he has meddled with my family. But you . . ."

"He knows a great deal about us." Her voice was calm. It sobered him.

"What are you saying?"

"About Gustav."

"Gustav . . . Biener?"

"Yes."

"What did he say?"

"Just that he knows I was working for Gustav. Reporting to him about you."

Rukovoi laughed abruptly, longer and louder than was called for. He heard himself and stopped. "And he is blackmailing you?" he asked her.

"I suppose he thought he was. He doesn't know that you know about Gustav or that I broke with him because of you. Still, it frightens me how much he knows."

"I must remember never to underestimate Mr. Gregory Moore." He stared into a candle flame, hypnotized for a moment. "It is not how much one knows. It is how much one *seems* to know."

He took her hand and pulled gently. They stood up. He put his arms around her.

"You are wonderful, Natalia. I love you more than anyone. More than anything. More than my life. I do not say it to you often enough."

She nestled her head in the hollow of his shoulder. After a time, she said, "Alexander. He told me you were trying to kill him. Is that true? Is that what you are doing?"

He held her tighter. One hand moved on her hair, stroking her head and the back of her neck.

"You said you would find a way out," she went on. "That is not what you meant, is it?"

"It is not something for you to be concerned about," he said into her hair.

She pulled away from him and went to stare into the empty fireplace, her arms wrapped around her.

Tentatively, he moved close to her, put his hands on her shoulders. "What is it, my love?"

"It is not so simple, Alexander. I am not interested in loving a murderer."

His hands fell from her shoulders. She turned to him. The candlelight glowed deep in her eyes. He thought he had never seen anyone so beautiful.

"There is no need for suspicion, Natalia."

She moved a step toward him. Again, he took her in his arms.

"I wish," she said. "I wish . . ."

His lips brushed her cheek.

"But wishing is for children," she went on in a barely audible voice. "Isn't that what you said?"

10

Moore was taking the champagne out of his refrigerator when the doorbell rang. He shoved the bottle down in the icebucket he had improvised from a glass salad bowl and hurried to answer.

He threw the door open. Joan was standing there, grinning. He was grinning, too. Neither of them moved.

"Christ, it's good to see you," he said. He opened his arms and she threw herself at him.

He lifted her off her feet. She was light in his arms, like a dream.

"Hey!" she gasped. "Put me down, you crazy grizzly. I can't breathe."

He swung her from side to side, bending backward to lift her higher. They laughed together.

She blew in his ear. Wriggled. Nipped at his neck.

"I vant to trink your blood," she japed.

Still laughing, he put her down and stood there appreciating her: Her face, lightly tanned, was animated by her broad, wild grin and the happy light in her deep brown eyes; her collarbones—the world's most beautiful, he had always maintained—made a graceful line over the scoop neck of the yellow silk dress that hung softly against her, gathered by a small belt that emphasized the narrowness of her waist. The color was perfect for her; it set off her suntan and made her short cap of dark hair seem more dramatic.

He wondered when and where she had been in the sun long enough to get even a light tan; he saw at once that the answer was not likely to make him happy.

He took her in his arms again. Finally, he stepped back and said, "Welcome."

"Thank you." She turned back to the hall and picked up her purse and a shopping bag.

"Living room?" she asked as she came into the apartment.

"Sure. I've got some champagne in the kitchen. I'll go get it, and I'll meet you."

In the living room, he popped the cork and poured for both of them.

"To returning," he said, lifting his glass.

"Oh, yes. Definitely. To returning." She drank, her eyes on his.

She sat down on the white couch. He stood. On the chair next to him was a small stack of gift-wrapped boxes.

"Looks like you bought out London."

"Not just London. Rome, too. And Cannes."

"Rome and Cannes? Not bad for less than a week, on a business trip, no less."

"It *was* business. We were tracking down a source."

"Such intrigue!" He was smiling, but he was not amused.

"It was. Really. We were in Geneva, too. I didn't believe it some of the time. After all, we were just being reporters. . . . I wish you could have been there. You would have loved it."

"I'll bet."

"Greg," she said reproachfully.

He was surprised by how upset she seemed. "Sorry. Just a joke." He looked at the boxes. "Well, do I get to see what you bought?"

"Sure. They're for you. Well, most of them are."

There was a leather folder from Rome and an ornately tooled leather box. From Cannes, there was a tiny black monokini, so little cloth he could close his fist around it.

He bent over and kissed her. "You're a nut," he said. "A lovely, thoughtful nut, but a nut, nonetheless."

"And that's why you love me," she said.

Inexplicably, he thought he detected nervousness in her voice. He had the sudden conviction it was important to change the subject.

"Meantime," he said, "you have to tell me more about your trip. How did it go?"

"Very interesting," she said with a comically exaggerated cat-that-ate-the-canary expression. "Very interesting indeed."

"Do tell."

"Don't get your hopes too high—I still don't have all the hard facts. But I do have some fascinating tidbits. Peter was already working on the story; he had a lot of information. And all that running around got us some more."

"Enough to draw any conclusions?" Moore asked eagerly.

"Well, one for sure. It's not only the Russians who are behind our troubles."

She stopped, enjoying the suspense she had created.

"That's all for now. It takes a while to tell and I want you to open your other present, first."

He had saved the biggest box for last. He unwrapped

the dull gold paper carefully, sensing that the gift should be approached with a certain amount of ceremony. The paper covered a plain blue box. He opened it and pulled the white tissue paper back. Under it was a silk dressing gown, deep red, like the best port wine. He felt the cloth, lifted the gown slightly to admire the design and the stitching.

"It's beautiful," he said. It was, but he was afraid it would always make him think of the lavender one she had been given on her last trip to London.

"Take it out of the box," she said.

Puzzled, he did. There was another one under it—a smaller one of rich, dark blue, almost black.

"That one's for me," she told him. "I needed one, too."

"I don't understand."

"I returned the other one I had. The lavender one."

"You returned it?"

"I didn't like wearing it with you. So there was no point in keeping it." She finished the champagne in her glass.

"Greg . . ." She stopped, shook her head. "Hell. This is going to be harder than I thought."

He sat down next to her. "What is it?"

"Well . . . it's . . ." She took both his hands in hers and turned them over. Lifted them one at a time to her mouth and kissed his palms. "If only I could read the future. It would make life so much easier." Her eyes searched his face.

"It's a lousy business we're in. It doesn't lend itself to easy futures for anybody."

"It's our future I care about."

"I'll tell you what," he said with an attempt at

lightness. "Why don't we chuck the whole thing? Retire. We could do something else. Open a little restaurant, say. A café. The *Kleine Konditorei* of Georgetown."

"Georgetown? Ugh!"

"All right. Not Georgetown. The hip, young West Side of Manhattan?"

"No."

"Sausalito?"

"Now you're talking."

"It's settled, then." He kissed her.

"Greg. . . . There's something serious."

"I kind of figured there was. All right. Shoot." He regretted the word as soon as he'd said it.

She was too preoccupied to notice. "I did some thinking on this trip," she began. "About you and me. When I got to London, I discovered I wasn't . . . happy to see Peter the way I used to be. I kept thinking of you. I couldn't . . . We didn't . . ." She stopped, embarrassed. Looked for another way to approach it. "Anyway, Peter knew right away something was wrong. He was very good about it, really. We had a couple of terrific talks on the beach." She smiled, with some irony. "Someday, maybe you ought to thank him. If it turns out to be something you feel grateful for, that is."

He reached out and touched her hair, her shoulder. Took her hand. She squeezed his.

"Anyway, what I want to say is that I think we ought to talk about this arrangement of ours."

He started to speak, but she anticipated him.

"No. Wait a minute. I want to get this all out while I can. I know we agreed we wouldn't mortgage the present to some imaginary future, but I'm not talking about the future. I'm talking about right now. And right now I love you. . . . And I don't want anybody else. So, as of now I'm not seeing anybody else anymore. Just you. Don't get me wrong—I'm not asking you to do the same thing. I'd like it, sure, but I don't think I ought to ask you for it."

"You've got it."

"What?"

"I said, you've got it. In fact, you've had it for a long time."

"But . . ."

He put a finger to her mouth. "Hush now."

Without warning, she opened her mouth and engulfed his finger. She wrapped her lips around it and slid them up and down the length of his finger with a rhythmic motion of her head and shoulders.

He closed his eyes and concentrated on the velvet of her lips on his finger, the hot wetness of the inside of her mouth. Her tongue moved on his fingertip.

He opened his eyes and with his free hand caressed her face and neck, her elegant collarbones, her hair. He kissed her eyelids, her forehead.

She released his finger and he put his arms around her. They kissed, increasingly tangled together on the couch.

She pushed him away and struggled to sit up.

"What's the matter?" he asked her.

"We ought to go into the bedroom and take our time. After all, it's a special occasion of sorts."

He was grinning again. "You're absolutely right."

He picked up the champagne bottle and the glasses and they walked slowly to the bedroom. She put her arm around his waist and leaned against him.

He set the wine and glasses on the bedside table and moved to switch on the lamp. Her hand diverted his. She led him in the darkness to the window and pulled up the blinds. He stood next to her, looking out.

"It's such a beautiful night," she said.

"It is." Trees and park spread before them, illuminated by a silvery moonglow. Beyond the trees were the scattered lights of houses, almost a quarter mile away.

He turned her gently so they were face to face. His fingers ran lightly over her eyebrows, her cheeks, her neck. He kissed the corners of her mouth.

With the tip of her tongue, she traced a line around the margin of his lips.

Slowly, he unbuttoned the front of her dress and lowered his head to kiss the hollow of her throat. She slipped her hands under his shirt and pressed them against his chest.

He slipped the dress from her shoulders, kissed them lightly. Her breasts were bare. He took a nipple with his lips, teased it awake with his teeth and tongue. She moaned.

He stood back and undid her belt. He dropped it on the floor and lifted her dress over her head and onto a chair.

She fumbled with the buttons of his shirt, worked it off his back. She unbuckled his belt, groped for his zipper, pushed his pants down.

They were overwhelmed by urgency as they struggled with stockings and shoes until finally they both stood naked in the moonlight.

He took her hand and led her to the bed. They sank down onto it, still watching each other. When his hands began to move on her body, it was as if he was learning her all over again. Their lips touched; their breath mingled in their mouths.

He wrapped his arms around her, pressed the length of his body to hers. He buried his face in her neck.

She moved beneath him. They rolled over and she was on top, staring down at him, smiling. She ground her hips against his.

Suddenly, she jerked off him and across the wide bed, away from the window. The motion alarmed him. He rolled after her, calling her name.

He was on top of her when he saw the dark pool spreading under her neck and shoulders. He kept going, over her and off the bed onto the floor.

Something hit her body, shifting it on the bed. Her arm spilled off the edge; her fingers brushed his naked back. He screamed.

He waited, paralyzed, behind the bed for minutes, then scuttled along the floor to the window and dropped the blinds. It was dark in the room, but he did not turn on the light.

He went to her and took her in his arms, held her, sitting on the bed, rocking slightly back and forth. Occasionally, sounds escaped him—moans and whimpers, and a kind of crooning, as if he were comforting her. He sat there all night, holding her.

When the dawn came he could see her and he fled into the living room. The blood on his arms and legs and chest was more than he could bear. He stood under the shower for half an hour and then stumbled back out into the living room. Partway through drying himself he forgot what he was doing and stood staring at the unwrapped packages on the white couch, not knowing what they were.

It was almost noon when he called Jordan Robbins. He barely managed to stammer out his name.

Moore sat in a corner while Robbins and the others scurried about the apartment. Robbins made him turn away when the body was carried out. A doctor talked to him, looked him over, and gave him a sedative.

The next morning, Moore woke up on the convertible couch in the living room of the safe house. He felt numb. Robbins was there.

"How you doin'?"

"Lousy."

"Go take a shower. I'll put the bed back and make you some coffee."

The shower washed away some of Moore's sense of being drugged, but when he came back into the living room he was still blank and disoriented.

Robbins handed him a steaming mug of coffee.

"Here. Double strength this morning."

Moore stood there holding the mug.

"Sit down, sit down," Robbins said. "No need to be formal with us." He gave Moore a gentle shove toward the convertible couch.

The coffee slowly brought Moore back to himself. When he remembered why he was there, his hand shook and he spilled coffee on the rug.

"Don't worry about it," Robbins told him.

He concentrated on the coffee, drank half of what was left, then put it aside. For five minutes he sat in silence. Then he said, "Okay. I'm ready to talk about it."

"You're sure?"

Moore hesitated an instant before he said, "Yes."

Robbins sat down opposite him. "Can you tell me what happened?"

"You know what happened. We were in bed. Somebody was out there, shooting in, and they killed her."

"That's it, then."

"Isn't it enough?"

"God, yes. I'm sorry, Greg. I didn't mean . . ."

"Okay. It's all right."

There was an uncomfortable silence.

"This makes three tries," Moore said.

"Say again?" Robbins was clearly bewildered.

"It's the third attempt on my life. Somebody took a shot at me in Washington, and somebody else tried to push me in front of a *U-bahn* at the *Kärtnerplatz* station."

"Holy shit! Why didn't you tell me?"

"There was no point." Moore's voice was dull.

"Maybe I would have taken you more seriously about your Russian."

"It wasn't your decision. Wilson knew about the one in Washington, and that didn't help me any."

Robbins nodded. "You never were exactly a blabbermouth, were you?"

Moore heard bitterness in Robbins's tone, but he did not pursue it. He said, "This time was a lot more professional than the first two. And a lot closer, too."

"What do you mean?"

Moore put his head in his hands for a moment, then looked up. "That sniper must have been—what?—about three hundred fifty yards away? Four hundred? That's pretty good shooting. He only missed by about six inches. Missed *me*."

He stood up and walked slowly around the room,

as if he were intent on circumnavigating it, then sat down again.

"I don't know," he said. "Maybe he didn't miss. Or didn't think he missed. Joan's hair was about the same color and length as mine, and we're about the same size. In the dark, who knows, maybe he thought she was me." He slammed his fist into the arm of the couch. "Goddamnit! It should have been me."

"Come on, Greg," Robbins implored. "Take it easy." He stood next to Moore, put a hand on his shoulder.

Moore shook him off and stood up. Went to the window to look out and moved suddenly away, shaking. When he could, he began to pace.

"What the hell good am I to anybody? Jesus Christ. I smear dirt on people. Ruin their lives. Make them betray what they believe in. For what? So Wilson can tell me to go home and forget it? So some congressman can write the whole Company off as a loss? And now, my crowning achievement—Joan is . . . Joan is dead. Because she was . . . stupid enough to love me."

He stood looking blankly across the room.

Robbins waited until Moore went back to the couch and sat down again before he asked, "You figure it was your Russian?"

"What?"

"You think it was your Russian who set it up?"

Moore rubbed his face with both hands. "No. I . . . No. I'm his best protection, I told you that. He wouldn't kill me."

"Yeah. But look, figure it this way—suppose he thinks if he kills you he's going to earn enough points to cancel out whatever it is you've got on him."

"No."

"Desperate men do crazy things, Greg. And maybe he has some ace in the hole you don't know about." Robbins brushed a lock of blond hair off his forehead. "What I'd like to know is what makes you think you can trust him."

Moore closed his eyes and leaned back on the couch. He was very tired.

11

Joan's parents came to Vienna for the body. They
wanted to bury their daughter in her hometown, an
affluent western Pennsylvania village rapidly being
assimilated into Pittsburgh's suburban sprawl.

Moore did not know how to behave with them. He
felt responsible for her death, guilty for having de-
prived them of their daughter, although he knew that
she had long ago separated from them almost entirely
and had had no use for the mercenary shallowness
with which she had been raised. And he was sickened
by the continual need to talk only of her magazine-
writer cover job and the phony one-car accident that
had been trumped up to explain her death.

It seemed obscene that she was being dragged back
to a place she despised, where no one who cared about
her or who had mattered in her life would attend the
funeral or be able to visit her grave. But he had no
status. There was nothing he could do but stand by
and watch as the arrangements were made.

At night, he got drunk. He did his drinking alone,
not wanting consolation from anyone who was available
to give it. On the third day after Joan's death, he sent
a telegram to Peter Harris, giving him the news. It
seemed like the right thing to do.

The next night, he stopped drinking after his fourth
vodka. He drove unsteadily around the city, servicing

the drops he and Rukovoi used, leaving a message that requested a meeting in two days, at four-fifteen in the afternoon.

———

At four o'clock, he walked through the Theresien Bridge gate of the Schönbrunn Palace gardens and strolled up a narrow mall between parallel rows of trees. It was humid and overcast, but the mall was studded with tourists.

At the end of the mall was what looked like a stone staircase leading to a gazebo. As Moore approached it, he could see more of it—it seemed to grow. He was seeing an end-on perspective of the Gloriette, a towering pavilion of Baroque columns and arches set at the crown of a steep hill. Its central, tiled walkway offered a view down over a reflecting pool, gardens, and the gaudy yellow palace itself; beyond the palace spread a panorama of the city, rising to meet the bleak sky.

Rukovoi met him behind the stone base of the Gloriette, between a water fountain and a green wooden stand that sold soft drinks and sausages.

They walked a sand-colored gravel path. The Gloriette loomed above them at their right. It was two stories from the path to the level where the columns began.

"You said there was an emergency," Rukovoi began testily. "I do not understand how you are having so many emergencies. And you are being very foolish, to speak with people in public so often."

"All right, Alex. Enough of that."

"You must not give me orders." Rukovoi was angry. "When we first met, I thought you were skillful. You said you would tell no one I was working for you, and that was important to me. But if we continue to meet in public, we will be seen. Our secret will be lost."

Moore's face hardened, but he said nothing.

When they had walked the length of the Gloriette, they paused. Ahead of them a path led into a stand of evergreens. Moore started along it.

"I have a story to tell you, Alex, so hang onto your righteous indignation until I'm done."

Suppressed anger flared in Rukovoi's eyes.

Moore glanced quickly around. There was no one on the path with them.

"There was a woman who worked with me in the Vienna office," he said. "She had a press cover; she did free-lance magazine work, mostly—Americans abroad, multinational business outlook, Terrorist of the Month. She may even have covered the Foundation. Joan Wheeler?"

Rukovoi's forehead wrinkled. "I do not know her. Why are you telling me this?"

"We were in love with each other, Joan Wheeler and I," Moore said. He stopped walking. It was cool among the trees. There was a sense of being isolated from the tourists only a few yards away.

"We were in love, but now she's dead. Somebody took a shot at me a few nights ago. He missed by just enough to put the bullet into Joan's neck. It was a nasty bullet. It shattered her spinal cord and cut a lot of veins and arteries. We were in bed at the time." His mouth was dry, his voice a papery whisper.

There was a long silence.

"I am sorry, Gregory, to have been angry with you, before. I did not know your unhappiness."

Another silence.

Rukovoi said, "We should not involve the women in these things. They must be left alone."

The reference to Natalia was unmistakable. Moore was surprised that she had told Rukovoi about their conversation, and then realized that it was consistent with the way she did things.

"That's beside the point, and you know it. As long as somebody's trying to kill me, we don't have time to worry about anything else.... You said you were going to look into it. What have you learned?"

"I have learned nothing that is specifically about you. But there is information which may be related to this shooting."

"What is it?"

"I received a message from Moscow two days ago. A man brought it to me in a sealed envelope placed inside a second sealed envelope. The man was coming here to Vienna for the Heavy Machinery Board. . . . Imagine. We have so much technology—we have ways to send messages instantly, computers to make codes— and because of all this technology, if a message is private and secret, it must be carried in person, the same way people have been sending messages for a thousand years."

"At least the messengers don't have to travel by horseback anymore. What was in your envelopes?"

"It was about my assignment to work on the political operation here in Vienna. General Nevelsky reacted very strongly when he learned of it. He thinks it is a threat to his success."

"Isn't it?"

"Not by itself; not at this time. After a longer time has passed, yes, it is a threat. Our careers must cross.

Also, the interests of those who support us in Moscow must cross. There will be open conflict."

"And you think this is tied to the people who are shooting at me and trying to push me in front of trains?"

"Yes. My friend in Moscow who sent me the message says Nevelsky is opposing me openly now, and opposing my new duties here in Vienna. He is talking about you, as well. He is saying there is no value to my claim that you wish to work for us. He is saying it is not true." Rukovoi continued along the path. "It is because you have given me no information."

"And that's because of *Mordzh* and this mess in Washington. If you want me to protect you, you'll have to be patient."

"It is not *my* patience that is in question. You will have to give me something before long, whether you can arrange for it properly at your headquarters or not. Otherwise, even my friends will begin to doubt me."

"All right. I see your point." Moore stopped. A young couple was coming up the path toward them. He was tall and Nordic; she was tiny, Oriental. They were holding hands, paying more attention to each other than to where they were going.

Moore looked away from them. "Why don't we head down toward the palace?" he suggested, and without waiting for a response started back along the path, out of the trees.

"It could be Nevelsky, then," Moore said as they passed the broad, dark reflecting pool. Its sky-gray water shimmered with fat goldfish.

"Yes. If he does not truly believe his accusation and does not think he can convince the people in Moscow, killing you is another way to keep you from helping my career. And, as I have said, if he knows the truth about us, he might kill you and then expose me. Although in some ways I think it is best for him to expose both of us."

"Unless . . ." Moore interposed. "Unless by exposing you he would also have to expose Walrus."

"Yes. To prove my treason, he must have a source of evidence. Otherwise, he could not disgrace me publicly."

"So it might still be easiest for him just to kill me."

"Yes."

They were at the brow of a hill. Moore stopped to let a woman in a flower-print dress push a baby stroller past them and up onto the flat pathway that surrounded the reflecting pool. He checked to be sure there was no one else near them before they started down the hill.

Moore wondered whether it could be Rukovoi who was behind the murder attempts, after all. Suppose he knew something about what was happening in Washington and Langley that canceled the danger to him inherent in Moore's death. But how likely was that? Even if there was a Russian mole, or a family of moles, in the CIA, there was a limit to how much they could know and to how widely their reports would be disseminated within the KGB. Rukovoi would not be in line for information on the CIA's bureaucratic infighting. As the Russian himself had been saying, there wasn't much security in modern communications, so truly delicate intelligence was handled with special care.

Full circle again, Moore reflected.

He said, "If it is Nevelsky who's after my hide, is

there anything you can do about it? You or your friends in Moscow?"

"I do not know. Perhaps."

"You've got to try. To protect yourself."

"I understand."

Two small boys in short pants came bounding down the steep path, yelling and giggling, one chasing the other. They were followed at a distance by their parents, walking slowly, wearing matching looks of fatigue.

Rukovoi let the family get several yards beyond them. "Perhaps Nevelsky is helping us, when he is so obviously fighting against me."

"How?"

"If Nevelsky is trying to kill you and deprive the country of your services only in order to gain advantage over me, my friends in Moscow will see that it is made known."

"Good. Let them get as much mileage out of it as they can. How long will it take you to get a message back to them?"

"The man who brought the envelopes will return to Moscow in three days."

"There's no way to do it sooner?"

"No."

"Damn it."

By the time they reached the garish yellow-tinted palace with its green wooden shutters, they had made plans to keep in regular touch through the drops they had been using and two new ones. Moore asked for an updated report on the status of the KGB political operation in Austria, although he had no idea what he would do with it, now.

Rukovoi walked off along a pathway leading into

the palace gardens. Moore turned the other way and started through the broad arched passageway that led to the forecourt and the street.

Halfway through the passageway, Moore felt a gnawing of apprehension. He felt oddly alone, and more was missing than just Rukovoi. It was as if the number of human presences moving with him had been reduced by at least two.

He had no idea what lay behind the feeling, but as he continued out onto the street and along the front of the palace toward the railroad station he became convinced that someone, perhaps more than one, had been following them.

———

The phone rang at Moore's Teletronics office. He picked it up.

"Mr. Walsh wishes you to his office," his secretary told him.

"Did he say why, or if I should bring anything?"

"No. He is asking if you are alone. I say yes. He is telling me please to ask will Mr. Moore come to Mr. Walsh's office."

"Okay. Thanks."

Walking down the hall, he wondered what Walsh wanted. It could be almost anything. Moore had no idea how many balls he had fumbled since the shooting.

The European Division President was at his desk, reading. Moore had a perfect view of Walsh's wavy silver hair among the gold-plated lamps and pen holders and picture frames arrayed on the inlaid desk top.

Walsh pushed his gold-rimmed reading glasses up onto his forehead and looked at Moore.

"Yes, uh, Greg," he said, bringing himself into focus with apparent effort. "Sit down. Please."

Moore took an armchair at one side of the room.

Walsh cleared his throat. "Yes. Well. I don't really know how to say this." He stopped.

Moore waited.

Walsh cleared his throat again. He took his glasses off and studied them. "I'm afraid we can't use you anymore," he said.

"You're firing me?" Against all logic, Moore found that he was surprised. He had known Joan was right when she predicted this, but somehow he had never fully accepted the notion. In the eighteen months he had been with Teletronics, he had come to like the job for itself, apart from its value as a cover for his other activities.

Walsh put his glasses on the desk top. "Yes. You could say that. I'm letting you go." He still had not looked up.

Moore was on his feet, at the desk. "Goddamnit, what for! You're not going to tell me I don't do a good job." He knew he was right. He was one of Walsh's best people, even when he was not putting in a full day.

Walsh pushed himself deep into his high-backed chair. "No . . . I . . ."

Moore backed up a half step. In response, Walsh sat forward again.

"You need somebody in that job," Moore said. "You can't do without me. Maybe you don't need me full time, but we could work that out."

"Well . . . no," Walsh said. He massaged the bridge of his nose. "There's really nothing for us to work out."

"That's not how I see it. You can't just call me in

here and say, 'Get your ass out of here.' Who's going to pick up the pieces? What's going to happen to all my accounts and my contacts?"

Walsh stared at the desk. "Uh. You know, Greg, I really don't want to do this. I'm the first to admit you do a good job for us. And you're . . . you're a good man." He finally looked up. "You have to understand: I don't have any choice. Not really. I only hired you in the first place because of your . . . unusual recommendation."

"I do understand. Believe me. But even if I sever my other connections, I'm still a valuable employee to you."

Walsh began playing with his glasses again. Moore watched him move the bows in and out.

"Greg, there's really no point in our carrying this conversation any further. There's nothing I can do about it. It's been made clear to me where my duty lies."

"Your duty! Is that what they told you? It was your *duty*?"

"That's right." Now Walsh was indignant. "What's wrong with that?"

Moore stared at him. There was nothing more to be said. He turned and walked out of the office.

Rukovoi settled into the corner of Natalia's living-room couch and swirled his after-dinner cognac in its snifter. Natalia picked up her own brandy glass and sank down on the couch next to him.

"Do you want to talk to me about it?" she asked. She touched his hand. "You know I am glad to listen."

"It is Moore, of course," he said. "Nothing has

worked out the way I planned. From the very beginning, it has gone wrong."

She tucked her legs under her on the couch so she could face him directly. He gazed into the empty marble fireplace as he spoke.

"At first, for my own purposes, I told him about what State Security was planning here in Vienna. I disagreed with the operation; I did not understand it properly then, and it seemed without point to me. Also, it was Nevelsky's operation, and not mine." He turned to her, looking for some sign of understanding. She nodded, her eyes on his.

He went back to staring at the fireplace. "Then, when I went to Moscow, everything changed. I learned more. I saw that the operation here in Austria was not wrong. It became my operation as much as Nevelsky's. It was a large step for me."

"A step toward a permanent position in Moscow." She could not hold it back.

"No. I . . ."

"Alexander. We are adults. I understand what you want."

"I want many things. They do not all . . . They are not all consistent." He glanced at her. "I would have been here for a long while . . ."

She touched his hand again. "It's all right, Alexander. I apologize for interrupting you." Her voice was tightly controlled.

He said, "The operation here is important to me. But I cannot ignore Gregory Moore's warnings. Even if he is exaggerating, some of what he says is correct, I am sure. It is possible for the operation to cause a disaster."

"What will you do?"

"I must warn Moscow. The risk is too great for me to keep this to myself. But I must be very careful what I say."

"Or they would know you told Gregory Moore about the operation."

"Yes." He watched a candle flicker. "I feel as if I have built a cage for myself. The things I did at first, to delay meeting Moore's demands, have turned into traps. The Walrus is a trap I made for myself. At the beginning, Moore thought I was inventing the Walrus as a way not to be working for him." Rukovoi's mouth pulled into a thin line that was not a smile. "In a way, you see, he was right. I had told him about the Walrus to make him go slowly with me. So I tried to persuade him that the Walrus was real, and I think I succeeded, but it has not helped me. It has only given Moore more information than he should have."

"There is a Walrus, then?"

He shrugged. "If the stories are correct. In Moscow I heard things that made me wonder if there is only one Walrus. I think there could be several people, and they are all referred to as the Walrus. Perhaps it is the whole operation that is called Walrus."

"Several?" She was intrigued. "Imagine. Do you know how many?"

He looked at her sharply. "No, Natalia. I do not know how many."

"Oh!" she said, startled. "I did not mean . . ." She laughed, stopped abruptly. "I apologize. I am not laughing at you. It is only . . . I was not trying to pry information out of you for sinister purposes."

He leaned over and kissed her.

"It is I who should apologize," he confessed. "I am seeing a conspiracy everywhere I look."

"Not here," she said. "My days of intrigue ended long ago."

"Yes. But I am happy that you had them. Otherwise we would not be together now." He sighed. "These Walruses could be very dangerous for me."

"How?"

"Gregory Moore is known as an operative who has successfully recruited Communists as agents. If counter-espionage is part of the Walrus's job, Moore will be someone they know about. One of them will learn that Moore has a new Russian agent. That much is all right. There are many in Moscow who know I am in contact with Moore. They think I am going to feed him false information. But if the Walrus learns I am giving Moore real information, then he will know I am working for Moore. You see, that is why I wanted Moore to know about the Walrus, at first, so Moore would be afraid we might be discovered. . . . Now I am the one who is afraid."

She cupped his face with her hand, touched her lips to his. "But why should you tell Gregory Moore anything that is the truth?"

"Ah. You see, that is truly my problem: Gregory Moore is not a fool. He will check what I tell him. As long as he can believe I am working for him, he will be my strongest supporter. He wants only for me to have success, because it is my success that makes me important to him."

"Yes. . . ."

"I think that to insure my success he will even give me information about his own government and about the CIA."

"And so you would give him information about your government, because in that way you could later get more information from him."

"Which he will give me so that I can be promoted still higher . . ."

"So you can give him still more information."

"Yes. Exactly."

"Why do you not simply trade the information you need?"

"It is all secret information. We cannot exchange it openly."

She sighed. "I suppose it makes sense."

Her glass was empty. "Do you want more brandy?" she asked him.

"Yes. Please."

She uncoiled herself from the couch and poured cognac for both of them.

"This talk makes me dizzy," she said when she was settled next to him again.

"Yes. It is a difficult game to play. I must weigh the information I give against the information I hope to get. I must decide what the Americans' reaction will be to the information I give, so that I can avoid things which will increase the discord between the two countries."

"If you believe that there should be no discord."

"What sane person believes otherwise? It is not in the interest of the Soviet Union to have a nuclear war. Not even with China. There must be some better way to prosper in security. . . ."

"Yes."

"And there is something else that is important. I think that Gregory Moore is different from most of the others in the CIA. One of them once said that they see the world as a game of poker. They know what cards are in their hands, but they can only guess what cards we are holding. Even so, they play with great bravado. If it suits their purpose, they bluff. And they try to guess if we, too, are bluffing. . . . But this is not the only way to see the world. I think for Gregory Moore it is more like chess. When you play chess, you always know all of your opponent's moves, and he knows all of yours. You have to guess his strategy; you have to find the pattern in what he is doing, if there is a pattern. But you do nothing simply because you are ignorant. If you make a mistake, it is because you are stupid or you lack skill." He sipped his brandy. "For Gregory Moore, to operate without information is like playing chess with half the board covered. You are bound to make mistakes, and they are all mistakes that you do not have to make if you can see the whole board."

"And you, Alex? What do you think?"

"That is what I think. Politics and power are more like chess than they are like poker. In chess, you can use misdirection. You can feint. You can sacrifice pieces for future gain. This makes sense in the world. But it is foolhardy to play at world affairs as if it were poker, with your sleeves rolled up and a cigar in your teeth. I think Moore must understand that we agree about this. It is the only thing that would make me valuable to him."

"So, in the end, he will have what he wants."

"If I become as important as he expects me to, he will have contact high in the government of the Soviet Union. In five years, or ten. Yes, he will have that. But he will not necessarily have what he wants. . . . When I am more important, it may be possible for me to walk away from Mr. Moore, because if he exposes me I will be in a position to explain to others in the government what happened."

"But . . . if they learn you have betrayed them, you will be tainted forever."

"Yes. That is why I need to be careful what information I am giving to Moore. And I will have to do something to show that I am cooperating with Moore only because I think we can learn from him."

"Even so . . ."

"You must not worry." He put his brandy glass on the rug and reached out for her. She came into his arms and nestled against him.

"It is all such a nightmare."

"It cannot last." He held her, hoping she believed his reassurance better than he did.

He looked at his watch. "I have to leave. There is a program running on the computer at the Foundation. My results are due in half an hour."

"Will you come back later?"

He shook his head. "I do not know how long I will have to work."

"When I am tired, I will go to sleep. But please come back here. I want you near me. I am worried."

He held her again, tighter. He kissed her. "All right," he said. "I shall come back."

Scattered lights from apartment windows turned the courtyard of the old palace into a rectangle of overlapping shadows. Rukovoi paused at the bottom of the steps. The multitude of grays, some transparent and some impenetrable, was at once bewitching and forbidding.

He started across the courtyard and caught a hint of motion under one of the trees. He remembered—it seemed long ago—sitting in Natalia's breakfast room looking down into the courtyard, watching a little girl in a red jacket sitting under that same tree. His head turned toward it. He saw a small man, neatly dressed, his face obscured by shadow.

Rukovoi walked faster, then slowed. The conversation with Natalia had made him nervous, he told himself; this was no more than a chance encounter, no reason to be afraid.

The man's path crossed his just inside the passageway that led to the street door. In the light cast by the lamps suspended from the vaulted ceiling, Rukovoi could see the other more clearly. He looked familiar.

He confirmed the familiarity at once. *"Guten abend, Herr Doktor,"* he said simply. His German was coarse, even in the few words.

Associations flashed through Rukovoi's mind; he was sure it was important for him to remember this man.

The man put his hand under his jacket. The motion and the gray courtyard they had just left combined to bring a picture into Rukovoi's mind. A gray office. A sense of unpleasantness and anxiety. Lenin staring down from the wall. The little man was . . . Dybenko! Nevelsky's assassin.

Before Rukovoi could move, Dybenko's hand came out from under his coat, holding a silenced pistol. He shot Rukovoi twice in the chest and once in the middle of the forehead. Already dead, Rukovoi staggered backward under the impact; his body hit the wall and collapsed into an inert bundle.

Dybenko put the gun back under his coat and continued along the passageway. He emerged under the carved lion's head and closed the door carefully behind him before setting off down the street.

12

The day after Walsh fired him, Moore took a long walk through the Inner City, trying to sort out where he stood and what he could do next. He was fighting a two-front war, and every time he lost a battle it hurt him on both fronts.

Rukovoi was the key to all of it, and the trouble was that Rukovoi himself was a puzzle. Sometimes Moore felt he could trust the Russian; but there were other times when Moore sensed that Rukovoi was playing a far more complicated and devious game than he let on.

One thing became clear to Moore as he tried to map the terrain of his situation: He had no more room to maneuver. He was on his own and he had to pick a strategy and follow it through before events got away from him.

He kept coming back to Rukovoi. It was a calculated risk, but he was going to have to rely on the Russian.

When Moore got back to the hotel he had been living at since Joan's murder, there was a message from Robbins: "Hawthorne wants to see you. Call him. Important."

Moore was at the embassy an hour later; he found Hawthorne surprisingly cordial: a muted version of his old football-player, insurance-salesman self.

"Can we get you some coffee? Tea?" Hawthorne asked.

"Coffee."

Hawthorne pressed an intercom button. "How do you like it?"

"Black."

"Betty, can you get us two coffees, please? My usual, and a black for Mr. Moore." He came around the desk. "Have a seat." He dropped himself into a leather wing chair.

Moore sat on the couch, wondering what was coming.

"Nice day," Hawthorne commented.

"Yeah. But you didn't get me here to talk about the weather."

"Nope. But I didn't want to jump right into business, either. We're people after all."

There was a knock at the door.

"Come in."

A slim woman in a shapeless dress came into the office carrying a small tray with two mugs of coffee. She put one of the mugs on the low table in front of Moore and handed the other to Hawthorne.

"Thank you, Betty."

She left as quietly as she had come in.

Hawthorne drank some coffee and put the mug on the table. "That girl makes a mean cup of coffee. Probably pretty hot in the sack, too, once you get past those dresses she wears. And that dumb short haircut. Why women do that to themselves, I'll never know. . . . Oh! Sorry. I guess your . . . I mean, I didn't . . ."

Moore said nothing.

Hawthorne leaned back in his chair, seeming to gather himself together.

"I'm sorry, Greg. I didn't mean to be so tactless. I guess it's been a pretty tough week for you, losing your lady like that and then having your big asset killed, too."

Moore sat forward. "What are you talking about?"

Hawthorne seemed not to have heard the question. "Listen, I have to tell you how much I respect what you did. We all do. Nobody ever guessed it might be Alexander Rukovoi. But once we knew, we went back over his file. I have to hand it to you—it makes all the sense in the world to try for him. And actually turning him. Well, I'd sure love to know how you did it."

Moore was at once furious and baffled. "How the hell . . ."

"Now, Greg . . ."

"You bastards. You goddamn bastards. It was you who followed us."

"It wasn't me."

"And now you're telling me he's dead?"

"Oh, yeah. My turn to be sorry again. I thought you knew."

Moore stared at Hawthorne. Nothing seemed real anymore. "What . . . how . . . how did it happen?"

"Shot. Three times. Last night, in the courtyard of the Palais von Hildebrandt."

"Oh, Christ. . . . Look, Roger, I hope this isn't some kind of asshole game you're playing."

"What kind of game could it be? The man's dead. I didn't make it up, if that's what you mean."

"Who shot him?"

Hawthorne shook his head. "We're not sure. Best guess is the KGB."

Moore picked up the mug in front of him. He wanted to throw it across the room or use it to make a pulp of Hawthorne's All-American features.

"You probably got him killed, following us. Why the hell couldn't you just leave it alone? Goddamnit."

"Maybe you should be grateful," Hawthorne told

him. "The other side was after you, and they seem to have settled for Rukovoi instead."

"Yeah. Sure. That's really how they work."

Hawthorne looked across the room. His fingers drummed on the arm of his chair. His blue eyes flicked back to Moore, then away.

"Well, tell me," Hawthorne said finally, in what was meant to be a casual tone. "Now that your big asset has been terminated, will you at long last fold up your tent like a nice Arab and steal off into the night?"

"I'm damned if I understand you, Roger. You sound as if you're glad it worked out this way."

Hawthorne erupted. "You fucking prima donna! You think this is an easy job? You think I wouldn't rather keep these assets than watch them go down the drain?" He stood up; his face was mottled with fury. "If you'd look around, you'd see it's all those goddamn bleeding heart, knee-jerk shithead politicians that are doing this, and they're doing it to all of us, not just you. Now, get the hell out of my office." He took a long breath. When he started talking again, he had himself under control. "I was going to give you a timetable for rolling up the rest of your network and getting back to Washington, but considering everything—take a day off to digest the news and we'll talk about the rest of it tomorrow."

Moore pulled himself to his feet and walked to the door.

"I'm sorry about your job at Teletronics," Hawthorne said. "I didn't have any choice."

Moore walked slowly back to his hotel. His mind was blank.

At the hotel, he walked up the three flights of stairs

to his room. He was beginning to focus again: He had to rebuild his whole world, and he had very little to work with. Without even the possibility of an alliance with Rukovoi, he was really alone.

He lay down on the narrow bed and stared at the pattern of sunlight and shadow that dappled the ceiling, trying to think. He fell asleep almost immediately.

When he woke up, the sun had gone behind the buildings across the street, and the room was a uniform gray. He looked at the clock built into the bedside cabinet. It was 4:30. Outside, there would be sun and a bustle of activity. The *Konditorein* would be jammed with Viennese and tourists having coffee and pastries and whipped cream.

Moore picked up the phone and asked the hotel operator to get him a number in London. While he waited for the call to go through, he went into the bathroom and splashed cold water on his face. The phone rang while he was rubbing his face dry.

"*Herr* Moore, I have London."

"Thank you."

"London? Go ahead, *bitte*."

Moore waited. There were clicks and hums on the line and the faint sounds of other conversations.

"Gregory Moore?" asked a strong male voice with an Oxbridge accent.

"Yes. Speaking. Is this Peter Harris?"

"The same."

"How are you?"

"As well as can be expected. The news about Joan took me rather off guard. But I did appreciate your sending the wire. . . . I imagine it was all a good deal worse for you."

"Yeah. I'm still a little numb."

"I sympathize, but surely you didn't call to commiserate."

Their connection went thin. A distant man gabbled excitedly in French about commodity prices.

"Gregory, are you there?"

"I'm here, all right. And so is half of Europe." The connection improved as suddenly as it had worsened. "I called about . . . what Joan came to see you about."

"I thought that might be it. Did she . . . Did she have an opportunity to tell you any of the things we learned, she and I?"

"No. Not really. Just that there were others involved besides . . . the visiting team."

"Just so. Just so. Look, we can't very well talk about this on the phone, can we? Why don't you hop up here and I'll fill you in."

"I don't know if I can get away. Can you come here?"

"Well, I suppose it's possible. I could juggle a few things, and dream up a story to do while I was there. All right, then. On one condition."

"What?"

"If I help you, you help me. When we get the story worked out, I want to break it."

"Absolutely. I'll help you however I can."

"That's fine. I'll be there within three days. I'll let you know exactly when. How do I get you?"

Moore gave him the hotel's phone number and cable address.

"Right. I'll see you in two or three days, then."

"Thanks, Peter. Take care."

Moore hung up. Two people had died and the Agency was in a shambles. It was all connected, and he was going to find out how, and why.

The only remnant of his earlier depression was a physical staleness. He stripped and exercised until sweat coated his body and splashed onto the carpeting. He took a shower, shaved, and put on a clean suit. He became suddenly aware of what a luxury it was. Now that he was unemployed, he would have to be careful how much he sent to the hotel valet.

Natalia von Hildebrandt did not answer the door when Moore rang the first time, nor the second. He said a silent prayer to no particular deity and pressed the bell again. After a minute, he heard footsteps.

She was wearing a black dress with no jewelry. Dark stockings. Plain black shoes. Her red hair was tied back, and she had not put on any makeup. Moore was struck by the deep lines of fatigue in her face.

When she saw who was there, she swung the door closed. Moore's foot stopped it in the middle of its arc.

"Please, Natalia. It's important."

"Get out of here. Murderer."

"They tried to kill me, too."

A muscle twitched under her eye. "I don't care about you. I don't know how I ever did. It is because of you that Alex is dead."

She pushed on the door. Moore shifted his weight to block it more firmly.

"They killed my . . . my girl friend, my lover, too, the same as they killed Alex. And now I think you and I are in danger."

"I do not want to hear about it." Her voice was shrill, less controlled.

"If you could give me some information, maybe I could find out who killed him."

"What difference can it make now? He is dead. I

want nothing to do with you. With any of you. I have had enough, do you understand?"

Again she shoved on the door. This time Moore let it close.

———

For the second time that day, he wandered the Inner City. Gradually, as darkness wrapped the buildings, the streets emptied. It was time for the opera, or dinner. Time to tend to home and family.

He found himself standing in front of the outer door of the building that held the safe-house apartment. He stared at it for a long time, and then he fished in his pockets for his keys and unlocked the door.

There was only a dim light in the passageway. His footsteps echoed from the ceiling. He crossed the courtyard and went up the stairs.

He hesitated before ringing the bell. When there was no answer, he unlocked the door and went in.

He was not prepared to find the place stripped almost bare. The boxes of files were gone, and so were the two typewriters, the radio, and most of the furniture. He went into the kitchen. In one of the cabinets he found a jar of Nescafé, two mugs, a spoon, and a bottle opener. There were five large bottles of Gold Star in the refrigerator.

He turned out the lights and went into the living room. He stood carefully at the side of the window. The street below looked deserted.

He pulled the shade down and drew the drapes, then sat in the darkness, in the heavy armchair that was one of the few pieces of furniture left in the apartment, thinking about what to do next.

He left the apartment and went downstairs to the

steel door that protected the entrance to Robbins's target range. He tried his key. It did not fit.

He felt a surge of anger, then resignation. The range had been against regulations—Robbins had claimed to have inherited it, but Moore had always suspected it had been Robbins's private toy from the beginning. It made sense that he would shut it down as soon as he knew he had to break up the office.

Moore went back up to the street and walked the short block to his hotel. In his room, he pulled his suitcase from under the bed, opened it, and released the concealed catches of the false bottom. He took out a soft leather case; it held an old .380 automatic. He had taken it from a Czech, an STB man he had run into years before on one of his assignments for Briggs. It was a rare thing in the Agency to be authorized to carry a gun, so he had kept it in reserve for an emergency. Until now he had never needed it.

Back in the apartment, Moore stood in the middle of the living room, staring at the phone resting on the carpet, its cord coiling back to the bare wall. It took him several minutes to work himself up to make the phone call. As he listened to the phone ring, his doubts grew stronger. His whole line of reasoning was based on guesswork. He wondered if he should hang up and think it out again.

There was a click at the other end.

"Hello," Robbins said.

"Jordie? It's Greg." No time for cold feet now. "I'm at the place. Can you come over?"

"Look, I'm kind of worn out. I thought I'd have a quiet drink and take it easy, go to bed early. . . . Is this important?"

"Yeah. I think it is."

"Well, shit. All right. I'll be over in, oh, say half an hour."

"I'll be here."

Moore hung up. His hands felt clammy.

He paced. Went into the kitchen and opened a beer, poured some into one of the coffee mugs and walked around with it. He took a swallow. It was not what he wanted; he put the mug on the windowsill.

He surveyed the living room. Bare as it was, it was too cluttered for his purposes. He pushed the couch against the wall under the window, moved the standing lamp into a corner, and pushed the armchair into the middle of the long wall. It made the room look bigger and barer.

He took his gun out, checked that it was loaded, checked that there was a round in the chamber. Afraid that it might jam after going so many years unused, he worked the slide repeatedly, ejecting one bullet after another onto the armchair. He reloaded the magazine, jacked a bullet into the chamber, and left the gun cocked, with the safety on, when he tucked it under his belt.

He sat down in the armchair and waited. The noise of a key in the lock brought him to full alertness.

———

Robbins came into the room and stopped short.

Moore was standing next to the chair, pointing a gun at him.

"What's doing, Greg?"

"Give me your gun."

"Come on, man. What is this? Cops and robbers? Wild West? Since when do we carry guns?"

"Cut the shit, Jordie."

Robbins hesitated. His body tensed; his weight shifted slightly.

"Don't," Moore warned.

Robbins shrugged. "I guess not."

Moving slowly, he opened his jacket wide and used a thumb and forefinger to draw his gun from its belt holster. It was the .357 Magnum revolver from the range downstairs; he held it out, dangling, toward Moore, who grabbed it and dropped it on the chair next to him.

"Stand over there." Moore jerked his head toward the space he had cleared in the middle of the room, but his eyes stayed locked on Robbins and his gun did not waver.

Robbins moved slowly in the direction Moore had indicated.

"A little more," Moore told him. Then, "All right. There."

"Are you going to tell me what this is all about?"

"It's about your killing Joan."

"My what!"

"It took me a while," Moore said levelly, "but I finally got it straight. Joan wasn't killed by accident. That shot was meant for her, not me."

"But . . . why?"

"To shut her up. To keep her from doing anything with what she'd learned."

"Then she did learn something from her friend the reporter? About the leaks?"

Moore did not answer.

"And you're saying that's why she had to be killed?" Robbins asked, going along with it.

"That's right."

"By *me*?"

Again, Moore said nothing, waiting.

"Why would I . . ." Robbins left the rest unsaid.

After a moment, Moore said, "Joan told me one interesting thing before she was killed. She said she was sure the Russians weren't the only ones behind the leaks."

"Who else? Did she say?"

"She never got a chance to. But if you look at it all hard enough, one thing's pretty clear—whoever was behind those leaks, they had to have help inside the Company. Not much. Just a couple of people would have been enough. But they needed someone on the inside."

"And you think I'm part of it?" Robbins asked, incredulity heavy in his voice. "You think I'm working for the Russians? And that's why I . . . killed Joan?"

"You're the only one who could have set her up like that. It was a well-planned operation, not something thrown together on the spur of the moment. Nobody else had enough information to make it happen that place, that night. To make it look like an attempt on me. That was the really brilliant part of it. Until today, I was sure the bullets were for me. . . . You knew what Joan was doing and when she was due back. It had to be you, behind it."

Robbins looked at the floor, then at Moore. For a moment, he seemed about to argue, but he said only, "What next?"

"I'm going to call the embassy and get somebody over here."

Robbins nodded. "Then the thumbscrews?"

"I hope not," Moore said. He picked the Magnum off the seat of the armchair and tucked his own automatic under his belt. Quickly, he checked the heavy

revolver to be sure it was loaded, then he moved crab-
wise to the phone, keeping his attention focused on
Robbins, the gun aimed at his chest, while he dialed.

The night-duty man answered.

"This is Gregory Moore. I need to talk to Roger
Hawthorne. Emergency."

"I'm sorry sir, but Mr. Hawthorne's gone for the day.
Perhaps if you called back in the morning."

"Oh, shit," Moore said and followed it with a code
phrase. In the middle of the room, Robbins smiled.

"Thank you, sir," the night-duty man said. "But Mr.
Hawthorne really is off for the day."

"Find him."

"I can't do that."

"You damn well can, and hurry."

"Can't somebody else help you?"

"No. I need the boss."

"Well, uh, you know, Mr. Wilson is in Vienna. I
think he may still be here at the embassy."

Moore went cold. "Really? When did he get into
town?"

"I can't say. I'm sorry. Do you want to talk to him?"

"That's all right. Just get me Hawthorne."

"But . . ."

"I said, this is an emergency. I don't want any more
shit. Just do it. If anybody comes down on you later,
tell them I was talking crazy. I threatened to kill
people."

Listening, Robbins smiled again.

Moore said, "That's the truth, too, sonny. If you
don't get your ass in gear. I'm likely to do just that."

The smile left Robbins's face.

While he waited, Moore stood up, holding the
receiver to his ear with his left hand while his right

kept the Magnum pointed at Robbins. The body of the phone dangled a foot off the floor at the end of the receiver cord.

Hawthorne came on the line, all business. He listened to what Moore had to say and told him he would send a car right over.

13

Moore motioned Robbins to the armchair and went to stand across the room from him, leaning against the wall out of line with the window—covered or not, it made him nervous. From where he stood, he could see Robbins and, by turning his head, the apartment door.

Robbins sat tensely in the chair, his hands on its arms, his back pressed against the upholstery.

As the minutes passed, the gun grew heavy in Moore's hand. The strain of watching Robbins began to tell on him.

The abrupt knock on the door startled both of them.

"Who's there?" Moore shouted.

"The milkman," a German-accented voice answered through the door.

"Come back Tuesday."

"Tomorrow is better," the voice objected.

Moore reached out and pressed a button next to the light switch. There was a ragged buzz from the entranceway, and the door clicked open.

A man came in. He was round-faced, about six feet tall, and he walked with a slight limp. He was carrying a tiny Ingraham M-11 submachine gun, four pounds of the most deadly weapon ever designed.

Moore glanced at the newcomer, then returned his full attention to Robbins. Something about that first glimpse stuck in Moore's mind. He took a second look at the round-faced man.

The M-11 was pointing at Moore, not Robbins.

Moore heard Robbins get up and whirled to cover him. Spun back to the newcomer. Too late. There was no way now to recapture the initiative. If he had shot one of them as soon as he had sensed what was happening . . .

He relaxed. Looked at the newcomer more closely. Moore did not remember where he had seen the face before, but he was sure he had.

"Better give me the guns, Greg," Robbins said.

Moore did as he was told. Robbins tucked the automatic under his belt and pointed the Magnum at Moore.

"All right," Robbins told the man with the sub-machine gun. "You can go."

"I was told to bring him."

"Go ahead," Robbins insisted. "I'll bring him. I'll take the responsibility."

The man did not move.

"Tell you what to do," Robbins said. "Have them send the kid back with the Merc. Tell him to park downstairs by the *Krugerstrasse* exit and wait for us there."

The man nodded stiffly, put the tiny submachine gun under his jacket, and left.

Robbins waved his free hand toward the armchair. "Have a seat. It's a comfortable chair."

Moore crossed the empty room and sat down.

"I was right, then," he said.

"Except for one thing. It had nothing to do with the Russians."

"Then who?"

"Nobody else. Just us guys."

"It's internal?"

Robbins nodded.

"Rukovoi thought there might be something like that," Moore observed. "A purge inside the CIA."

"I wouldn't call it a purge, exactly."

"Whatever you call it, it's destroying the Agency. How can you gain by that?"

Robbins grinned. "Publicly, it's destroying the Agency."

"But in secret, business as usual," Moore said, beginning to understand.

"Business *better* than usual." Robbins shook his head in wonderment. "You know, the amazing thing is that in a way you understood it all, right from the beginning. The Agency can't really be dismantled. And more important, the covert work can't stop. Not in this day and age."

"So you're setting it up for the public to think all the dirty work had been abolished. But the truth is that you'll keep it going, this time in total secret."

Robbins grinned. "Think of it: no more second-guessing by every jerk on Capitol Hill. No more running from reporters. All we'll have to do is the real job we were hired for. . . . And the truth is, we have the Russians to thank for opening our eyes on how to do it."

"What do you mean?"

"Well, you were right about that, too. They did start it. The KGB thought they were being very clever, leaking some naughty things we'd done, picking a time when the leaks would do us the most damage. They had just about shot their wad on it, when a couple of people figured out that if we pushed the Russians' idea a little further, ourselves, we had a chance to end up in a much better position. And it looks like it's working out fine." He smiled. "You never know, do you?"

Moore said nothing.

"I still think you ought to come aboard," Robbins urged him. "There aren't many as good as you are. We could use you." He glanced down at the Magnum. "I don't want to have to hold a gun on you."

"Then put it away," Moore suggested drily.

"The trouble is, if you're not going to come aboard, we're going to have to kill you."

"Like you killed Rukovoi?"

"Are you nuts? We didn't kill Rukovoi. You were certainly right about him: He would have made a terrific asset."

Moore digested the denial and knew that the most important question was still unanswered.

"You didn't kill Rukovoi. But you did kill Joan."

Robbins did not answer.

Moore said: "This is so important that you'd kill your friends for it?"

"I didn't kill her."

"But you went along with it. You set her up. And you're ready to kill *me* yourself, right now."

"We can't let the truth come out, not at this point. It would ruin everything. If Joan and you'd got to work on what she learned, and if the two of you weren't coming on board with us—well, we couldn't let that happen. I mean, suppose you let it slip to your friend Rukovoi . . ."

"Rukovoi is dead."

"He wasn't then."

"It's a hell of a way to operate."

"It's working. And who'd ever guess the CIA was

responsible for its own destruction? I'm telling you, when we're done testing everybody and we've got everything organized, we're going to be able to do the job better than it's ever been done before."

"So that's what all the trips to Washington were about. But nobody bothered to test me when I went back."

"We're only testing the people we think might work out. When you were in Washington, you weren't on the list."

"Lucky me. And what's all the testing about?"

"Attitudes. Loyalty. We're getting rid of a lot of penetrations. Russians, French, Israeli. That place was a regular sieve."

"And what about the old-timers? Collins? Wilson? They're on the never-been-tested list, aren't they?"

"Come off it, Greg. They've been around a long time. Thirty years? More? They're almost charter members."

"Still, if you're testing *everybody*, I'd think . . ."

"I don't know what you think you're getting at . . ." Robbins spoke rapidly, as if he could not reject the implication quickly enough.

"Oh, don't you?"

Robbins's body tensed, but his voice stayed level. "Look . . . maybe I'm going at this the wrong way. Will you give me a chance to explain?"

Moore took a deep breath. "Okay, sure."

Robbins holstered the Magnum.

"Wilson wanted to kill you, you know, to get his hands on your big-deal secret asset. Who was still a secret then, by the way. Wilson was behind that crazy black kid in Washington. And the business on the subway platform, too."

"Son of a bitch. And now he's in Vienna."

Robbins was surprised. "How'd you . . . Oh. The phone call to the embassy. That guy ought to button his lip. Yeah, he's in Vienna."

"Why?"

Robbins snorted. "For you, believe it or not. Hawthorne wasn't handling it well enough for Wilson, and there was a lot of excitement about finding out who your Russian was and how to take him over from you. I don't know: I thought it was crazy. I was kind of coordinating things in Central Europe for Wilson; I told him he was wasting his time, but he wouldn't listen."

"You're coming up in the world."

"Yeah. You could say that."

"And Wilson's out to bottle and pickle me."

"No. That's the whole point. Not anymore. And I was the one who convinced him to go easy on you. I put myself on the line for you, Greg. I really did. I was sure that once you really understood, you'd agree with us." He shook his head. "And now Rukovoi's dead anyway, so that part doesn't matter. But we'd still like to have you with us." He paused, studying Moore, looking for some point of contact between them.

He said, "We've known each other a bunch of years now, Greg. You ought to at least hear me out. I'm telling you, you've got the wrong idea about this."

Moore sighed, nodded, closed his eyes. "Yeah. Maybe I do. . . ." He rubbed his head.

He launched himself out of the chair, propelling Robbins backward, bouncing him off the wall.

As he and Robbins came off the wall, Moore pushed

Robbins away, braced himself, and lashed out with one foot. A shout pure and savage burst from him as his toe glanced off the inside of Robbins's thigh and sank into his groin.

Robbins bent over, keening with pain, his arms folded across his stomach. All Moore could see was Joan. He felt at once icy and aflame with fury. As Robbins crumpled to the floor, Moore kicked again, wildly. His foot caught Robbins in the chest and flipped him onto his back. He lay there in a ball, whimpering.

Moore turned away. His stomach knotted. Sour fluids rose in the back of his throat. He swallowed, fought to keep from being sick.

He turned back to Robbins, who was rocking back and forth now, still whimpering. Moore came up behind him, straightened him out roughly, and pulled the guns from his belt. When Moore let go, Robbins curled up again, but not as tightly. The whimpering had stopped.

Moore ran from the apartment. On his way down the stairs, he tucked the automatic under his belt, but he kept the Magnum in his hand until he had crossed the courtyard and was out of the passageway and onto *Annagasse*.

He walked as briskly as he could without attracting attention from the flashy crowd of young people gathered outside the after-hours club next to the old church of St. Anne. The *Kärtnerstrasse* had never seemed so far away.

The broad pedestrian walkway glowed dimly with light from its angularly modern streetlamps.

Moore walked as if in a dream. His legs felt stiff and his body was awkward as he strained to move quickly while at the same time remaining part of the relaxed pedestrian traffic. He was dimly aware of a crowd a few blocks ahead, in the open area next to the ornate bulk of the State Opera House and the entrance to the *Kärtnerplatz* underground mall. He passed the Hotel Sacher: there were three cabs in the taxi rank and a dozen people under the off-white awning waiting to get into them.

Across the street, the plaza was aswarm with people, many more than could be coming from the opera. The light changed. Moore crossed the street and pushed his way through the milling crowd.

The escalators were frozen in place. A few people were on their way down; more were coming up. Moore bulled past the congestion at the head of the escalators and started down, taking the ribbed steel steps two at a time. He felt less restrained now. No one would notice that he was hurrying—running for a tram or a bus or a train was a Viennese tradition.

The underground plaza was in chaos, so packed with people that Moore could barely get off the escalator. He pushed forward, oblivious to the protests of those he shoved and elbowed, trying to get to the subway. All he could think of was the need to be as far away from Robbins as possible, to be out of the city so he would have room to run. Being held back by the crowd inflamed his impatience at first; only gradually did he become more aware of his surroundings.

No one seemed to be going anywhere. The people around him were stationary, except for small eddies of destinationless motion. The underground plaza was more like a crowded bar than the main passage to a train station.

Fifty feet from the escalator, he ran into a solid wall of people, sitting on the floor. They were all young—university students and hangers-on—and they bore a variety of placards and banners, sticking up on poles among them. It was the anti-nuclear-power group again: They made a carpet of youthful faces between Moore and the glowing overhead signs, rectangles of red and violet that marked the way to *Linie U1* and *Linie U2*.

There was no way of going any farther. Moore turned and pushed his way back to the periphery of the plaza, moved around its circumference, occasionally colliding with someone. He was disoriented now—he could no longer tell which of the stairways or motionless escalators led up to the point he wanted.

By luck, he chose the right one. He bounded up a stairway and found himself on a pedestrian island in the middle of the Ring Boulevard. He joined the long queue of people waiting at the *Strassenbahn* stop.

He looked around nervously. There was a lot of traffic, but no sign of a streetcar. He wondered what Robbins was doing. Would he call the embassy? He would have to. Then what? Was the Mercedes waiting downstairs for him by now?

Moore's eyes went to the street the car would emerge from if they were coming after him. The intersection was empty. As far as he could see down the block, there were no headlights, no cars moving. He traced the route they would follow, up the *Kärtnerring* toward the Opera House. There was a double line of cars stopped at the first light, a block away. In the far row, almost obscured by a small van, Moore spotted what looked like a familiar shape. The dark color was hard to identify in the artificial light. The van inched forward. The car it had hidden was a Mercedes, almost certainly Robbins's car.

Moore slid out of his place in the queue and put the line of waiting people between him and the Mercedes. When he got to the shelter of the news-stand, he looked up and down the Ring for a streetcar. Nothing.

At the end of a small island was a group of people crossing the Ring. Moore pushed into its center and moved with it. In his anxiety, he almost collided with a bicycle being pushed by a man of about sixty in lederhosen and knee socks.

Moore glanced apprehensively over his shoulder in the direction of the Mercedes, on the other side of the Ring. He let the bicycle move past him, and as they reached the sidewalk he came up behind the man pushing it. No one seemed to be watching. Moore curled the fingers of his right hand into his palm and swung quickly. The clublike heel of his fist struck the man behind the ear. His hat toppled off. Moore caught him as he fell and lowered him to the pavement, catching the bicycle at the last minute.

Before anyone had reacted, he was on the bike, pedaling away. He heard a shout behind him, then another. He pedaled harder, not wasting the momentum it would take to turn and see what was happening.

He had gone about two blocks along the *Kärtner-ring*, away from the Opera, when he heard the blare of automobile horns, the squeal of tires. He glanced over his shoulder. There was a jumble of cars around the island. Cars were stopped in both directions, and the Mercedes was crosswise in the broad avenue, trying to complete a U-turn. They had seen him.

Moore crouched over the handlebars and pumped the pedals as hard as he could. He felt for the brake handles, squeezed them once, lightly, to see how they worked. He looked for a way to change gears, saw only a pair of silver levers mounted on the bike's tubular frame. He took one hand off the handlebars to change to a faster gear; he had never used a ten-speed bike, and it was an awkward motion for him. The bike wobbled, thrown off balance. He grabbed desperately for the handlebar. The wobbling became a wide veering: the bike swooped left and right, taking up most of the road as he fought to get it back under control.

The street brightened. He could see his own shadow stretching out in front of him, cast by the headlights of a car.

An intersection was just ahead. *Johannesgasse.* Moore jerked the handlebars right, steering between two parked cars, and bounced over the curb onto the sidewalk. He pedaled diagonally across the corner, nicked a parked car as he jounced back onto the street, headed across *Johannesgasse*, praying that the main park gate was open.

It was closed. He turned at the last moment, barking his knee on the gate's wrought-iron uprights. Oblivious to the pain, he swung through the small parking lot behind the Kursalon. He almost missed seeing the small, open gate—it was shaded from the streetlights and only ajar by about two feet. He squeezed both brake handles and made the tightest turn he could. The bike heeled precariously, almost went over. Fending off the gate with one hand and squeezing through, Moore heard behind him the protesting scream of the Mercedes's brakes and tires as the car slammed to a halt. Then the report of a car door closing.

Moore pedaled furiously. He was on a sweeping curve that skirted the end of the Kursalon, which loomed a ghostly white at his left. The path swung around toward the band kiosk and the outdoor café.

The broad lawn beyond the band kiosk glowed faintly with moonlight. Moore could go no farther in this direction—there was no cover. He banked the bike sharply, and pedaled along the walkway that led to the statue of Johann Strauss, who stood as always, playing his violin, framed by an ornate arch of white stone.

Behind the statue, Moore squeezed the brake handles and jumped from the bike, lowering it quietly to the ground. He swung around to face the path he had left and the gate that had let him into the park, pulling the Magnum from his belt.

A figure came into view. Tall and blond, moving quickly, head turning right and left—searching. Robbins. His hands were close together in front of his chest, obscuring what he was holding.

Approaching the band kiosk, Robbins slowed and then stopped. He peered toward the Kursalon, surveying the forest of empty white tables that spread between him and the building. He turned and examined the band kiosk, moved carefully to its stairs and mounted them.

Moore watched, crouched behind the base of the statue, as Robbins used the band kiosk for a vantage point to take in the lawn and the paths that bordered it. His arms rested easily on the kiosk rail. Now Moore could see the M-11, this one with the stubby black silencer, could visualize how easily Robbins could sweep it over the lawn, spraying bullets like a garden hose.

Robbins's head turned abruptly toward the statue of Strauss. He was motionless for a moment, and then he backed away from the rail and left the kiosk.

Moore stood up. His pulse pounded in his ears, loud and regular. He could barely breathe.

Robbins came into view at the edge of the path. He was moving carefully, slightly crouched, keeping close to the hedges and trees.

Moore raised the Magnum in both hands and sighted along the barrel. The muzzle was just below Strauss's bronze violin.

Moore squeezed the trigger. Again. The gun bucked in his hands. His ears rang.

He turned and ran, forgetting the bicycle, forgetting everything but the image of Robbins jerking backward when the first bullet took him in the head, being knocked flat by the second bullet's impact with his chest.

Moore was panting when he reached the other end of the park. It was brighter: the moonlight and the streetlamps were augmented by light from the towering Hilton Hotel that straddled the end of the park.

Moore took off his jacket and brushed away the twigs and leaves he had snagged on his run from the statue. He blotted his face dry on the lining.

He picked up the Magnum and started for the hotel, then realized what he was doing. He found a spot of soft earth near a recently tended hedge, wiped the Magnum carefully on the bottom of his jacket, then pushed the gun down into the rich soil and scooped dirt on top of it.

When he stood up, the world went black. He stood where he was, breathing slowly, until his head cleared. He readjusted the automatic at the small of his back and again started toward the hotel.

14

There was an empty cab at the taxi stand in front of the Hilton. He got in. The driver studied him curiously in the rearview mirror.

"Where are you liking to go?" he asked.

Moore snapped back to reality. In his best German, he asked, "What did you say?"

"My apologies, sir," the cabby said, in German now. "Where do you wish to go?"

"Ah." Moore was not sure. "The Hofburg, please."

"Excuse me, sir, but the Hofburg is not open at night."

"Thank you. I merely wish to walk around the outer walls. It is a pleasant evening." Moore was sweating. He hoped the driver would not notice.

"Yes, it is a good night for walking," the cabby agreed. He put the car in gear and eased it away from the hotel.

Moore watched the cab until it was out of sight before he started walking. He knew, now, where he was going and why he had given the old imperial palace as a destination. It put him near the place he really wanted. The only question was, how was he going to get in?

He stood for a quarter hour in the parking lot next to the statue of a mounted emperor, watching the traffic, the pedestrians, and the immense arch-shaped doors across the road from him, with their prominent carved lions' heads. In a sense, it had all begun here, in just this way; he found it hard to believe it had only been three months since the night he sat in the Mercedes, watching these same doors, waiting for Rukovoi.

Moore left the parking lot and crossed the street. He tried the brass doorknob under the right-hand lion's head. The door was locked. The lock looked simple enough. He was no expert at picking locks, but he'd had the training. He took out his key chain, chose a long, thin piece of metal that looked like a pipe cleaner, and put it to work.

It took him longer than he expected, almost ten minutes, with two near misses, to get the lock open.

He swung the door back, stepped into the passageway, and quickly closed the door behind him. He wiped his forehead, ran his fingers through his hair, and brushed off his jacket again before he walked across the courtyard and went up the stairs.

This time, when Natalia answered the door, he forced his way in before she had a chance to recognize him and react. He slammed the door behind him and locked it.

She was livid. "Get out of my house!"

He took the automatic from under his jacket. It was not pointed at her, but it consumed all her attention.

"I have nowhere else to go," he said.

"Why did you come here?"

"I killed a man tonight."

She wrapped her arms around herself, shuddered. "Are you proud of yourself?"

"No."

"Why do you tell me?"

"I don't know, Natalia. I'm tired. I need to stop and think. There's no one else I can trust. So I came here."

After a moment, she said, "Whom did you kill?"

"A man who was about to kill me. Who I thought was my friend, once. The man who was responsible for my lover's being murdered."

"And Alex?"

"No. I don't think he killed Alex. But if I had waited another minute, I would be dead now. At Strauss's feet."

"In the *Stadtpark*?"

He nodded.

"Listen to us!" she exclaimed. "The trivia of murder. How was your day at the office? Whom did you kill today?" She laughed—high-pitched and shrill.

Moore waited for her to stop. Noticed the gun still in his hand and tucked it away.

"What do you propose to do now?" she asked him. Her voice was closer to normal.

"I learned something today from the man I killed. I can't let it go by—it's too important. I've got to learn more, and then I've got to get to the right people with it. If I can figure out who the right people are, that is, and if I can keep from getting killed in the meantime."

"Can I ask what it is?"

"It wouldn't be a good idea for you to know. It's too dangerous. It killed my friend Joan. It almost killed me. And I think that, indirectly, it's what killed Alex, too."

"But you said it wasn't the same man. . . ."

"I know. It wasn't. But I think. . . . Never mind. It's too complicated, and I'm not sure I'm right, anyway."

"You are protecting me?"

"Yes, I guess so, in a way."

"Alexander was like that. He would not talk about the intelligence part of his work, not because he did not trust me—we had straightened all that out over Gustav Biener—but because he was afraid I would be in danger if I knew more. . . . Toward the end, it was different. He talked much more. I don't know why. Except if he . . . if he had a premonition of his death, and he was telling me as much as he did in order to prevent the information he had from being lost."

Moore felt suddenly weak. He leaned against the wall.

"Are you all right?"

"I'd like to sit down for a while. Eat something, maybe."

"Of course. Come with me to the kitchen."

He sat at a wooden drop-leaf table at least a hundred years old while she put cold meat and cheese on a platter and filled a basket with slices of French bread.

She put the food on the table. "Wine? Beer?"

"Do you have any mineral water?"

"*Römerquelle*, I think."

"Please."

He took a slice of ham and some cheese and bread and discovered that he was very hungry. Natalia poured him a glass of mineral water, and sat opposite him watching him eat.

"You can't stay here," she said. "It's too dangerous. For both of us. Anyone who knows you well will think of coming here to look for you, eventually."

"You're right." He drained the glass of mineral water.

"You said it was a friend who tried to kill you?"

He was making himself a sandwich. He stopped. "In a way, yes."

"Is he the only one?"

"No."

She poured him more mineral water. "And the others? Are they your friends as well?"

"Colleagues is more like it."

She waited for him to elaborate. When he did not, she said, "I see."

He finished making the sandwich. "Is there something I can wrap this in?"

She rummaged in a large drawer, took out a waxed bakery bag. She emptied it and handed it to him.

"Thanks." He put the sandwich in it.

"Who killed Alex?"

"The KGB. Internal Security, or maybe Department V."

She absorbed the information without comment.

Standing up, Moore drank the second glass of mineral water. He stuffed the sandwich into a pocket of his jacket.

She asked, "What will the KGB do about you?"

"Kill me, I suppose."

"You are running from your friends and your enemies."

"I'm a popular guy. And you're right—if I don't get out of here, it's going to rub off on you."

He started for the door.

"One more thing," he said. "Do you have any money you can spare? I'm not in a position to do any banking for a while."

"You presume a great deal."

For a moment, the weariness was back. "It's very

simple, Natalia. If you help me, maybe I'll get to live long enough to find out who killed Alex. Maybe I can make them pay a little. If you don't help me, I'm dead."

"I'm sorry, Gregory. You understand, I have had a great deal of pain at your hands recently."

"I understand."

She hesitated, as if she was about to say more, but only turned and went for her handbag. She took out some bills.

"I don't know how much it is, but it's all I have here."

"I appreciate it."

On their way to the door, she asked, "What will you do now?"

"Find somebody to protect me from both sides while I get the information I need and try to stop what I think is happening."

He put his hands on her shoulders and kissed her cheek. "Thanks again, Natalia. And be very careful for a while, please."

He opened the door and started for the stairs.

"Gregory!"

He stopped.

"Where will you spend the night?"

He shrugged.

"Wait here a minute."

She ducked back into the apartment and returned in a few minutes. She gave him a sealed envelope with a name and address on it in an elegant hand.

"Here. You will go to the Principessa Mazzini. She is very old and frail, but she owes me many favors. She lives in an ancient house, with many basements. I have not seen them all, but she has told me there are more levels to the house underground than aboveground. The people used to hide there from the Turks. And before them, from the Romans. If you need to hide, she will let you stay there. It is not a place you should remain more than a few days: She is likely to become nervous about you. But for a short time, she is reliable."

He put the note in his jacket pocket. "Thank you."

She grimaced. "I hate it all. And I have not forgiven you for Alex. But too many have died. . . ."

––––––––

The building looked to Moore as if it had been there forever. It was set back from the street, surrounded by a high wall and a heavy iron gate. A brass plate set into the wall held a large brass button. Moore pressed it. A man in a business suit came out, took Natalia's letter, and left Moore standing outside the gate. He leaned against the wall so he could look up and down the dark street. He saw no one.

The man came back and let him in, without a word. Moore followed him into the house. The only light in the marble-floored entrance hall came from a pair of thick candles in four-foot brass candlesticks. Moore had the impression of wood all around him, ornately carved. To his left a broad staircase swept up to the next story, at least sixteen feet over the ground floor. But his attention was taken up by the woman in the wheelchair in front of him, and the tall man in white jacket and white trousers who hovered next to her.

The woman studied Moore for a long while before she spoke. She had large, watery blue eyes behind immense, thick glasses. She was covered from neck to toe by a richly patterned dress, and there were white gloves on her hands. The skin of her face was pale and infinitely wrinkled.

"I will honor the request of the Countess von

Hildebrandt," she said in an antique and precise Viennese German. Her voice was surprisingly strong. "If your need for concealment is not urgent, there is an empty servant's room you may use. Otherwise, you are welcome to what quarters you can find in the third subbasement. You will be perfectly safe there."

"Thank you. I think the servant's room will do for tonight."

He wondered if he was being foolish, but he could not face the thought of cowering in a dungeon. It was less than three hours since he had killed Robbins— the thought chilled him—and no one was likely to have followed him this far.

"It is just as well. I doubt you would find the basement pleasant." She turned to the man in white. "Ludwig, I wish to have you call Hans. He will show this gentleman to his room."

"Yes, Your Highness." He walked off down the hall.

"Hans is my majordomo," she said to Moore. "If you were to tell him that I have suggested you use room number six, he would take you there. If you have any other needs, Hans will see to them. There is no need for you to thank me. I am doing this not for you but for the Countess von Hildebrandt, whom I admire in spite of her disastrous taste in men and her penchant for inappropriate liaisons." A smile added more wrinkles to her face. "You see, young man, old as I am, I am not immune to change. I have become quite outspoken, even to strangers, precisely in the modern manner. You may tell the countess, if you see her again, that I deplore her Russian."

"Her Russian is dead, Your Highness."

"Is he? How lucky for Natalia. Good night, young

man. I would appreciate it if you were to arrive at a civil hour, the next time you come. I sleep very little, but I do not like to receive people this late."

"Yes, ma'am." Moore bowed; it seemed perfectly natural. "Thank you."

"Good night." She pressed a button on her armrest and the wheelchair hummed away down the hall.

Moments later, a door opened in the hallway and a man in a black cutaway coat and a wing collar appeared.

"I am Hans," he said. "How can I help you?"

"The principessa suggested that you show me room number six."

"Yes, sir. Follow me, please."

They went along a wood-paneled hall and then down a flight of stone steps. The corridors below ground were stone, with stone floors, illuminated by large, globular lights hanging at intervals from the ceiling. It was cold, especially in contrast to the softness of the night, but it was not uncomfortable. Moore was surprised to find that room number six had plaster walls and carpeting on the floor. Except for a vent in the top of the door, there were no openings in the walls or ceiling. In one corner there was a dehumidifier; he turned it on. The only furniture was a bed, a chair, and a small, open clothesrack. The bed was not made, but there were sheets and a blanket piled at the foot of it.

As Moore made the bed, he reflected that he was doubly glad he had not chosen the third subbasement. Even this was far too much like a dungeon for his taste. There was no danger he would ignore Natalia's warning and overstay his welcome.

In the morning, Hans brought him coffee and showed him where to find a shower and a toilet.

He was feeling stale and stiff and claustrophobic. He started the day by exercising for an hour. When he was done, he showered and shaved and went upstairs. He followed the directions Hans had given him to a small dining room overlooking a garden at the back of the house. A man in white—not the one he had seen the night before—served him coffee and rolls and asked if he wanted anything else.

"A pen and some paper."

"Yes, sir." He returned with them almost at once.

While Moore sipped his coffee and nibbled at the rolls, he made a list. He wrote the first entries quickly:

> England
> France
> West Germany
> Sweden
> Switzerland

Then, after some deliberation:

> China

And:

> South Africa
> Israel
> Egypt

He stared at the list for several minutes, and then he began to cross out names, starting with China, then Egypt and Israel, then England, then West Germany. That left France, Sweden, Switzerland, and South Africa. He crossed out Switzerland. Then he crossed out South Africa and wrote Israel again.

He ran the pen back and forth over the whole page and crumpled it up. On the second sheet, he wrote

France

and next to it

Leclerq

The last time he had worked alone for J. P. Briggs, Moore had been at the border of Germany and Alsace. American and French interests had been different enough to make the *Deuxième Bureau* more an adversary than an ally, and Renée Louis Leclerq had given Moore his share of trouble and more. The two men had developed a grudging professional respect for each other; Moore was sure Leclerq would remember him and hear him out before reporting the contact to his superiors.

He finished his coffee. The man in white, who had been standing in a corner so unobtrusively that Moore had not been aware of him, refilled the cup. Moore buttered a roll, and wrote

Cable Peter Harris (call?)

He underlined the notations, folded the sheet of paper in half, and put it in his jacket pocket. He finished his second cup of coffee and his roll and asked the man in white how he could find the front door.

"A minute, please," the man said, and hurried off. He returned with Hans.

"Are you leaving, sir?" the majordomo asked.

"Yes."

"Will you be returning tonight?"

"I don't know, Hans. I doubt it."

"Yes, sir." He reached into the inside pocket of his morning coat and handed Moore an envelope.

"The principessa instructed me to give you this when you left. It is at the request of the Countess von Hildebrandt. The principessa also instructed me to say that you were not to concern yourself about this. It is a matter between the principessa and the countess."

"Whatever you say, Hans. Thank you."

"I will show you the door," Hans said, and left the room. Moore followed; he had the impression that Hans did not approve of him.

Outside, Moore looked into the envelope. It was money: one-thousand-schilling notes. There were a dozen of them.

At night it had not bothered him to be in the old Russian sector, but now, in the daylight, he found himself looking over his shoulder as if he were in imminent danger of being recognized and attacked by one of the Russians who lived here, in the property their countrymen had so capitalistically accumulated in the forties and fifties.

Once he had decided that the French were the ones who were the most likely to be able to help him and to protect him, among the few he could turn to without feeling like a traitor, his plans had become much clearer. He simply had to walk into the French Embassy and, with a moderate amount of discretion, let the right people know why he was there. He was sure that once he mentioned Leclerq they would not send him away without hearing him out. Nor would they turn him over to the Americans, as some other allies might. In fact, the likelihood was that they would be overjoyed to have him.

Nevertheless, as he approached the French Embassy, Moore became steadily tenser and almost unbearably alert—aware of every sound and motion around him. It was an oppressive day, hot for the season and very humid, a foretaste of the summer.

Two blocks from the embassy, Moore stopped dead. Across the street from him, among the cars parked diagonally to the curb, was a dark green Mercedes, about ten years old.

He looked up and down the street, saw a woman wheeling a baby in a stroller and another woman, much older, carrying a shopping bag. He crossed to the Mercedes. It was the same car; he was sure of it.

He turned around and walked back the way he had come. As he walked, he visualized Wilson and Hawthorne and several faceless others meeting in Hawthorne's office at the embassy, speculating about where Gregory Moore might turn up next. They would have called Langley to get someone to go through his file. He remembered belatedly that he had made no secret of his hope that the relationship with Leclerq might prove useful. It was all there in his final report on the Alsatian assignment, and he had even filed a separate memo on it.

That left him with the second of his alternatives—to try to reach Peter Harris, who might already be on his way to Vienna. Which meant the telephone was the best way to get him, if he could be reached at all.

Moore remembered seeing a phone booth on his way from the principessa's, but he did not remember where, and when he tried to retrace his route, he found he could not.

He stopped on a street corner, uncertain where he was, unsure of which way to go. He was lost. He had not felt that way since he was a child and had been separated from his parents while they were all sight-seeing in Chicago. But here he would find no police-man to give him sympathy, an ice cream cone, and eventually a ride to his hotel.

He stood on the corner, frozen. It was minutes before he had himself well enough under control to start moving again. He knew he could not be too far from the Ring. The sky was overcast, but not so badly that he could not guess at the position of the sun. He turned his back to it and started walking.

Before he reached the Ring, he saw an empty cab. He flagged it and got in.

"*Postgasse*," he told the driver.

They had not gone far when he reconsidered. If they had thought to cover the French Embassy, they would certainly be watching the post office. Or would they bother? It was old-fashioned to go to the post office these days: There were booths all over the city that could be used for foreign calls. And they had a limited number of people they could spread around Vienna looking for him. Still, it was not worth the risk. Where else could he go? The Teletronics office? Walsh was back in Frankfort, and he could probably get someone to let him use a phone. But that seemed even more dangerous than the post office.

It occurred to him that Hawthorne, or Wilson, or whoever was running the show, could solve his man-power problem by putting the police on Moore's trail as Robbins's murderer. At first, when Moore thought about it, it seemed unlikely: the Austrians would not take kindly to the idea of American spies shooting at each other in a public park. But he saw that there was another way for Wilson to handle it. He could go to someone in Austrian counterintelligence—Gustav Biener, probably—and, being properly embarrassed and apologetic about it, explain that there was a renegade American agent on the loose, one who had already killed both an American and a Russian. It was neat, and it would probably work. The police could be kept out of it and Wilson might even be able to arrange for the Austrians simply to hand him over if they found him.

"Driver," Moore said, "I've changed my mind." He gave a street number that was a few blocks from the Mazzini palace. He needed to sit still and think, somewhere that was off the streets and out of the public eye. Hans would not be happy to see him, but he was reasonably sure the principessa would take him in for one more day, or a few hours.

He paid the driver and started to walk. At the corner before the palace, a man got out of a parked car; he was large and square and he wore a suit of a dull blue-gray cloth that Moore was sure was only woven in Soviet-Bloc countries.

Moore turned sharply to walk back the other way and almost ran into another man, short and slender and as nondescript as anyone Moore had ever seen.

"Please. Mr. Moore," the short man said in English with a heavy Russian accent. "We do not wish to hurt you. We wish only to talk to you." He was pointing a small, silenced gun at Moore.

Before he could decide whether to believe the little Russian or to sell his life dearly on the spot, the bigger man reached around from behind him and pinned his arms to his sides.

The short man slipped the gun into his pocket and

took out a hypodermic syringe. He circled to Moore's side, out of kicking range, and plunged the needle into Moore's shoulder. It put him to sleep almost at once.

———

Moore woke up slowly. He was lying on a lumpy couch in a large, almost empty room. On one gray wall was a huge portrait of Lenin. Moore had the feeling the sharp-eyed, sharp-bearded Bolshevik was staring at him. He wondered vaguely what had been in the syringe and whether it had all worn off yet. He turned his head and a small construction crew began to drill in the back of his skull. He closed his eyes and fell asleep.

He woke up. He was still in the gray room and Lenin was still staring at him. This time, he could turn his head without waking up the construction crew.

He sat up slowly. There was some pounding in his head, but it did not last. His mouth was dry. He looked around the room and saw that he was not alone.

In one corner there was a massive old desk. Sitting at the desk was a man in a gray suit and a darker gray shirt. He had pale skin and a sharp face set off by dark hair and eyebrows. From what Moore could see of him, he was cadaverously thin.

"Hello, Mr. Moore," he said. "I am General Gherman Nevelsky."

15

Moore tried to measure his own mental condition. He had no yardstick: He felt groggy, but otherwise he thought his mind was working well enough—assuming that Nevelsky was not an hallucination.

Nevelsky picked up a phone, said a few words of Russian, and hung up. The door opened and a woman came in. She was about Moore's height, and he guessed she outweighed him by twenty pounds. There was a long braid of blonde hair wrapped around her head like a crown, and her cheeks were rosy in a way that spoke of vigorous exercise.

Behind her was another woman, shorter and older, carrying a stenotype machine. They pulled two wooden chairs up next to the desk and sat down. The blonde, sitting next to Nevelsky, conferred with him in whispered Russian while the other woman set up her machine.

Watching them, Moore wondered why he was taking it all so calmly. Maybe his mind wasn't working so well, after all. Even that thought was not enough to produce more than a mild stab of apprehension. So he was sure: Thanks to the miracles of the Soviet pharmaceutical collective, he was about to be named Mr. Congeniality. It made him want to giggle, but he suppressed the urge.

"Mr. Moore," the blonde said, "my name is Olga,

and I am General Nevelsky's interpreter." Her voice was low and even, with only the faintest trace of an accent. Like the rest of her, Moore thought—pleasant.

"I will explain to you our methods. General Nevelsky prefers to have me speak English for him. While we speak Anna will take down what we say. It will be carefully transcribed and translated. Anna is an excellent recorder." The two women smiled at each other. "She will make no mistakes. When I ask you questions, you may give your answer by speaking to me or to General Nevelsky. This depends on your comfort. By our experience from the past, it will be easier for you if you pretend that this is a conversation between you and me. Do you understand?"

"Yes." He was struck by how smooth she was. Just pretend you're having a conversation with me. Between that and the happy drug, things could probably get very friendly and . . . pleasant.

"Do you have any questions?"

"One."

"Yes? Go ahead, please."

"How did I get here?"

Nevelsky leaned forward in his seat; his head was next to hers. Moore could barely tell that he was speaking.

"We learned of your whereabouts from the Countess von Hildebrandt," Olga said. "Two of our employees visited with her, and they discovered she had been badly abused by members of your organization. She said they had threatened to kill her. For her own protection, she agreed to come here."

Through the drug, Moore could glimpse the truth that was likely to lie behind that story. It Natalia was here for her own protection, she had come to protect herself from what the Russians would have done to her if she had not come. As for her being threatened and abused by Wilson or his people, Moore saw no reason to doubt it.

"And she told you about me?" He addressed the question to Nevelsky, who whispered again to Olga.

"She told us that your life was in danger. Here, you are both safe."

Step right up and take a ride on the tiger, Moore thought. What I need now is a bent nail to grind into my palm or some other reminder of reality. But it all seemed like a game to him.

He seized on the thought. A game. Let's make it a game. Heads you win, tails I lose. No, that's wrong. But maybe . . .

"Mr. Moore?" It was Olga.

"Yes?"

"Have I answered your question?"

"Yes, I think so. I'd like to see the countess, if I could."

A hesitation. "Of course. She is resting now. And we have questions for you to answer. I am sure you will be able to see her. Later tonight, or tomorrow."

At the word "tonight," Moore looked around the room and realized how dark it was. Dusk was slipping over the city.

"So," Olga said. "Shall we go ahead now?"

"Please."

There was a long silence. Moore was vaguely aware that Olga was listening to Nevelsky.

"Have you know the countess long?"

"A few years." It was not the kind of question he had expected. A point for them.

"You know her well?"

"Who knows another person well?"

"I'm sorry? . . . Oh, yes, I understand. But that is not what I meant to ask you. Let me say—have you been close with the countess?"

"Have been. Yes. Have been."

"Yes. Mr. Moore, it would be easier for everyone if you did not play word games."

"Word games? Sorry. Didn't meant to. Just answering questions." He allowed himself a smile. "Okay?"

"Good. I'm sure it will be much better, now. Did you know of the countess's relationship with Alexander Rukovoi?"

"Oh, sure. Great couple."

"Did you use it as a way to get information from Rukovoi?"

"No. The countess and I haven't been close for a while, you know. We're just friends. I wouldn't . . . Oh, no. And she wouldn't do that."

"Why do you say that?"

"That's a very loyal lady."

"Loyal?"

"Of course. You think she'd talk about her lover like that? Never."

"I see." She conferred briefly with Nevelsky. For a moment, the steno machine was silent.

"But you did get information from Alexander Rukovoi?"

"Well, yes, sure."

"What kind of information?"

"Very little. I gave him as much as I got."

"Why was that?"

"That was our arrangement. I was supposed to give him information."

"And he was supposed to give you information?"

"He had to, or else I couldn't give him any." Moore shifted on the couch. It was very uncomfortable. It made him think again of having a bent nail to help him keep in touch with reality.

"Didn't you make up a story about defecting? Excuse me. There was a story that you would defect from the CIA and give information to Rukovoi. That was a false story, isn't it so?"

"There were a lot of false stories."

"That one is the one I am asking about."

"In a way it was false, in a way it wasn't. Why do you think my boys are after me the way they are?"

"I will ask the questions, Mr. Moore." There was the slightest edge to her voice.

A point for our side, Moore thought. He said, "Go right ahead. Ask away."

"You said the story was false, in a way. How was it false?"

"Well, I couldn't defect outright, not right away, or how could I learn anything to tell Alex?" He waved a hand. "Wait, wait. I'm sorry. Didn't mean to ask a question."

"That's all right. Now, tell me: How was your story false?"

"I told you."

"Let me ask in other words. Alexander Rukovoi reported that you would remain in your job at the CIA so that you could give him information. Is that true?"

"Yes."

"You would give him true information?"

"Yes."

"Why?"

"It was good for him. It would make him a big shot."

"And that was your only reason, to make him a big shot?"

"Who said that?"

"You did."

"No, I didn't."

Olga sighed. Moore heard frustration in the sound.

"*Was* it your only reason?"

"Yes," he admitted. He had to bite his tongue to keep from saying more.

Nevelsky whispered in Olga's ear.

"You did not intend to be an agent for Rukovoi, then?" she asked.

"Well . . ."

"He was to work for you, and the rest was a ruse to fool his superiors. Is that how it was?"

"Yes."

"You did not intend to defect, then?"

"No. Not then."

"Not then?"

"Things have changed." *Did it!* he thought. *That wasn't so hard.*

"Explain, please."

"I'm not so popular with the CIA these days. I don't get on too well with the people I work with, or maybe I should say the people I used to work with."

"Yes. You killed one of them, didn't you?"

They got that from Natalia, he thought. They must have really got to her. Can't blame her, though—this is some powerful stuff they shoot you up with.

"Gregory?"

"Sorry. I was drifting. It's nice to be able to relax."

"Yes. Real friends make you feel good. Is there anything we can get for you? Some food?"

"How about some vodka? I'll bet you have terrific vodka."

"It is better to wait for vodka. After we have finished talking will be a better time."

Bad interaction between alcohol and drug, Moore noted, inordinately pleased with himself for having picked up some information.

"Whom did you kill?" Olga asked him.

"Jordie Robbins." That was an easy one, probably a test. He was sure they knew.

"Why?"

"He was about to shoot me."

"Why?"

"Because I was . . . disloyal."

"Were you really disloyal?"

"Jordie sure thought so. So did Wilson, for that matter."

Nevelsky leaned forward again. Moore had noticed that the gaunt general had been participating only occasionally in the questioning. The woman had to be very good and very well rehearsed for him to give her her head that way. It occurred to Moore that she had to be more than just an interpreter. That business about real friends, for instance, and offering him food. . . .

"Who is Wilson?" she asked.

"Come on, you've got to know Wilson. He's a big deal at Langley. Collins's right-hand man. Hatchet man, too. Don't tell me you don't know him."

She let it drop. "If you were not going to defect, why did they think you were disloyal?"

"We had some disagreements on policy. Violent disagreements. It looked like I was coming out on the bad end of it. I was washed up there."

"Washed up? What is washed up?"

"Finished. *Kaput*."

"Is that why you decided to defect?"

"You could say that."

"When did you decide?"

"It's hard to say. I didn't really decide. People started to shoot at me."

"I see." She spoke with Nevelsky for a minute. "Gregory, we understand there is to be a reorganization of the Central Intelligence Agency. Have you heard about it?"

"A little. It was one of the things I got in trouble about."

"Can you tell me, please, what you know about this reorganization?"

"Sure. They're going to break up the Agency into a lot of pieces and put most of the pieces under the control of other organizations."

"What sort of . . . pieces . . . will there be?"

"It's too early to tell, exactly, until the Congress moves on it."

"Can you tell me how you think it will be done?"

"Yes. I suppose."

"Please do. I would be very interested."

Moore shifted on the couch again. He stamped his foot on the floor.

"Gregory? What is it?"

"Foot's asleep."

"I'm sorry. I do not understand."

"Foot's asleep. You know. Pins and needles. Numb."

"If you would tell us more about the reorganization of the CIA, we could allow your whole body to be asleep."

He laughed. He couldn't help it.

"Gregory!" she said sharply, like a schoolteacher.

"I'm sorry. I didn't mean to." His childlike feeling of contrition was real. More than anything else so far, it horrified him.

"Tell me about the CIA now, Gregory."

"Yes, ma'am." God, how suggestible can you get? "Please, would somebody turn a light on? It's awfully dark in here."

There was the click of a switch and two lights came on. The brighter one, hanging from the ceiling over Moore's head, cast a circle of light on the couch. He had a clear view of himself and the threadbare red satin upholstery and the worn Oriental rug. The other lamp stood on the floor across the room and threw most of its light on the stenographer. Enough of a glow reached Olga to make her look appealing in an earthmother sort of way. Nevelsky, beside and behind her, was lost in shadow.

"You were going to tell me about the CIA, Gregory," Olga reminded him. Her voice was softer, more intimate.

"I really don't know much."

"Try. For me."

"All right. They say there's going to be a new department of national analyses. They'll work out of the State Department, with a desk for each country." Even under the lulling influence of the drug, he felt a tickle of apprehension; his mind was not clear enough for him to weigh the importance of the information he was giving Nevelsky. He told himself it was trivial and part of the game he was playing, but he was not sure if that was true or simply a drug-induced rationalization.

"There'll be a satellite data analysis department," he went on, sensing Olga's annoyance at his pause. "The Air Force wants that one, but I think they're going to end up independent. A foreign nationals department, for interviewing people, I suppose. It's a long list. Maybe it would be easier if I wrote it down for you sometime."

She smiled encouragingly. "That's a good idea. Tell me, Gregory, why did you decide to defect?"

"You asked me that."

"I know. But I want you to tell me again."

"I didn't like what was going on."

"But it was after you started to work with Alexander Rukovoi."

"I haven't liked what was going on for years."

"You haven't answered the question."

"I'm getting tired. I thought I answered the question before."

There was a pause. He heard the buzz of Nevelsky's voice.

"We are going to stop now, Gregory," Olga said. "It has been a hard day for you. You must sleep if you are tired. I am going to send in a nurse who will take you to a more comfortable room where you can be by yourself. She will give you something to help you sleep. We can talk again tomorrow."

A woman in a nurse's uniform led him to a cubicle that contained a narrow iron-frame bed and no other furniture. A white hospital smock hung over the bedframe. The woman motioned to indicate that he should put on the smock, and left. He sat on the edge of the bed. He was enjoying his little game, when he could keep his mind on it. It bothered him vaguely that he was not concentrating as well as he wanted to.

The woman came back, carrying a steel tray that

held a hypodermic syringe. She saw him sitting on the bed and shouted at him in Russian. She pulled on his arm. He sat where he was, not resisting, but not cooperating. She let go of him, snatched up the smock, and threw it at him, yelling again. He smiled and started to put the smock on over his shirt. She shouted once more and ran from the room.

When she returned she had with her the big man in the blue suit who had been half of the team that first picked Moore up. He grabbed Moore under the arms and lifted him to his feet.

Moore cheerfully let himself be undressed, doing nothing to help. During the process of getting Moore's clothes off him and the smock on, the big man lost his patience and began to throw Moore around. It hurt, but it made Moore happy. It was a major victory.

Once he was in bed, the woman gave him his shot. The big man stood by to make sure there was no more trouble.

As he was falling asleep, Moore wondered quite calmly how badly the drug would damage his brain.

The next morning, they were back in the broad gray room again. It was no cheerier and not much brighter in the morning than it had been at dusk. Moore fixed his eyes firmly on the portrait of Lenin and tried to remember the rules of his game.

Olga asked about his health and whether he had slept well, then got to the point: "Today, I would like to talk about the CIA's agents in the Department of State Security or in any other intelligence agency in the Soviet Union. Do you know of such agents?"

"Penkovsky."

"No. No." She smiled, but Moore thought she was already annoyed. "I do not mean so many years ago. Do you know of any others, more recently?"

"Nosenko. Shadrin."

"Not defectors of that sort. I am talking of agents who are working in the Soviet Union now, and reporting to the CIA."

"I don't know any. They say we can't do it."

This resulted in a long conference between Olga and Nevelsky. Moore passed the time by making faces at the stenographer. It was something he had not done since grade school. It was great fun, and it made her visibly uncomfortable.

"What are you doing?" Olga said in her schoolteacher voice.

He grinned. "Playing with Anna." In spite of his pleasure, there was a petulant defensiveness in his response to the challenge. He suspected that they had given him a stronger dose of the drug than they had the night before.

"This is not the time to play. We have more to talk about."

"Okay."

"Tell us what you know about Soviet agents in the CIA."

"I don't know much about that. I never met one, that I know about." He brightened. "But I was going to be one, sort of."

Nevelsky leaned forward and whispered urgently in Olga's ear. She said, "Yes, that is what you told us yesterday. But you were going to get information from Alexander Rukovoi that way, weren't you?"

"We were going to trade."

"But you were giving him false information."

"Sometimes."

Nevelsky leaned forward again. "Only sometimes?"

"Yes."

"Why would you tell him the truth?"

Grinning: "I'm a defector."

"Why would you tell him the truth?"

Petulant: "I told you. I'm a defector."

"But you were going to get information from him. You just said that." She sounded angry. He could not tell if it was real or a device.

"Yes."

"That is not the act of a defector."

"Well, I couldn't let my superiors know what I was doing, so I had to pretend."

"Stop it, Gregory! Stop lying. It is not good to lie to your friends."

"I'm sorry. I'm sorry. I wasn't lying, really." He had to fight to hold back the tears. He felt as if his mind were being ripped into two halves, one that was participating in the conversation—a compliant eight year old—and another that was just watching, sometimes horrified, sometimes uncaring, sometimes enjoying itself tremendously.

"You were getting information from Alexander Rukovoi," Olga said. "Tell me the truth."

"Yes."

"But a few minutes ago you said you did not know any agents for the Americans in Soviet intelligence."

"You said, now."

"Yes."

"Rukovoi is dead, now."

Nevelsky spoke. This time Moore heard the words clearly. Nevelsky had had enough.

"You have made General Nevelsky angry," Olga said.

"I'm sorry."

"Why are you acting this way?"

"It's a game."

Nevelsky stood up, furious, leaning over the desk toward Moore. "No! Is not game! *Eta ochin seryozny.* Is very serious."

Moore laughed. Victory.

Nevelsky came around the desk. Olga trailed after him, talking to him urgently. He stopped. "*Nyet!*" he told her forcefully. He walked over to Moore.

From close, Nevelsky looked even thinner. Childhood images flashed through Moore's mind: Plastic man, stretched very thin; Jack and the Beanstalk, with a human beanstalk; Jack Sprat. But there was something overridingly sinister about Nevelsky that canceled those images.

Olga stood next to him. She, too, looked different from close up. Not as warm, but considerably more intelligent.

Nevelsky spoke in rapid Russian, clearly intended for Moore. Olga looked at the KGB man sharply, a silent rebuke which he did not see.

She said, "General Nevelsky is saying if you do not cooperate in our conversation, there are other ways for us to learn from you what we wish to know."

Moore nodded. "Good. That's fine."

"*Shtaw?*" Nevelsky asked, unbelieving. "What?"

"It's okay with me."

Nevelsky stared at him.

"Do you know what you are saying, Gregory?" Olga asked.

"All I know is whatever you've got me on, I don't like it. Maybe we can come to an understanding, but not this way."

"I think you are making a mistake," she chided.

"I told you, I'll take my chances. I don't like feeling this way."

"There are worse things."

Suddenly Moore was afraid. He told himself it was the drug talking—he was suggestible and Olga had been offering scary suggestions. But whatever the reason for it, the fact remained that he was afraid. He had just enough control to know that he could not afford to reveal it.

"Enough," Nevelsky said. He spoke briefly to Olga and stalked from the room.

"You have your wish," she said. "You will be taken back to your room. You will stay there all of today. Food will be brought. Tomorrow you will have physical activity. Tomorrow night, perhaps you will be given the vodka you asked for. After that, the next day, General Nevelsky will speak to you again. I may be there, or there may be another interpreter."

"What about Natalia?" he asked. "The countess? You said I could see her."

She shook her head. "Another day." She seemed perplexed that he could have believed her.

When they locked him in his room, he sat on the bed, struggling to keep himself oriented. Physical activity tomorrow, Olga had said. Maybe some motion would help flush the drug from his system. There was enough room between the bed and the wall for him to do sit-ups and push-ups. He got down on the floor and started. His heart began to pound wildly. He got up carefully and walked back and forth next to the bed, breathing deeply, afraid to lie down too abruptly and afraid to make things worse by continued exertion.

Finally his heart calmed down. He sat on the bed again.

His mind kept slipping off into a dopey euphoria. After a while he stopped fighting it.

Two days later, he was in the gray room again, feeling much stronger and more clear-headed. He was sitting on the lumpy red couch. Nevelsky was standing at a long cabinet across the room, pouring himself a drink. Olga had been replaced by a man. He was no more than twenty-five, Moore guessed, with fair skin and blond hair and a large, irregular strawberry birthmark on his neck and cheek. He was sitting in a wooden chair next to the old desk, the same chair that Olga had used. There was no stenographer in the room.

Nevelsky closed the liquor cabinet and turned to Moore. *"Ne mozhno eegrats,"* he said sternly.

"You must not to play games," the blond translated.

Nevelsky went on in Russian, speaking for the interpreter's benefit, but watching Moore. The interpreter began to translate after Nevelsky's fifth or sixth word.

"We know there is a purge going on at the CIA. We have some information about what is happening, but we would like to have more. If you will help us, we will be grateful. There is nothing for you to go back to. You will be dead . . . excuse me, you would be dead now, if we did not save your life by bringing you here. The CIA is searching for you in all of Vienna. They have the assistance of the Austrian intelligence service. If you help us, we will be your friends. Do not help us and you will be . . . finished."

Nevelsky's eyes burned into Moore's. *"Pahneemayete lee vwee?* You are understanding?" It was more a threat than a question.

"I understand some of it. You'll have to be more

specific, though. I need to know exactly what you want. Some things I can do for you, some things I can't. And you'll have to tell me what's in it for me."

Nevelsky reacted with a mixture of anger and incredulity. He barked something at the interpreter.

"General Nevelsky says you must not to bargain with him. You are in his power, here. He will tell you what he wants, and you will do it."

Moore leaned back on the couch and studied Nevelsky. "That's wrong, General, and you know it. You can treat me like an enemy or a prisoner of war. You can drug me to the eyeballs or hang me by my thumbs or wire a dynamo to my tender parts. But whatever you get will be a struggle for you, and you won't be sure how much of it is true. Even if it's all true, you won't get any more than I know right now, and I certainly won't be any use to you for any other purpose, like disinformation, for instance. Or, instead of that, you can try a little harder to convince me I'm doomed without you, and we can dicker for a while, and in the end you'll have hired yourself an agent, if we can figure out a way to keep me alive in Washington. And I think we can."

Nevelsky said nothing.

"Well, General, the ball's in your court. Your choice. If you want to start with the bamboo slivers, let's get to it."

Still Nevelsky said nothing. He drank from the glass he was holding. The drink was a clear liquid—a small mineral water, Moore thought, or a very large vodka.

Nevelsky began to speak.

The interpreter said, "You must not think you are clever. If I . . . if the general agrees with what you are saying, he will watch you carefully. He will know always where you are and what you are doing. If you betray him you will be killed, or you will be brought to dungeon . . . to a dungeon the same as the one you describe."

"All right," Moore said. "That's understood. But I'm a lot more valuable to you out where I can learn something than I am if you chain me to the wall."

Nevelsky drank again. He drummed his long fingers on the glass; his eyes were on Moore, but his ax-blade face wore an abstracted look. Abruptly, he crossed to the desk, picked up a phone, and spoke a few words.

A man in uniform came into the office, pulling a gun from a stiff holster.

Nevelsky spoke to him and to Moore.

"Go to your room," the interpreter said.

The uniformed man waved the gun at Moore for emphasis. He followed Moore into the hall, the gun trained on his back.

An hour later, Moore was back in the gray room. Nevelsky began at once to ask questions about the way the Agency was organized.

"Wait a minute," Moore objected. "We're not up to this, yet. I still don't know what's in it for me."

"*Zhizn*," Nevelsky said. "Life."

"Not enough," Moore said, frightened by his own audacity.

"What want you?" Nevelsky asked.

"First of all, I'll need protection. And money. And I want Natalia von Hildebrandt."

"*Nyet.*"

Moore folded his arms across his chest. He could feel his heart beating.

"Money, *nyet*," Nevelsky said. "Countess, *nyet.*"

"How the hell do you expect me to get to Washington without money? Or to do anything once I'm there?" He waited for a response. When there was none, he went on. It was an effort for him to keep his voice level and strong. "And what good is Natalia to you? She can't know anything of value, not beyond what she must have told you already."

Nevelsky spoke to the interpreter, who was again sitting in the wooden chair, erect and motionless. He translated: "She is valuable to our enemies. We do not wish her to be able to speak to them."

"How much damage could she do? Besides, she's a very discreet lady."

Nevelsky's lip curled with contempt as he spoke. The interpreter said, "She is discreet at dinner parties. She spoke freely here."

Moore's hopes sank. He was committed to following through with his challenge to Nevelsky, but it was beginning to look like a bad gamble.

Nevelsky was studying him again. He stared back, trying for a mixture of confidence and defiance.

Nevelsky said something. The interpreter was silent. Nevelsky turned to him and spoke again, more sharply. The interpreter blushed, said something in Russian to Nevelsky, then spoke to Moore. "My apologies. I did not hear the general. He wishes to know—is this woman . . . she is important to you?"

"Yes. She is very important."

"You will have responsibility for her?"

"Will I what? Oh, sure. I'll take responsibility for her."

"On your life?" Nevelsky asked.

"Yes."

Nevelsky nodded, spoke rapidly to the interpreter.

"The general says that he will discuss the woman

with you later. First, he says, you must answer his questions. If he is satisfied with what you say, perhaps he will . . . he will arrange some plans for you. First, you must answer his questions. He repeats this."

Moore had hoped for better, but he sensed that it was time to say yes.

For hours he sat on the couch and answered questions. He tried to hold himself to public information. He tried to slant his answers away from sensitive areas without seeming evasive. It was not always possible. Nevelsky was sharp, and he knew what he wanted. Moore assumed that everything he was saying was going down on tape, to be translated and minutely analyzed. He hoped he was buying something with it.

Finally, Nevelsky stopped asking questions. He walked over to the couch.

After a long moment, he said, "You are standing now."

Moore stood. Without fuss or preamble, Nevelsky made a fist and hit him in the groin. He doubled over, clutching himself.

"You are *standing!*"

Dimly, Moore understood. He pressed his hands against his thighs and levered himself upright. The effort and the pain brought out beads of sweat on his forehead.

Nevelsky hit him again, in the same place. The pain was tremendous. He fell over sideways onto the couch.

"Standing!" Nevelsky shouted.

Moore wanted to retch. Laboriously, he pushed himself off the couch and tottered to his feet. *Not again*, he prayed silently.

Nevelsky hit him again. He crumpled. Nevelsky left him lying on the floor.

Much later, the woman in the nurse's uniform came and helped him to his room and put him to bed.

———

The next day, after he had showered and been given a heavy breakfast, they gave him a new suit and led him again to the gray room.

Nevelsky was there, alone.

"You go to Washington now," he said. "We give you instructions. Follow instructions, you have life. Not follow, you are dying. *Pahneemayete?*"

"I understand."

Nevelsky did not move. His head was cocked to one side, his cold eyes fixed on Moore, weighing, assessing.

Without a word Nevelsky turned and left the room.

Moore waited. The portrait of Lenin made him uneasy. He went to the cabinet along the wall to see if he could open it. Early as it was, it seemed like a good time for a drink. The cabinet was locked.

The door opened behind him. He whirled. Froze.

Natalia was standing in the doorway.

Her hair was limp and dull and she wore no makeup. Under one eye was a broad multicolored swelling. A drab print dress, the product of some People's Clothing Factory, hung awkwardly on her.

"Gregory?" Her voice was weak, uncertain.

He went to her and put his arms around her. Her body, leaning against his, felt frail and vulnerable.

"Are you all right?"

"I don't know," she said.

He patted her head. "It's going to be okay. You'll get some rest, some food, some new clothes. You'll feel a lot better, you'll see."

"But . . ."

"I know. I know. Don't worry about a thing. There'll be time for explanations later."

He held her at arm's length and looked at her. She seemed totally bewildered. He kissed her cheek. "For now, you just leave everything to me."

"All right," she said docilely. "I'll do what you say."

He took her in his arms again. "Good," he said. It was hard for him to speak. "That's good."

In the embassy garage, they were put in the back seat of an Audi sedan with Swiss license plates. The young interpreter handed Moore two thick envelopes.

"Here are passports and tickets for you to travel. Also, money. You must to buy clothing and a suitcase. This car will take you to Geneva. Aeroplane goes to London from Geneva. In London, you will stay three days. A man will come to you there. He will have instructions and money. Your driver knows nothing. You must not to ask him questions."

He slammed the car door and waved as they pulled away.

16

Natalia slept in the car, slumped over with her head against the window and one arm bent under her awkwardly. Moore sat looking out his own window at the Austrian countryside. He felt neither tired nor drugged, but he did not have the energy to focus on what was coming. The problems ahead were too far away for him even to guess their shapes. He was content to be hypnotized by the passing stripe of highway, the cars flashing by, trees, mountains, sky.

He drifted into a kind of half-world, neither dream nor reminiscence, his thoughts directed by the rhythms of the car and the passing scenery and by the heat and shape of Natalia's body on the seat next to him.

They had first met not in Vienna but in Prague. Moore had been acting as contact man for the CIA in an exchange of information with Austrian intelligence, and Gustav Biener had been assigned on the Austrian side. Biener had not wanted the exchange to take place in Vienna. His reasons, Moore learned later, had more to do with avoiding his wife than with security. Moore had agreed on Gstaad; he had been surprised to find that Biener's advance man was an elegant Viennese countess.

After Natalia had identified herself, she and Moore had spent two delightful days together on the slopes, until Biener himself arrived. Then Moore's time was consumed by work, and Natalia's by Biener, so they had seen little of each other. But she had stayed in Moore's mind, and as soon as he had been able to put a few days together he had called her and invited her to join him at St. Moritz.

It had been idyllic. Even at a distance of almost four years, the snatches of it that came back to him were clear and vivid. That the flame had not burned more than a few months had hurt and bewildered him at the time, but now it seemed reasonable. The difference in their ages had seemed first a challenge and then a kick, but it had gone poorly with the differences in their backgrounds. He had felt very adult—seasoned but not yet at the peak of his powers—but in retrospect he could see how childish he must have seemed to her at times. When she had finally run out of patience, he had taken it badly; later he came to see that it had been inevitable, and not due to her unreasonableness. It seemed possible that if he had been a little older, or more experienced, things might have worked out differently, but that was not a kind of speculation he indulged in. What had happened, had happened. The only thing he could influence was the future.

Natalia stirred beside him. Her face was puffy. She rubbed her arm where she had been lying on it.

"Where are we?"

"Somewhere between Linz and Salzburg."

"Was I asleep long?"

"A couple of hours."

She looked at the driver, then out the window, then at Moore. "I feel lost."

"How's your head?"

"Outside, it hurts. I must have hit it on the window

while I was sleeping. Inside . . . my mind is wrapped in cotton wool."

They sat in silence. She brushed at herself, squirmed so she could straighten her dress. "That awful young man was right. We must go shopping in Geneva."

He wanted to ask her how they had treated her, but he was reluctant to disturb the quiet mood, and there was the driver to think of.

"We'll shop all day," he agreed. "One store after another."

"When do you think we will get there?"

"Tonight sometime, if we don't stop."

"Do you think the driver can tell us?"

"You must not to ask him questions," Moore quoted.

"Yes. I had forgotten."

It was very late when the driver pulled into the yard of a farmhouse in southwestern Switzerland.

A stout, gray-haired woman came to the door and ushered them in and upstairs to a large bedroom with twin beds and down comforters. The mountain light was clear and crisp; Moore was grateful to have the soft cover to insulate him. He slept soundly until the stout woman woke him and told him, in barely intelligible Swiss German, that there was coffee downstairs and a shower at the end of the hall. Natalia's bed was empty. The stout woman anticipated his question: Madame had already showered and was downstairs having coffee.

———

The driver took them into the heart of Geneva and pulled over to the curb. He got out of the car and opened the rear door.

"I think he wants us to get out," Moore suggested.

"Here?"

"Looks that way. End of the line."

"Where do we go from here?"

"We have plane tickets to London, remember? For tomorrow. But it looks like we'll have to arrange our own tour of Geneva." He got out of the car and held out his hand to her. "Let's go. Our driver is getting impatient." He helped her from the car.

"Friendly, wasn't he?" Moore commented as the car drove away.

"Gregory, can you be serious for a minute?"

"Right now, I doubt it."

"Please."

"Sorry. I thought as long as we're in transit we ought to enjoy ourselves. While we can."

"We have to talk."

"Conceded. How about this—why don't we do some of that shopping we talked about and find ourselves a hotel, and then, after we've cleaned up and had a nice dinner, like two civilized people, we can catch up on our week and think about the next one."

"You can be a very perplexing man, Gregory."

"Keep 'em guessing, I always say."

She looked up the street, as if seeing the shops and the handsome, well-dressed Genevans for the first time. "It would be a welcome change, to feel civilized again."

"I'm afraid it's going to be our last chance for a while," he said, serious after all.

"We don't have our own passports, credit cards, nothing like that," Moore said over coffee. "And I'm not sure how smart it would be to advertise our whereabouts, anyway. So until we hear different, we have to assume this is all the money we've got. It's a question we ought to raise with whoever meets us in London."

"What do you think they will tell us to do?" She had bought a white linen dress; she wore it with a green scarf that almost matched her eyes. The softness of the candlelight hid the marks of grief and pain and fatigue on her face.

"The way I read Nevelsky," Moore said, "he's more interested in making trouble than in learning things. I suspect he wants me to go back and throw sand in everybody's eyes."

"Throw sand . . . ?"

"Make it hard for them to see. Confuse things."

"I see."

"It's consistent with the kind of questions he asked you—about where I really stood, and what Alex really thought I was up to."

She had been reserved about describing her treatment at the Soviet Embassy, but Moore knew enough about the Russians to be able to fill in most of the unpleasant details. He thought it was a testament to her strength that she had not broken down completely. And yet the information Nevelsky had pulled from her was relatively minor.

"He wasn't pressing for every last detail; unless you left a lot out of what you told me, I'd say he was just checking the general layout of things, trying to guess where there might be some bodies buried."

"I left nothing out that I know of."

"No reason why you should. We're on the same side. For the moment, anyway."

"For the moment?"

He could see that he had rocked her. He said, "I

seem to remember something about how much you hated me not so very long ago."

The pained surprise on her face was replaced by anger. "Yes. Because you killed Alexander."

"Okay. The question is, can we be allies in spite of it? We have to be able to trust each other, at least until this is over. I can't be worrying that you'll think of Alex one day and decide you hate me too much to help."

"I understand. You do not have to worry. For all the pain you have caused, I will be your ally until we have finished all of this."

———

Heathrow was clogged with travelers when they arrived the next afternoon. They waited patiently to have their money changed, in no hurry to get on to the next step.

When they had their thin packets of pound notes, they got a luggage cart for the two carry-on suitcases they had bought in Geneva and started out on a long and confusing underground journey up and down ramps, along tiled corridors, and over moving walkways, in search of the bus to the British Airways terminal at Victoria Station.

When they finally found the departure point, there was no bus. Moore took advantage of the wait to make a phone call. A woman answered.

"Hello," Moore said. "I'm trying to reach Peter Harris."

There was a silence. Even over the phone, Moore could sense the woman's discomfort.

"Who is this, please?"

"I'm a friend . . ."

"Can you tell me your name, please?"

Moore hesitated, but there was only one thing to do. "My name is Gregory Moore. Who are you?"

"I'm Peter's sister, Gwynn. I don't think I've met you, Mr. Moore."

"Probably not. I'm kind of a business acquaintance of Peter's. And I really do have to reach him. It's important. A matter of life and death, you might say."

"I don't doubt it, Mr. Moore." There was a catch in her voice. "I'm afraid you're too late, however. Peter's already dead."

He felt no surprise, only a deepening of his sense of frustration and futility. "I'm sorry. I didn't mean to . . ."

"It's quite all right."

"How long ago? How did it happen?"

"He was flying to Vienna, for a story. It was last week. He went down not far from the St. Gotthard Pass."

"He was by himself?"

"Yes. He did that frequently when he had short assignments on the Continent."

"Do you know why he crashed?"

"The Swiss authorities said the plane was out of fuel."

"He ran out of gas? Does that make sense?"

Icily: "He's never done it before."

"No. I'm sorry. Of course not. I meant . . ."

"Yes, Mr. Moore, I know what you meant. It is a thought I've had myself. If you could shed some light on that possibility—suggest a motive, for instance—I should be grateful."

He hesitated. "No. I'm sorry, I wish I could."

"In that case, Mr. Moore, you'll understand it if I say good-bye." She hung up.

Moore walked back to the bus stop. The bus was there; Natalia was aboard. He joined her.

"Was he in?" she asked.

"He's dead."

"Dead!" She looked around to see if she had been heard. There was only a scattering of passengers; none of them seemed to be paying any attention to them.

"How?"

"He was flying to Vienna in a light plane. Somebody fiddled with his fuel gauge and he crashed in the Alps."

The bus door hissed closed and the bus swung smoothly away from the curb.

They did not talk on the way into the city.

The hotel the Russians had picked for them was off the Strand, up the hill toward Drury Lane. When the clerk gave the bellman their key, he handed Moore a slim white envelope.

"A message, sir."

"Can you tell me who left it?"

"No, 'fraid not, sir. Wasn't on duty at the time, y'see."

"Do you know who was?"

"No, sir, can't say as I do."

"All right. Thanks anyway."

"Yes, sir. Glad to be of service."

They had a double room on the top floor. Two oval windows, like ornate portholes, gave views of Bush House to the east and, to the north, the steeples of the Law Courts. Moore tipped the bellman and, when he had left, opened the envelope. It contained a colorful single-page brochure of the kind that fill the racks at travel agencies. This one described the beauty and educational value of a boat trip down the Thames to Greenwich. In the margin next to the description of Greenwich Observatory, someone had penned the notation "1403." Moore assumed it was a time, not a year or a room number. He handed the brochure to Natalia and began to unpack his bag.

It was an unusually cold afternoon for late June, with a turbulent sky. The excursion boat cut through the foamy rollers that striped the dull slate water of the river.

At Greenwich, they walked up from the dock, past the old square-riggers aswarm with tourists. Signs showed the way to the National Maritime Museum and the observatory.

Halfway up the long, green hill, Natalia looked behind them.

"Gregory," she gasped. "Look."

He stopped and turned. It was remarkable. Allowing for differences of national character, they could be at Schönbrunn.

The similarity was even more striking from the top of the hill, looking down from next to the small brick observatory. The hill fell away sharply at first, then more gradually, crisscrossed by a long switchback path. And then, beyond a broad lawn, there was Greenwich Palace and the Queen's House. The vista was muted and pastel in contrast to the view in Vienna, the palace a sedate off-white to Schönbrunn's garish green and yellow, but that seemed appropriate to Moore. This was England, not the home of operatic excess and *schlag* with everything. Even so, he felt eerily dislocated, and surprised by the aversion he felt to the thought of Vienna.

"Excuse me, sir." It was a short, round man; a

woman in a flowery dress stood behind him, holding hands with a little girl of about six.

Moore looked at his watch. It was 2:03.

"Could you please take a picture of me and the missus?" His accent was flat; Midlands, Moore decided, out of no particular expertise.

He took the man's camera, listened to his explanation of how it worked, and then waited while the man arranged himself and his family at the rail with the hill and the palace behind them. Moore winked at Natalia, who was standing to one side, confused.

After Moore took the picture, the man hurried back to him, all smiles.

"Thank you. Can I do the same for you? Take a picture of you and your missus, I mean. I could send it to you. Nice souvenir, don't you think?"

"Yes. But . . . no thanks, anyway."

"You sure, now?" He turned to his wife and daughter. "Marian, love, would you come over and say hello to the nice people? . . . She's a little shy, you know," he apologized. "Come on. The nice man took your picture. Ought to say thank you, for that."

"It's all right. There's no need."

"Now, never you mind, Mr. Moore. I'm raising her, and she's going to learn her manners. Kids today—it's a bleeding shame the way they act to their elders." To the girl: "Come on, now. You just come right over here and say thank you."

She did and, to Moore's amazement, curtsied prettily. Her father beamed. "That's right, now. That's the way a good girl does it. Daddy's proud of you. Now, you and your mother run off and look at the observatory."

He watched them go before turning back to Moore. "Surprised to hear your name, were you?"

"Very."

"That your countess, over there?"

"Yes."

"Doesn't look like one."

You don't look like what you are, either, Moore thought. He said nothing.

"You're going to New York tomorrow," the plump Englishman told him. "I've got plane tickets for you. Hotel room. Money. There's a credit card, too. But a little word to the wise—don't use it but when you need to. Got that?"

Moore nodded.

"All right, then. You fly to New York, stay over the night, then bright and early you get up and take the train to Washington. I've got some documents for you, too. All in a left-luggage locker. You've a very simple job when you get to the States. All you have to do is see that these documents are put into the right hands. I don't know what that means, myself, but I'm told you will."

"I don't have a clue."

"Of course you don't," the Englishman snarled. "Not now. Wait till you see the bleeding papers. Sometimes I wonder where they get the dumb bleeders they send me for briefing. Now look—all you have to do is see the papers get put to the proper use. And they told me you have some special kind of knowledge. Something about a conspiracy, I believe. Do you by any chance have some idea what *that* might mean?"

"Yes."

"Well, God save our noble Queen, the man knows

something. What you're to do, besides the papers, is to spread that knowledge of yours as widely as you can. Especially, they told me, in high places. Is that all clear?"

"Yes." The instructions were clear enough; Moore was not sure about the motivation for them. He assumed he would understand better when he saw the papers that had been left for him.

"That's all," the Englishman said. He held out his hand. Moore took it. "You sure I can't take your picture, you and the countess?"

"No. That's all right. Thanks."

"Right then, cheerio." He let go of Moore's hand. "Good luck to you." He went off toward the observatory.

Moore looked at his hand. The Englishman had given him the key to a baggage locker at Victoria Station.

There was a black vinyl attaché case in the locker. Moore did not open it until they were back in their hotel room. It held the promised plane tickets, a pre-paid room voucher for the Biltmore Hotel, five hundred dollars in used twenties, and a credit card made out to Stanley Greenspan, the name on the phony American passport he had been given in Vienna. And there was a tan, nine-by-twelve kraft-paper envelope. Moore opened the clasp and slid out a sheaf of papers. He flipped through them—typewritten lists of dates and places and short, single-spaced paragraphs, photocopied bills and receipts; two photographs, murky but decipherable.

He read the top of the first page aloud: " 'Meetings

between Martin Wilson and members of the Committee for State Security (KGB), 1975 and before.'"
The second page was headed: "Meetings between Martin Wilson and members of the Committee for State Security (KGB) 1976." There were other pages—one for each year since 1976.

He handed the papers to Natalia, who looked through them. She was about to comment when a sudden realization made him grab her arm, shake his head forcefully, and press a forefinger to his lips.

"Gregory? What?"

He shook his head again. "Let's go for a walk."

"But . . . Oh. I see. Yes, I would like that."

He repacked the attaché case and carried it with him when they left the room.

They joined the stream of homebound commuters walking over Waterloo Bridge, but turned off to walk down the modern concrete steps leading to a broad plaza in front of the National Theatre, overlooking the Thames.

When they were settled on one of the benches, Moore took the papers from the attaché case again and they read them together.

"What do you think this means?" she asked him.

"I don't know. It's not what I expected."

"Is it real?"

"That's a good question. I'm not sure I know the answer." He glanced over everything again. "If it's a fake, it's a very impressive job. I think for now we have to assume it's real."

"If it is real, it means this Martin Wilson is working for the Russians."

"That's what it looks like."

"How can that be? If he is their man, why are they asking you to expose him?"

It was a question that occupied Moore all the way to New York. He could come up with only one answer that made sense—the KGB's goal was to disrupt the CIA as badly as possible. If they knew that Collins was engineering a dismantling of the Agency so he could rebuild it in his own image—and with Wilson as their agent they must have known about it—the KGB would serve itself best by letting Collins build up a good head of steam and then, when he was going full speed, making sure that he was thoroughly discredited. If the timing was right—with the major revelations coming after the CIA had been emasculated by Collins's maneuvering and the Congressional reaction to it—the net effect of Collins's downfall would be to leave the United States with its main intelligence apparatus reduced to useless fragments, and no immediate way to glue them back together.

Moore's assignment was simple: he was to be the instrument by which the KGB delivered its coup de grâce. The things Moore could tell, based on Robbins's version of what Collins was really up to, would block Collins's plans and start his fall. Exposing Wilson as a Soviet agent would give Collins a last push toward ruin: Whatever credibility Collins might retain would be destroyed by the news that his most trusted lieutenant was a KGB man.

It was, Moore thought, a beautifully worked-out strategy.

As the plane settled toward a landing and he looked out over the glittering skyline of Manhattan and then the orange-studded gridwork of nighttime Long Island,

Moore thought about his own role in what was to come. He had no qualms about bringing down Collins and Wilson. What bothered him was the negative effect his revelations might have on the intelligence community's ability to do work that was valid and important. He hoped he could mitigate that by getting the exposé under way quickly.

One other thing bothered him: the certainty that Collins and Wilson would now be more eager than ever to see Gregory Moore buried in the deepest possible hole. That carried danger not only for him, but for the woman sleeping next to him.

———

There was a phone in the customs hall. While they were waiting to be cleared, Moore called Washington. He got an answering service; the operator told him that Congressman Grogan was out for the evening. Moore left no message. He rejoined Natalia on the customs line.

As their turn approached, Moore became increasingly nervous, although they had already gone through passport control and been stamped into the country.

The customs inspector said, "Good evening. How are you?"

"Awful," Moore told him. "I just missed an important business call."

"Sorry to hear it. Anything to declare?"

"No."

"Been away long?"

Natalia answered for him. "Two weeks." Moore had never before been so conscious of her accent.

"That's nice. Good length for a trip." The inspector looked them over. "Would you open your bags, please?"

He went through everything with a relaxed thoroughness. When he got to the attaché case, Moore wondered if he would open the envelope and, if he did, what would he make of its contents.

He picked up the envelope, hefted it. "This the business you missed the call about?"

Moore nodded.

The inspector dropped the envelope back into the attaché case. "Hope it works out for you." He toed a switch and the conveyor belt carried the bags past him to the end of the counter. "That's it," he said. "Welcome home."

They checked into the Biltmore, and Moore went downstairs for a walk. He found a phone booth just off the main hall of Grand Central Station. Grogan was still out.

Moore hung up and walked into the station, letting his eyes wander over the vaulted blue ceiling patterned with stars and constellations. Ahead of him, the Kodak billboard was an immense color transparency of a Pennsylvania Dutch farm, its barn painted with gaily patterned hex discs.

Pennsylvania. Congresswoman Carolyn Carlson.

He sent her a telegram: IN TOWN WILL CALL. URGENT TALK ABOUT WIDGETS. LIFESAVER.

In the morning, they took an early Metroliner to Washington.

"Where are we going now?" Natalia asked him as they crossed Union Station's vast, arched-roofed reception gallery.

"Follow me," he said. He led her out of the station and across a busy traffic circle, heading for the white stone and brown glass façade of the SEC Building.

A block from the SEC, he said, "Right here. Near transportation and the Capitol. Not near anyplace where we might run into Wilson or Collins."

The hotel lobby was clean, but the furniture was old and worn; the carpet was threadbare. Even new, none of it had been attractive.

The old man behind the desk had a halo of frizzy gray hair and a seamed brown face. There were teeth missing in his warm smile.

"Okay, folks, what'll you have today?"

"A room for two, please."

"Got one here with a double bed. That okay?" He grinned.

"No twin beds?" Moore asked him.

The grin faltered. "I don't think there is." He checked. "Nope. Just the one double is all. Summertime, you know. Get all filled up."

Moore looked at Natalia.

"If it is the only room . . ."

The room was small, almost all bed. A narrow unit along one wall was dresser, desk, and television stand. "I've got some phone calls to make," Moore said. "I can't use the hotel phone."

"May I come with you?"

Moore considered it. "Maybe it's a good idea."

"Thank you, sir," she said bitingly.

They went back to Union Station to find a phone booth. He carried the attaché case; it was becoming part of his hand.

Grogan was not in his office. Carolyn Carlson was in hers; she took his call.

"Hello, Mr. Moore. How is the widget business these days?"

"It's lousy, I'm afraid, and getting worse. I think it's very important for you to hear about it. Immediately."

"It's the end of the session. There's no time here that's more hectic."

"I wouldn't make a request like this if it wasn't absolutely urgent."

"You know how I feel about widgets. You're not going to change my mind."

"I have information that you've got to hear. For your sake. For the sake of what you're trying to do."

She laughed. "Don't tell me you've changed *your* mind?"

"Can I see you? You and Grogan. I've been calling him but I can't get through."

"When do you want to see us?"

"Whenever you can make it. As soon as possible."

"I think tonight might be a good time. Let me confirm it with Bill, first. Can you call back this afternoon?"

"What time?"

"Make it four o'clock."

"Is everything all right?" Natalia asked him when he came out of the booth.

"All set."

"Gregory. I would like to talk with you."

"Sounds serious."

"Yes. In a way, it is serious."

"All right. But we can't talk here."

"I suppose not." She thought for a moment; her face brightened. "This is my first visit to Washington," she said eagerly. "I would like to see the White House.

The Congress. All the monuments. We can talk while we are walking."

He took her shoulders. It was the first time he had touched her intentionally since Vienna.

"You're like a kid," he said, smiling. " 'Show me the pretty buildings, Daddy.' "

Her smile was tentative at first, but it almost took his breath away. He did not realize how long it had been since he had seen her smile.

"Perhaps not 'Daddy,' " she said.

"No. Perhaps not. But—I hate to say it—I'm afraid we'll have to postpone the sight-seeing for now."

"But . . ."

"I know. But. But the thing is, we can't hang around Washington. Not healthy. We're going over to that ticket window and buying a couple of tickets on the next train out of here. Wherever it's going."

It was going to Richmond. They sat in the back of the last car, a rickety old former clubcar with torn seats and unconvincing NO SMOKING signs that looked like bumper stickers. There was no one within half a dozen rows of them.

"Okay," he said. "What's on your mind?"

"I have only one question, Gregory. Why am I here? If we do not to speak to each other, except for you to tell me where to go and what to do, if I do not help you in any way—I should have stayed in Vienna."

"It wasn't an option, if you remember, your staying in Vienna."

"Yes, of course. I was not thinking. Did the Russians have some reason to send me with you, then?"

"I suspect they must have."

"What?"

"I can only guess: I'm going in there to try to convince my friends in Congress they should take action against the most important people in the CIA. That's why Nevelsky sent me back here. For evidence, I've got the papers he gave me, but they could be inventions and forgeries. The other thing I've got is my own story. A lot of what I'm going to be telling them has to do with Alex and the way the people back here dealt with me on that. And I'll be telling them some things Alex said about what he was doing and what the KGB was doing. It would be a big help to me if I had someone who could corroborate my story, and you seem to be the perfect person to do that. Considering that Alex isn't available."

She turned away. When she looked at him again, he thought he saw the brightness of tears in her eyes.

"You say it so easily. As if his death were some minor inconvenience."

He put a hand on hers. She pulled away.

"It's reality," he said. "Alexander Rukovoi was a good man. Maybe he was ten times the man I am, for most purposes. But he was assassinated by his own people and now he's gone. You can blame me, hate me for it, but the fact is I didn't do it. It was the last thing I wanted. . . . Frankly, I'm not entirely sure why they did it. Nevelsky had to be awfully worried about Alex to pick that way to neutralize him. You'd think he would be valuable to them alive, for debriefing, to see what he'd been up to and what my methods were."

He realized that she had tuned him out. She was staring out the grimy, scratched window at the barely visible pastures and farmland of Virginia.

It was many minutes before she faced him again. "I suppose you are right. You did not do it. But, if not for you, it would not have happened. It is something I will never forget. I may never forgive you for it entirely. But that does not mean I hate you. . . . Now we are forced together. We are in danger, and we have no one but each other." She closed her eyes and put her head in her hands. "I do not hate you."

He stroked her head. At his first touch she shuddered, but as he continued she sank toward him, leaned against his shoulder. He put his arm around her.

She said, "I am tired, Gregory. For the first time in my life, I feel . . . old. I need to be able to relax. If I cannot think of you as my friend, I am afraid I cannot stand the strain any longer."

17

At 4:10, Moore called Carolyn Carlson from Richmond. She asked him if he could meet her and Bill Grogan at Duke Ziebert's for a late dinner. She did not seem surprised when he told her that it was not that kind of conversation.

"What about my place?" she suggested.

"I don't know how safe that is either."

"Don't be silly. No one will know you'll be there unless you tell them. And I promise you, it's not bugged. I have it checked regularly."

"All right," he conceded. "Eight-thirty?"

"A little after nine would be better. Grogan and I will be hungry. I'll have some cold cuts and beer or something like that. That all right with you?"

"Fine."

She gave him the address. "Say nine-fifteen, then."

There was nothing for them to do but wait. He rented a car with his Stanley Greenspan credit card and they drove north on local roads to give Natalia a better look at Virginia than she'd had from the train.

Carolyn's address was in a resurgent section of Capitol Hill. Moore drove up and down the narrow residential streets under leaf-laden branches. He found a space he could wedge the car into, and they walked the three blocks to the townhouse apartment in anxious silence. Moore was alert for any sign that they were being followed; he found none.

The congresswoman answered her door in a cream-colored hostess gown; her neckline was open enough to show the curve of her breasts. Her dark hair hung heavy over one eye, and she had a rich suntan. Moore thought she looked even more striking than she had at the French Embassy party.

"Well, the widget salesman himself," she said, smiling warmly. "Do come in." When she saw that Moore was not alone, she covered her surprise immediately, but the warmth left her smile. "Hello. I don't believe we've met."

"Allow me," Moore said, momentarily bewildered by the stiff way the two women were reacting to each other. "Natalia, this is Congresswoman Carolyn Carlson. Carolyn, I'd like you to meet Natalia, the Countess von Hildebrandt."

They murmured the proper formal words to each other. Neither woman extended her hand.

Carolyn turned, her gown swirling around her, and swept down the hall to the living room. Moore and Natalia followed. Natalia paused a moment to straighten her skirt; the white linen dress was showing the effects of hours spent sitting on trains and in the car.

Grogan was slouched in an easy chair, in his shirt-sleeves with his tie loosened and his collar open. There was a tall glass of beer on the table at his elbow.

He lumbered to his feet. "Gregory. How are you?"

"That's what I'm here to tell you. How about you?"

"Not bad." He turned to Natalia. "My name is Bill Grogan. Greg didn't tell me he was bringing a beautiful woman with him."

She smiled. "Natalia von Hildebrandt." She held out her hand.

He took it, bowed slightly. "Charmed."

Carolyn was at a side table that held a platter of cold meats, a salad bowl, and a cutting board with a loaf of bread.

"I'm afraid I only ordered for three." Moore heard the faintest tinkle of ice in her voice.

Grogan said, "Give the nice people something to drink, Carolyn."

"How silly of me to forget. But I can count on you to set me straight, can't I, William?"

"Every time."

They spent another quarter hour on social preliminaries. Moore noticed through his mounting impatience that Carolyn somehow contrived never to speak directly to Natalia. He had the feeling that Natalia had noticed it as well.

Finally, Grogan said, "All right, Greg. Why don't you tell us what it is that brings us all together tonight."

Moore put his plate on the coffee table and took a last swallow of beer. "I think the way to approach this is for me to tell you the whole story, from before I was in Washington the last time. It'll be best if you let me finish before you ask questions. Get the whole story, and then we can go back and talk about the details."

"Sounds like you've got quite a story."

"Quite a story." Moore glanced at Natalia. She was sitting on the edge of an easy chair, her back stiff, her hands folded primly on her knees. He gave her a quick smile of encouragement.

He started with Rukovoi and the idea of getting a high-level Soviet penetration. When he referred to

Natalia as Rukovoi's "friend," Carolyn looked at her as if she were seeing her for the first time. Natalia kept her eyes on Moore.

No one interrupted until he described the attack on him and Carolyn at the restaurant in suburban Maryland.

"He was shooting at *you!*" Carolyn exclaimed.

"That's right. Maybe I saved your life that night, but if I did I owed it to you. You were only in danger because you were standing next to me."

"And that son of a bitch Wilson made it up, about my being the target."

"That's right. Frankly, I was a little surprised you bought the story so quickly."

"Why? Lord knows, I'm not above making a fool of myself." She glanced at Natalia.

Grogan asked, "Who was behind it?"

"I'll get to that in a minute. I'd like to go a little further, first."

Talking about Joan Wheeler was unexpectedly difficult for Moore. He had to stop, gather himself, and then go on. He left out the details of their last evening, but he emphasized the one conclusion Joan had given him about what she and Peter Harris had learned—that the Russians had been responsible, in part, for instigating the CIA exposé, but that they had not been alone.

Again, Carolyn could not contain herself. "You're saying it was the Russians who were behind the revelations?"

"That's right."

"Why would they do that?"

"To throw sand in the gears. Bring the machine to at least a temporary halt."

She leaned toward him accusingly. "You're saying I'm a dupe of the Russians, is that it?" She was furious.

"No. No. It's a lot more complicated than that. If you'd listen for another minute . . ."

She sat back. "Go ahead."

He took a breath, let it out slowly. Began: "After Joan told me that one thing, she clammed up. She said it was a long story and she wanted to tell it to me all at once." Now came the touchy part. "We went to bed," he said. "We hadn't seen each other for a while and we . . . well, we went to bed."

"I'm sure you're a healthy enough fellow," Carolyn commented bitingly.

He went on: "While we were in bed, someone shot her with a high-powered rifle. Shot her in the neck. Killed her, right there in my arms." He stopped. He was shaking.

"How awful," Carolyn breathed.

Grogan said, "Christ, Greg."

There was a long silence.

"Do you know who did it?" Grogan asked.

"Now I do. That's the second part of the story." He looked at the two legislators. They were waiting, ready.

He told them.

For over an hour after Moore finished the story, Carolyn Carlson's living room was bedlam: Both legislators were full of questions and confusion and disbelief, and every answer led to a new question. Natalia was drawn into the chaos to support Moore, to describe Rukovoi's attitude and actions. She repeated what Rukovoi had told her about Arkady and the Walrus and Nevelsky. Moore was astonished—she had never mentioned that part of it to him.

When the room finally subsided into silence, Carolyn looked at her watch. "My God. It's twelve-thirty. I don't know about any of you, but I could use a drink. You're welcome to join me."

No one refused. They sat drinking in silence, sorting out the evening's implications. Carolyn got up to refill their glasses. When she sat down again, she said, "All right, where do we go from here?"

Grogan looked up from his drink. "I think we go to the committee and tell them what we've learned, as best we can, and show them those papers the Russians gave Greg about dear old Marty Wilson. . . . Greg, I take it you'll let us have them."

Moore nodded. "I'll give you a copy."

"Okay. So we go up to the Hill and lay it all out for them. I imagine the next step after that will be to get Greg and the lovely countess up there to testify formally. Executive session. I don't want this going all over town before we've had a chance to deal with it." Elbows on his knees, he studied Moore. "I'd like you to go along with that, Greg. I'd like you to promise to keep this to yourself for a while."

"I'm sorry, Bill. I can't."

"The hell you say. If you think—"

Moore cut him off. "What I can do is promise not to go to the papers—any of those people: television, whatever. And not to talk to anybody else who might. But my life is in danger, and I'm sitting on the most important piece of information this town has seen in a long time."

"I'm not questioning any of that. Maybe what you should do is hole up . . ."

"Are you kidding? That's the worst thing I could do. If I'm going to stay alive, I've got to spread this far enough, to enough interested parties, so that getting rid of me wouldn't stop the process. But I promise you I'll be careful about it. Christ, I've been in the secrets business for a dozen years now. I'm not going to start talking to gossip columnists." *Just to KGB men.*

"No need to get upset, Greg." Grogan stood up. "I, for one, have picked up enough information here tonight to mull over for at least a week. And I've got to be able to explain it tomorrow. So, with all due respect, I'm going to toddle off home and go to bed."

Carolyn moved to walk him to the door. "I don't want to be inhospitable, but it is late, and I need to get my seven hours." Her eyes were on Moore.

Back at the hotel, Natalia said, "I think the beautiful congresswoman is fond of you, Gregory. She seemed relieved to think of me as the mistress of your Russian agent."

"Well . . ." he said. He pulled off his tie and hung it over the doorknob.

She paused, looking at the bed. "Is it a strain for you, having to be gallant with two older women at the same time?"

He turned to get to the closet and found he had to squeeze past her. He took her shoulders. "I don't mind at all. And as for the congresswoman . . ."

"Please, Gregory. You do not have to reassure me."

"I wasn't . . . Oh, hell. It's late. We're tired. Let's go to bed."

They lay on their backs in the darkness.

He said, "Natalia, you'll have to excuse me. I haven't been in the same bed with a woman since . . . since Joan. I don't know how I'd react. I'm not sure I want to find out, right now."

Her voice was soft: "We have been sleeping in the same room for days; to sleep in the same bed does not have to be different."

"No, but . . ."

"We were lovers, once, in the past. It does not mean that we must be lovers again." She rolled onto her side, away from him. "We do not have to decide now."

Later, she said, "I would like you to hold me. No more than that. For a minute. Only hold me."

She fell asleep in his arms. He lay there, intensely aware of her, until he, too, drifted into sleep.

In the morning, he went window shopping. In front of Garfinkle's he collided with a short, portly man with a Van Dyke beard. They apologized to each other profusely. The man gave no sign that he was aware of the slip of paper Moore had slipped into his vest pocket, but Moore was sure he knew it was there. It bore a short note—Grogan's name and Carolyn's, and the words "CIA official." Moore was sure it would be enough for Nevelsky, who undoubtedly had people watching him and Natalia, anyway.

Briggs met him at the cemetery again.

"I heard about Joan," Briggs said. "I'm sorry."

"Yeah. Thanks."

"It's never easy. You two were pretty close, weren't you?"

Moore stared.

"Don't be surprised. You know me. I like to keep up with things."

"We were close enough. Getting closer that night." Moore stopped. There was no point in wallowing in it. "What's been happening back here?" he asked.

"Since I saw you? A lot. A bunch of us have got together to try to turn this stupidity around. Ex-Company people, mostly. We've got a lobbying group and a public-information group." He shook his head. "Can you believe it? A public-information group. But it's the only way. We can't just sit still and let the politicians and bureaucrats dismantle the world's best intelligence apparatus." He grimaced. "Listen to me. I'm absorbing my own propaganda. The world's best! It's been a while since that was true." He looked searchingly at Moore. "More important than all this, what's been going on with you? What happened to your Russian? And did you figure out who's been shooting at you?"

"Not only at me. Joan, too."

"The same people who were gunning for you?"

"That's right."

"Who?"

"It's complicated."

"What isn't, in this business?"

Moore nodded.

"About the shooting," Briggs prompted.

"As far as I can tell, the man who approved the order was Martin Wilson."

Briggs stopped. "Just like that. Not the Russians. Martin Wilson."

"That's right. For Collins."

"Why?"

"Because we were getting too close to the truth, Joan and I."

Briggs studied him. "I guess you'd better start from the beginning."

"I guess."

They walked for a long time, side by side, among the gravestones. Briggs listened without comment.

As Moore spoke, he saw the older man's head lift and his back straighten. When Moore finished, Briggs stopped walking and turned to him with burning eyes.

"The bastards," he said in a simple, matter-of-fact tone. He smiled, but the fierceness did not leave his eyes. "Collins is no man to underestimate."

"No," Moore agreed.

Briggs's expression softened. "We may be on the right path, but we're not out of the woods yet. Right now, I'm most worried about you."

"What do you mean?"

Briggs began to walk again. "You're going to need protecting. Soon. Because you know what those buddies of yours in the Congress are going to do? They're going to get their committee together and talk all this over, and if they decide to take it anywhere—*if*, mind you— then the first thing they'll do is call in Collins and Wilson to get their side of it. There'll be an executive session, all very polite, and our boys Collins and Wilson will get the whole thing laid out for them, and plenty of opportunity to explain it away."

"No."

"Yes. That's just how it's going to work. When it's over, chances are the committee won't do a thing. But Collins is going to know you're in town, and he's going to know the countess is in town. And that you're both out for his hide. He's going to find you, Greg, make no mistake about that, and when he does he's going to fill you full of little holes."

"You paint a very vivid picture."

"It's a very real prospect. Very frightening."

"What do you suggest?"

Briggs thought before he answered. "Let me put a couple of men on your tail. They'll hang back, but they'll keep track of who else is there, and they'll be available in case of an emergency. Just one thing: In order to avoid scaring anybody away, they'll have to give you a fair amount of room. That means if you do a lot of zigging and zagging you may lose them."

"I'll keep it in mind. But I don't much like the idea of having to limit my movements." *Or worrying about your people tripping over the KGB.*

"Greg. Humor an old man. At least for a week or two, until we see how it's going to break."

"All right." KGB or no, Moore was relieved to have some support.

When he got back to the hotel, Natalia told him Grogan had called.

"I'm worried, Gregory. There was a . . . *Belastung* in his voice."

"Strain?"

"Strain, yes. And more than strain. Something is wrong, Gregory."

"I hope not," he said. He moved past her to the closet.

"What are you doing?"

"Packing." He threw his suitcase on the bed. "We're leaving here."

"I was right," she said. "Something is wrong."

"I don't want to take any chances."

"Congressman Grogan wants us to meet with his committee."

"Did he say when?"

"Tomorrow."

Moore stopped packing. "I've changed my mind. We'll leave our things here. I don't want to tell the world we're going away."

"I don't understand."

"I'll explain later. Right now, just throw some cosmetics together and a change of underwear, whatever you need for overnight. Carry what you can in your purse, and we'll put the rest in the attaché case. We can't hang around here."

He called Grogan from Union Station; using railroad station telephones was getting to be a habit.

"Did the countess give you my message?" Grogan asked.

"She did," Moore replied. He thought: *She's right, he does sound strained.*

Grogan said, "The committee has voted to request that you testify before an executive session. Both of you. We're meeting tomorrow in one of the committee rooms."

"Why do they want us to testify?"

"We talked about it last night. To fill in the spaces."

"Are you contemplating some kind of action?"

Grogan hesitated, "Well, you know, it's a complicated issue . . ."

"No."

"What do you mean, 'no'?"

"I mean no, it's not complicated, and no, we're not coming to any committee rooms."

For several seconds, there was no sound on the line but the hiss of circuit noise. "Greg, you can't . . . I mean, do you want us to do something about all this, or what?"

"Sure I do. But you're not going to get me near the Hill. I'm fonder of my life than that."

"You sound like you think I'm setting you up to be hit, like something out of *The Godfather*."

"I wouldn't have put it that way. Not quite." It was

hot in the phone booth. Moore opened the door and felt the refreshing breath of the air conditioning.

"Jesus, Greg, this isn't getting us anyplace. Are you coming or not?"

"We'll testify for you, but not on the Hill. Out of town."

Grogan hesitated again. "All right. Where?"

"Maryland somewhere."

"You've got to be more specific than that. We can't have a committee meeting just somewhere in Maryland."

"Let's do this—ten-thirty tomorrow, have coffee in the restaurant at the Hay-Adams. You know, the one that overlooks Lafayette Park."

"Upstairs from the lobby?"

"That's the one. I'll call you there. Then you can call the rest of the committee and tell them where to meet us. Just make sure they start out separately. The one thing I want to be sure of is that you don't all come in one big bunch, like a caravan. Maybe it would be best if you were all having breakfast out, a dozen different places, all over town."

"That's awfully complicated."

"I get complicated when my life's at stake."

"I don't understand. Last night you sounded pretty confident you could cover yourself. Now you're sounding like some kind of spy, with secret meetings and all. I really don't get it."

"Don't you?"

There was no response.

"Okay, Bill," Moore said. "I'll talk to you in the morning." He hung up and left the phone booth. Natalia looked at him questioningly. He put his arm

around her shoulder and squeezed. "Time to go for a
ride in the country."

They walked to the garage and redeemed the rental
car. On the way out of Washington, Moore wondered
how close a tab the Russians would keep on what
Stanley Greenspan was doing with his credit card. He
decided the rental car was probably safe for another
few days.

He drove out past Andrews Air Force Base and then
turned south. It was dark by the time they got to St.
Mary's City; they had to drive east toward Lexington
Park to find a motel.

Sitting on one of the beds in the uninviting room,
Natalia asked, "Why are we here?"

"To put ourselves out of harm's way."

"There is danger?"

"You know there is."

"What did the congressman want?"

"We're going to testify for his committee tomorrow."

She crossed her arms on her chest, hugged herself.
"I am afraid."

"Let's get some dinner. You'll feel better. We passed
a restaurant on the way that looked interesting."

He held out his hand to her. She took it but made
no move to get up. He pulled lightly; she countered it
with a pull of her own.

"I am not hungry."

He pulled harder. "Come on. Neither of us has eaten
since breakfast."

When they got to the restaurant, her appetite surprised both of them. It was her first real American
food—local shellfish, steak, salad, apple pie. Midway
through the meal, enjoying herself thoroughly, she
asked, "What is this place?"

"Around here? St. Mary's City? It's the first capital of Maryland. The original settlers landed here, in sixteen hundred and some. It's very picturesque, full of history. You'll see it in the morning."

On the way back to the motel, she said, "I am happy we came here. I did not think about our danger at all while we were eating. Thank you."

There were two double beds in the motel room. Without discussion, they turned back the covers on just one of them. For the second night, they fell asleep in each other's arms.

———

Moore woke up at dawn and gently disentangled himself. He dressed and went to stand in the coolness of the morning. There was a faint pink glow on the horizon; the sky was a blue so pale it was almost white.

They had an early breakfast in St. Mary's City and strolled among the old buildings for a few minutes before getting into the car and driving north. At ten-fifteen, Moore began to look for a place with a public phone. At ten-forty he pulled into a gas station and told the attendant to fill it up. He walked across the apron to an isolated phone booth with the glass knocked out of the door.

"I was beginning to wonder," Grogan snapped when he came to the phone.

"Accomac," Moore said.

"What?"

"Accomac, Virginia. It's at the south end of Delmarva, about midway between the Maryland line and the bridge."

"And that's where you want to have this meeting?"

"Nearby. It's a nice day. I thought we could go for a walk on the beach."

"You're crazy."

"Maybe. I'm driving a blue Cutlass. I'll be parked off the highway, on the southbound side, just past Accomac, at three this afternoon. Why don't you and your friends meet us there?"

"Greg, there's got to be a better way . . ."

"Three o'clock, south of Accomac. See you there." He hung up.

He paid for the gas and climbed back into the car. "All set," he said. "We're going for another ride. I'll show you the ocean."

On their way through Annapolis, he stopped and rented a second car.

"It's possible we'll have to split up," he explained.

"Separate?"

"Yes."

"Why?" She seemed hurt as well as perplexed.

"It's a feeling I have. Something Briggs said, and the way Grogan's been acting. If things get tight, I'll have to know you're someplace reasonably safe until we have a better idea of how this is all going to work out."

She started to protest.

"No arguments," he said. "We're on slippery ground right now. You have to accept that I'm doing the right thing for both of us. We don't have time to have a debate about it."

She took his hand and held it to her cheek for a second. "I will do as you say."

He gave her an envelope—motel stationery. "I wrote this this morning. It's a note to my college roommate. He's a big shot lawyer on Wall Street. They've got a fancy apartment and fancy friends, plenty of money, and no kids. They'll be delighted to have a countess staying with them for a while. Especially a beautiful, intelligent countess like you."

Before they started out again, he said, "You don't have to stay right behind me all the time. I'll make sure you don't get lost. And don't worry. Nobody's going to bother us, at least not for a while."

When they were on the highway again, Moore kept watch in the rearview mirror until he saw the silver Rabbit and the green Ford that had been behind them, off and on, since Washington. He hoped they were both Briggs's.

Moore stopped at a sporting goods store in Salisbury, the last town of any size before the vast open stretches of East Shore Virginia. Natalia pulled into the lot next to him and they went into the store together. She browsed while he bought a .30-caliber rifle and two boxes of ammunition, a quilted carrying case for the rifle, and a folding hunting knife with a blade that locked open. They were on their way out when Moore noticed a display of straw hats.

"Come here," he said. "I want you to try on a hat."

He picked the one with the biggest brim. It was a good two feet across, with a flat crown like a Panama hat. The hatband was a blue-and-white patterned kerchief; its ends were poked through holes in the brim—they dangled alongside her cheeks. She tied them in a bow under her chin and turned her head coquettishly back and forth.

"Beautiful," he said.

He paid for it and asked for a bag. They had to wait for the clerk to find one big enough.

From Salisbury, they drove straight down the East Shore to Cape Charles. The last thing before the

Chesapeake Bay Bridge-Tunnel was a cylindrical white building, windowless, with a truncated red-white-and-blue cone growing out of its center. There were large red letters on the second story of the white cylinder: AMERICA HOUSE.

Moore pulled into the driveway with Natalia close behind him. He stopped, got out, and walked back to her.

"I want to check in here for the night, but with your car, not mine. Follow me around back."

He parked the Cutlass and had her drive him to the office. Registering, he made a small production of looking out the window for the license number of the car, making sure the clerk looked, too, and saw the Annapolis rental car and Natalia.

They left the car in the space assigned to their room and climbed into the Cutlass. Moore swung back onto Route 13 and drove north. It was almost three; he took a chance on going faster than the rest of the traffic, anxious to be at the rendezvous on time.

18

The contingent from Washington did not arrive until almost three-thirty. There were three cars, all of them dark government sedans. They pulled up behind the Cutlass in a neat line.

So much for discretion, Moore thought. *I wonder how many of my friends and enemies followed them here.* He had made emergency provisions for getting off the peninsula but he was far from confident, now, that they would work.

Grogan got out of the lead car and walked over to where Moore and Natalia were leaning against the Cutlass's front fender.

"Well, here we are."

"That's it?" Moore asked.

Grogan twisted to survey his miniature convoy. "That's it. Eight committee members, two staff attorneys, two recorders. A fair-sized contingent." As an afterthought he added, "Carolyn couldn't come."

"Eight committee members," Moore said. "Out of what? Thirty-six?"

Grogan pushed gravel with his toe. "Thirty-eight."

"And where are the others?"

"Back in Washington, most of them. I guess."

"Well what the hell!" Moore exploded.

"Take it easy, Greg. A dozen congressfolk and staff schlepping out here to the beach, that's a lot for one renegade spy and one slightly tarnished countess. Begging your pardon, ma'am."

Moore was fuming. "Is that how things are, Bill? When did I get to be a renegade?"

"Look, I'm sorry about that. Sometimes I ought to watch my tongue better than I do. The damn air-conditioning in that car went on the blink, and I'm so hot and sweaty I'd probably snarl at Santa Claus."

"There's a breeze here."

"A little."

Moore pushed himself away from the car. "It's better by the ocean. Why don't we get going?"

He led them south a few miles, to a turnoff marked with a Virginia State road sign. The road went east all the way to the ocean; it ended at a small fishing village.

"This is swell," Grogan told him as they stood next to the cars. "Very picturesque. And now maybe you'll tell me what we do next."

"There's a restaurant at the end of the pier. Unless things have changed drastically in the past five years, they've got some pretty good seafood. I think we ought to go in there and have a quick bite to eat, to keep our strength up and our heads clear, but mostly to give us all a chance to get acquainted before we get down to the serious business. Then we can walk out on the dunes. I think I know a place we can talk in peace."

"I was right. You really are crazy, aren't you?"

"You see something wrong with all of this?"

There was a wisecrack on Grogan's tongue, but he swallowed it. "The truth is," he confessed, "I don't see anything wrong with it at all. It makes sense, in an odd sort of way. It's just . . . unorthodox."

The restaurant lived up to Moore's expectations. The table conversation did not.

The eight committee members who had made the trip were, on the face of it, a representative group. There were six men and two women, five Democrats and three Republicans, with a spectrum from right to left in both parties. What struck Moore most about them was how uneasy they were with him and Natalia. The legislators made no attempt to draw them out, to get to know them. It seemed bad investigative technique to Moore. Bad technique, or a sign they didn't care because they'd already made up their minds.

Moore was especially disturbed by the committee chairman, a white-haired veteran from Arkansas, who made a point of keeping himself as far from Moore and Natalia as he could, as if he were trying to avoid contamination.

As they all walked out over the dunes, Moore held Natalia's hand, to reassure both of them. About a quarter of a mile along the beach, they found the kind of place he'd had in mind. They all sat on the sand, amid tufts of spiny beach grass, with their backs to a low dune with enough natural curve to make the group a near semicircle. A dozen yards away, the sea lapped gently at the shore, its surf flattened by the barrier islands.

The first questions were asked by the committee chairman.

"Well, son, you got us out here, and we thank you for that, on a fine summer day like this, but we've got some serious business to transact. What I don't understand about all this—and I'm speaking to you honestly because I don't see the point in holding back—it seems to me, you got all involved with the Russkies, and you went to stay in their embassy for a while, and then out you come with a bunch of papers they gave you, and you tell us that the two most important men in the CIA are some kind of traitors. And if that's not enough, they're not even the same kind of traitors. One's a power-mad fascist who wants to take over all the dirty tricks and covert operations and not tell anybody anything about what he's up to. Not the Congress, for sure, and maybe not even the President. And the other one, the way I get it, is a Russian. Born there—isn't that what you told my colleague from Michigan, or have I got my stories mixed up? Well, never mind that: it doesn't matter. The only thing I'm asking you right now, son, what really bothers me, is how you figure we're supposed to believe you."

"Has the committee spoken to Mr. Collins or Mr. Wilson about this?"

The chairman bridled. "Now, look here, son, I didn't come all the way out here to get sand in my britches and take lip from you while I'm about it. So you hunker down and answer that question, you hear?"

"Yes, sir," Moore said, controlling himself. "The answer is—if you give us a fair hearing, I expect you to believe us."

The congressman leaned forward and looked down the arc of committee members. "Grogan, he give you this kind of shit, too?" To the recorders, jotting in their steno pads, he said, "Now, you don't want to write that down, like good folks. That kind of talk is not part of our record." To Moore: "If we give you a fair hearing? Is that what you said, just now?"

"Maybe I should explain what I mean," Moore said. "If you've already spoken with Collins and Wilson, then they've heard the substance of my case, and I have to assume they've made some attempt to rebut it.

Called me a liar. Implied I was a Russian agent, myself. So if you've heard them, I need to know what they said, to give me a chance to contradict them the way I'm sure they've already contradicted me. That's one thing I meant when I said I'd like to be sure I'm getting a fair hearing."

"Really?" the congressman said, his voice laden with sarcasm. "Is that what you meant?" His face was red under the shock of white hair. "Well, let me tell you something, son. You're not here to tell us what's fair and what isn't fair. You're here to tell us your story and answer our questions. Seems to me like a man who admits he shot a fellow employee of the Central Intelligence Agency ought to figure he's got better than a fair deal just if he's not sent straight back over the water to answer for his crimes."

Again, Moore bit back his anger. "What would you like me to tell you?"

"Maybe what we ought to do is start by finding out some things about you and where your story comes from. You have these papers from the KGB that you gave us to look at. You have this very pretty lady you brought with you. And she's been the mistress of a Russian spy. And an Austrian spy, I'm told. And it seems she was your mistress, too. Isn't that right, Countess?" He made the title into a sneering insult.

Her chin trembled, almost imperceptibly, but she conquered it. She said nothing.

Moore snapped, "That kind of talk is no help."

The old southerner looked around at the others. "Now he's telling me what's helpful and what isn't. This same fellow who turned against his superiors based on the word of some Communists and a fancy foreign whore? Now, what am I supposed to do about that?"

He paused to give weight to his rhetoric and then turned to Moore. When he spoke, his accent was milder and his tone more serious. "All right, son. I'll cut out the nonsense now, if you will. Are you ready to get down to business with us now, like a grown-up?"

"If you'll tell me whether the committee has spoken with Mr. Collins or Mr. Wilson."

"Shit, son, you just don't learn, do you?"

"Yes, we have," Grogan interjected. "Both of them."

"Grogan, whose side are you on?" the chairman shouted.

"There's no point in lying to them."

The chairman stiffened. "All right, Congressman, if you're so damn smart, then we'll just do this your way." To Moore, he said, "Yes, Mr. Moore, we did speak with Mr. Collins and Mr. Wilson about this. Unlike you, they were very cooperative, and they told us a lot of interesting stories. One story was about how, just yesterday morning, one of their people saw you making contact with a known agent of the KGB. Outside Garfinkle's, they said. I suppose maybe you were doing a little bargain hunting."

It went downhill from there, for almost two hours. Finally, they gave up on it and trooped through the sand to where they had left the cars.

The committee chairman got into one of the government sedans with another senior committee member and the two staff attorneys. They drove off northward.

Moore called Grogan aside.

"Bill, I've got a favor to ask you. No matter what the rest of the committee believes, I've been telling you the truth. Once I went to you and Carolyn, I was relatively safe. Collins and Wilson needed me alive for this meeting. It would have looked awfully suspicious if I'd died before I could talk to the committee, and I'm sure they knew it would come out this way. But now things are different. They're not going to want me going to anyone more receptive: They're going to want me dead. I think I have a way to get clear for a while, but to do it I need your help."

"Okay," Grogan said hesitantly. "What is it?"

"I want you to stay here and keep one of the cars. Get the others to go home in the other one."

"There's seven of them. They'll be awfully crowded in one car. And it's a hot trip, going back up. This sea breeze doesn't carry very far."

"They'll live. I may not. And Natalia may not."

"Aren't you being a hair melodramatic?"

The anger Moore had been holding back came to the surface. "You know, Grogan, once upon a time you had a mind of your own. And two good eyes and a decent conscience. What's happened? Has Washington fever done that much damage to your brain? Collins calls me a liar and the going gets a little rough, so you're ready to throw me to the wolves. Don't you see where that leads? Don't you care?"

Grogan studied his toes. "You're right." He slapped his gut. "Sometimes I forget the guy who's buried inside all this flab. Sometimes . . ." His eyes met Moore's. "You're getting a shitty deal on this one, you're right about that. Myself, I don't know what to believe right now. But if it's some running room you want, I guess I can't deny you that." He looked off to where the others were waiting. "This is going to take a little persuading. Wait here. I'll be right back."

Natalia came to stand next to Moore. He put his arm around her.

"What happened?" she asked. "Why did they talk that way to us?"

"It was a case of our word against Collins and Wilson's. They're big shots; we're not. We've had a lot of contact with Russians; they're pure. That's the ball game."

"Ball game?"

"Sorry. I meant—they win, we lose."

"What will happen?"

"I don't know."

Grogan came back. "All right. They don't like it, but they'll do it."

"Good. Thanks, Bill. The thing for them to do now is to get on the road, go out to Thirteen and head south. We'll follow them as far as the Bay Bridge."

"The bridge? That's the wrong way. They'll end up in Norfolk. Crowded like that . . ."

"I know. But it gives me some time when I know where they are and where they're going. I don't want to worry that they're going to gum me up somehow."

"They have a radio in the car."

"They do? Why don't you go and disconnect the microphone? From both cars."

"Greg, they won't . . ."

"Sure they will. They don't need it this trip, and you'll put it back in when you're in Washington."

Grogan went to argue with his colleagues again, then made a brief stop at the two government cars and returned with the microphones. A pair of black, coiled wires dangled, bouncing, from his fist.

"Thanks, Bill. I really appreciate it," Moore said. "Now, let's get going."

The two sedans pulled out onto the road. At the

highway they turned south. Driving the car with the broken air conditioner, with Natalia next to him and Grogan in the back seat, Moore followed the legislators to Cape Charles.

There was a turnoff immediately before the Bridge-Tunnel toll plaza. Moore pulled to the side of the road and watched the other car stop to pay its toll. There was a delay.

"Arguing about the overcrowding," Grogan ventured.

"Probably."

The sedan pulled past the toll gate and got onto the bridge road. Moore turned around and headed north.

Back at the fishing village Moore said, "I hate to do this, Bill, but I'm going to ask you one more favor."

Warily: "What's that?"

"I want you to make that same trip over the Bridge-Tunnel to Norfolk. And I want you to do it in our rental. Let us have the official car."

"They'd crucify me."

"They'll crucify you anyway. Say I held you at gunpoint."

Grogan shook his head. "Okay. I sure hope it does you some good."

Moore could see Natalia getting the attaché case and the rifle carrier and the rest of their purchases from the trunk of the Cutlass. "To tell you the truth, I don't think it will, in the end. I'm just hoping it'll give me enough time to get Natalia clear."

Grogan put a hand on Moore's shoulder, pressed it with a mixture of affection and encouragement. "It's a hell of a business. I wish . . ."

"So do I. Whatever it is. Let's go."

Grogan got into the Cutlass; Moore and Natalia, into the dark government sedan.

"Put on the hat," Moore said.

She fished it from the bag and tied it in place. Her red hair was invisible under the immense straw disk.

"Good," he said.

The two cars paced each other down the peninsula until Moore saw the silver Rabbit and the green Ford in his rearview mirror. Then he began to slack off on the accelerator and let Grogan pull ahead of him. He watched the two following cars. As they drew closer, he slowed more. The Rabbit pulled abreast of him. He turned his head toward Natalia.

"Look out the side window at the scenery," he told her. When he returned his eyes to the road, the Rabbit was a few feet in front of them. He could see the backs of two men's heads. They did not seem to be interested in the official sedan they had just passed.

He used the same maneuver with the green Ford. It went by as they were coming to America House.

Moore turned off into the motel parking lot and pulled up next to the car they had rented in Annapolis.

"I want you to get going right away. Drive straight down this road. It'll take you to Norfolk. Once you're there, get directions to the airport and take a plane for New York." He gave her two hundred dollars, almost all he had left. "They won't be looking for you by yourself. Not yet. You know what to do when you get to New York?"

"Yes. I have the address, and the note you gave me."

"Good. Better leave the hat with me."

She took it off and gave it to him.

For a long moment, she studied him. "I don't want to leave you, Gregory."

He kissed her softly. "I want you safely in New York so I don't have to worry about you."

She pulled his face back to hers with gentle finger-tips. Her kiss, like his, was soft, but it lingered. He could feel her mouth pulse against his.

Without a word, without looking at him again, she left the government sedan, slid behind the wheel of the rental car, and drove out of the parking lot.

He gave her five minutes before he started again.

19

Driving north, he wondered again if the Rabbit and the Ford he had put on Grogan's tail were Briggs's or if one or both of them had been sent by Collins or Wilson. He had no way of knowing how many factions were interested in him. Out of habit, he had been thinking of Collins and Wilson as one enemy, but that was not necessarily how things stood now. Not if Wilson was the Walrus.

Moore tried to imagine the conversation between Collins and Wilson when they left the committee room with Moore's accusations of Wilson fresh in Collins's mind. How would Wilson defend himself to Collins? Would Collins believe him? But he could come to no conclusion; besides, it was more important to think about his own next moves.

The general outline was clear. His first impulse had been to stay inside the government, to go to people he knew who were directly concerned with the issues he had to raise. Having failed in that, what he needed was as much exposure as he could get, to keep the whole affair from being buried and forgotten.

His problem now was security. He knew the people he wanted to see and what he wanted to say to them. For some purposes, it made sense to make the phone calls early, to get everything under way; yet if he was to stay out of Collins's or Wilson's hands, it would be wisest not to surface too early. He had to assume they were covering his most likely contact points. It would not take much manpower, because there were not many places for him to go: two newspapers and two or three newsmagazines, a handful of syndicated columnists. And there would be problems of corroboration. It was a very touchy story. Touchy, but irresistible, he hoped. It would help that two journalists had died, and that one of them had been a CIA operative. If he could get the story out into the world, it should develop on its own.

He was still plotting strategies and guessing their outcomes when he realized that in spite of the automatic evasive maneuvers that had been part of his driving ever since he left America House he had failed to shake a black pickup truck that had been appearing and disappearing behind him for almost two hours.

His mind snapped to full alert. He increased his speed slightly and got off the highway at the next interchange. He got on in the opposite direction, drove south one exit, and repeated the maneuver, coming back onto the road going north. For a minute he thought he was clean, and then the black pickup reappeared in his rearview mirror.

The identification was certain, then. But what were the pickup's intentions? So far, it seemed, nothing more than following, with no need to be subtle about it.

Moore kept going, the pickup always at the edge of his awareness. One way or the other, he had to shake it or he could not do anything in safety.

He was somewhere in the middle of the Delmarva peninsula, near the Delaware-Maryland border, he guessed. Off the highway, everything would be rural—back-country roads, farms, trees. The sun was going down; he had to decide whether to act before he lost the day's last light, or to wait until night, and hope the darkness would give him the cover he needed. He chose immediate action; he had spent too long on the receiving end.

He got off the highway and went east on a winding two-lane road. As he drove, he reached into the back seat for the rifle case and hauled it into the front of the car. It was almost impossibly awkward, but he managed to work the rifle out of the case as he drove.

He looked in the rearview mirror. Here, on a narrow road among the trees, night was much closer than on the broad, open highway. He could barely make out the pickup behind him.

He propped the rifle next to him, its butt on the center console and its barrel on the dashboard, and paid attention to his driving. Slowly, he opened a gap between himself and the pickup. It was more work than he would have liked: The government sedan was slow and awkward, and the truck behind him had obviously been souped up.

Finally he found what he was looking for: a series of bends in the road followed by a four-way intersection. He tensed, praying that the intersection would be clear.

At the last minute, as he entered the crossroads, he stabbed the brake pedal and swung the steering wheel left. The car slewed into the turn. Moore's foot went from brake to gas, coaxing the car to skid further. It came to rest broadside in the road, facing back the way he had come. He was reaching for the rifle as the pickup crossed the intersection. He hit the door handle and tumbled out. The sedan was still oscillating on its springs from the violence of the turn and stop.

Moore knelt in the road, raising the rifle to his shoulder, but the truck's taillights disappeared around another bend before he could get off a shot.

Moore jumped back into the sedan, threw the rifle onto the seat next to him, and gunned the car back toward the highway. He wondered if the truck carried a two-way radio, tried to remember if he had seen an antenna.

He was within sight of the highway when a pair of headlights appeared in his rearview mirror, coming up fast. He accelerated, checking the mirror frequently, so preoccupied with his pursuer that he did not see the car blocking the road at the turnoff to the highway until it was almost too late.

His foot came down on the brake almost of its own accord, and he twisted at the wheel. Again, the car slowed into a turn, scrubbing off speed as it skidded sideways. The second stunt turn was too much for it. The two outside tires blew. When the rims hit the pavement with a loud screech of metal and a shower of sparks, the front suspension buckled.

The car stopped as if it had hit a wall. Moore was thrown sideways across the front seat. His head rang. There was no light in the car. He groped on the floor, feeling for the rifle.

Suddenly everything was blinding light. He flung his arm over his eyes, but it was not enough. He heard sounds, indistinctly. It was as if the glare had impaired his hearing.

Hands grabbed him, pulled him from the car, shoved him up against the fender. He was searched, roughly.

He felt a hand in his pocket, grabbing the folding hunting knife, pulling it out. He heard the knife clatter to the pavement somewhere in the distance.

In the continuing glare, more hands tore him away from the car, shoved him forward, stumbling, to another car. Pushed him into the back. He fell across the seat; someone pushed his legs in awkwardly and slammed the door.

The car went forward, backward, forward again. It accelerated, went into a long, sweeping, uphill curve, and accelerated again. They were on the highway. Moore tried to sit up and found that he couldn't.

He persisted, fighting his sense of weakness and futility and recurring waves of nausea. Finally he made it to a sitting position. There was no one else in the back seat with him. There were two men in the front; the driver and Martin Wilson.

Wilson was turned so that he could watch Moore. He held a .357 Magnum revolver, propped on the seatback, pointed at Moore. It made Moore think of Vienna and Robbins.

"You just don't quit, do you, Greg?"

"Not when I'm on to a good thing." The thought was clear, but the words came out in fragments.

"I have a lot of respect for your ability to hang on in the face of opposition. I'm sorry I can't say the same for your judgment."

"Matter of opinion." Moore's voice was stronger.

"Not entirely." Wilson seemed amused. "There are some battles you should know not to fight, no matter how much spirit you have. I don't play chess against Bobby Fisher."

"I suppose not." Moore was silent for a while. "Where are we going?"

"Not far. I have a little place on the shore. You could call it a beach house. Very isolated. You know how it is—Washington is so unpleasant in the summer, and it's nice to be able to get away to someplace secluded and cool. You'd be surprised how important it can be to have true privacy from time to time."

"No, I wouldn't. I'm sure it's vital, for you."

Wilson adjusted the position of the Magnum, as if to remind Moore it was there. Neither of them said anything more until they had arrived.

It was a large cabin at the top of a steep hill. The approach was up a gravel path almost invisible from the country road they were on. The path itself was flanked by evergreens that loomed over them, dark against the night sky.

When they got out of the car, Moore heard the sea.

"You can't see it at night," Wilson said, "but just beyond the house is a cliff. It goes straight down to the water. There's a small beach down there, too, with a wooden staircase to get to it."

"It sounds lovely." Moore's shoulder ached where it had hit the steering wheel.

The driver opened the cabin door.

"Inside, please." Wilson motioned with the Magnum.

Moore went into a dark room. There was a click behind him and the lights came on.

It was a simple cabin—one large room, with kitchen appliances along one wall, and a few large pieces of Colonial-style furniture, most of it along the other three walls.

"David," Wilson said to the driver, who was standing in the doorway. "Go out and sit in the car. The others will be along soon. Let me know when they start up the path."

"You okay, with him?"

"I'm fine."

"Yell if you need me." David went out, closing the door behind him.

Moore looked around the room again, placing the furniture more firmly in his mind.

"Why are we here?" he asked.

"Why are *you* here? Instead of lying in a hole somewhere? That's what you mean, isn't it?"

"More or less."

"It's simple, really. There is the question of how you should be dealt with; unfortunately, the answer is not immediately clear. I can tell you that the strongest opinion so far is that you should be killed, so you needn't have any doubts about what I'll do if you suddenly forget your manners." He moved the gun again, slightly but meaningfully. "In the meantime, the decision is that you should be kept isolated but available. This seemed like a good place. I've been reasonably careful to keep anyone at the Company from knowing this cabin is mine. I doubt they even know it exists. So you will stay here until we know what to do with you."

"We?"

"Purely a way of speaking."

They stood watching each other.

Wilson broke the silence. "You know, I'm surprised at your childish faith in your friend Briggs. You've managed to doubt the rest of us."

"Go ahead," Moore said, interested.

"Consider the fascinating community of interest between one J. P. Briggs and one Gherman Nevelsky. Don't you think it's awfully convenient that General Nevelsky handed you a package of documents containing exactly what you need to destroy Mr. Briggs's primary rivals? That was the idea, wasn't it? Down with Collins and Wilson, up with Briggs. Nevelsky couldn't have done a better job for Briggs if he knew exactly what Briggs needed. So maybe he did know what Briggs needed. He could have, if Briggs was working for him. That makes a lot more sense than Nevelsky's blowing his own man, doesn't it?"

Moore was momentarily too stunned to speak.

"I don't blame you if you never thought of that," Wilson went on. "But now that it's on your mind, give it a little time to develop. And there's something else you might think about—why was Nevelsky in such an awful hurry to get rid of Rukovoi? If I were Nevelsky, I would have wanted to keep Rukovoi around for a while, so he could tell me about his relationship with Gregory Moore. A man like Rukovoi can be a lot of use that way. But Nevelsky had him killed. Why? I claim the answer is very simple. It's in the story you told Grogan. If Rukovoi really knew this mole, this Walrus, as he said he did, there was a chance he would eventually identify him for you. That would be a very pressing reason to kill Rukovoi, if Briggs was the mole."

Wilson took a cigar from his jacket, stripped away the cellophane with his teeth, and bit off the end. With the cigar clamped between his teeth, he fished in his pants pocket, then shifted the gun to his left hand to dig in the other pocket. Moore considered jumping him, decided the cigar maneuver was probably calculated to produce that response, and did nothing.

Wilson came up with a cigar lighter, transferred the gun back to his right hand, and lit his cigar.

"So here's Nevelsky," Wilson resumed. "His man in

the CIA is telling him that he's on the verge of being blown because of you and Rukovoi, and meanwhile some people over here are tearing up the hamstrung, spy-riddled old CIA and replacing it with something a lot tighter and more efficient and more effective, in the process leaving Nevelsky's man out of the game entirely. So what does Nevelsky do? He terminates Rukovoi and then picks you up, fills you full of nonsense, and turns you loose with just the evidence he thinks you need to destroy Briggs's opposition and reinstate him firmly at the top of the Company. If that isn't neat, I'd like to know what is."

"You spin a good yarn."

"It's more than a good yarn, Greg. It's the truth. If you think about it for a while, you'll see it's the only thing that fits. If you can put aside your personal grievances, that is, and look at the bigger picture for a change. That's the trouble with you guys in the field, you know. You have this worm's-eye view of what's going on in the world. You're so close to everything that it all looks clear and vivid to you. But all you see is one piece, and that's not enough."

"Why do you care? What difference does it make what I think?"

Wilson released a long plume of blue-gray smoke. At the end of it, he blew a perfect smoke ring. It was the closest thing to flamboyance Moore had ever seen in him.

"Ordinarily I wouldn't care. You've been a lot more trouble than you're worth, these last couple of months. But now this whole question of the KGB mole has come to a head because of you." He puffed on the cigar again. "The way things look, nobody's going to convict me of anything based on your evidence. At worst, it's going to slow us down some. But there's another way to look at it. It may be that Nevelsky and Briggs have outsmarted themselves. Because if you were to see the truth, and if you were to say so, I think we could nail the coffin shut on them." He smiled. There was no warmth in it. "Don't get me wrong, Greg. Nuisance that you are, I know that your heart's in the right place. Unfortunately it's led you to do some damaging things. In the old days they would have called it insubordination, at best. Terminated you, at worse. But times have changed. Not everybody can just soldier on in the face of all kinds of doubts. I can understand the impulse, even if I don't applaud your acting on it. All I'm asking by way of penance and contrition is that you think about what I've just been saying."

Moore started to speak. Wilson held up a hand. "No. Don't say anything. Just think."

Wilson hooked a chair leg with his foot and pulled the chair closer. He sat down, crossed his legs, and rested the gun butt on his knee, keeping the muzzle aimed at Moore's chest. "No hurry. We have plenty of time."

Moore wandered around the cabin. He looked out the window, sat on the bed, paced. Wilson's attention never flagged. The gun followed Moore everywhere he went.

He lay down on the bed with his hands behind his head and examined the ceiling for almost a quarter of an hour. Then sat up, swung his feet to the floor, and stood. Reached for the ceiling, touched his toes.

"Hey!" Wilson said.

Moore stopped in midstretch.

"Not so much motion."

"Sorry. I'm a little bit stiff."

"We'll worry about that later."

"Right." Moore looked at Wilson. He seemed no different from any of the times Moore had seen him. Distant. Cold. Gray.

"All right," Moore said. "I buy it. Nevelsky and Briggs were working together. Rukovoi was killed because Nevelsky thought Rukovoi was close to exposing the relationship between Nevelsky and Briggs. And Nevelsky gave me evidence against you not just to bring you down, but to help Briggs and to protect their relationship. That's what you were saying, isn't it?"

Wilson smiled. "More or less."

"It makes sense to me."

Wilson stood up, pushing the chair away as he did. The gun was unwavering. "I'm glad you came around to seeing the truth."

"So am I," Moore said.

"I'd like to get some of this down on tape, if you don't mind."

"I guess not. Why do you want it?"

"It would be very useful if we could put together an affidavit for you to sign—about Nevelsky and those papers he gave you, among other things."

Wilson shuffled sideways across the cabin to a breakfront cabinet that held a set of antique-replica dishes. Keeping the gun pointed at Moore, Wilson pulled open a drawer and took out a cassette recorder.

"Here we are," he said. He pitched the recorder easily to Moore, underhanded. Taken by surprise, Moore had to lunge to catch it.

"Why don't you sit down," Wilson suggested. "On the bed or somewhere. Make sure the machine is set up to record, and then we can get going."

"Okay." Moore turned toward the bed.

And kept turning, the recorder in his outstretched arm like a discus as he whipped around, releasing the recorder and diving blindly for the floor, rolling amidst the thunder of gunshots until he crashed into a wall and bounded, off balance, to his feet, moving back in the direction he had come from and closer to where Wilson had been and still was, his rimless glasses askew, blood on his face, the gun in his hand pointed now at the spot where Moore had hit the wall. Firing.

Moore kicked. The gun flew across the room, ricocheted from wall to stove to floor, going off when it hit and spinning crazily, a top gone mad.

Moore kicked again. Wilson clutched his midsection and doubled over, vomiting. Collapsed.

Feet pounded to the door. The knob turned.

Moore dove for the gun, pushing Wilson out of his way. His fingers closed on the cold metal as the door burst open. He rolled, the heavy gun not fully in his hand, not yet ready to fire, and found himself looking into the fat silencer of an M-11 submachine gun in the hands of J. P. Briggs.

"You all right?" Briggs asked, letting the M-11 dangle in one hand.

Moore stood up, still holding the revolver. "I guess so."

"What about him?" Briggs nudged Wilson with his toe.

"He's alive, if that's what you mean."

"Kind of a shame."

"You can't win 'em all."

"No. But you can want to."

Moore looked down at Wilson. "It's sort of a mess in here. You mind if we go outside?"

"Good idea."

Outside, among the pine trees, Briggs said, "I've had my eye on Mr. Wilson for a while now, in a casual sort of way. There were signs he had a little hideaway on the shore somewhere, but I hadn't got around to finding it. We followed some of his cronies tonight, and here we are. We took care of the cronies on our way in. Not a moment too soon, either."

"We?"

"You remember I told you about the organizations I was forming? Well, we do more than give lectures to ladies' teas."

Moore smiled. "I see."

"What happened up here?" Briggs wanted to know.

"Wilson told me about you and Nevelsky."

Briggs's hand tightened on the compact submachine gun. "What's that supposed to mean?"

"He had a fascinating story to tell. All about how you were Nevelsky's man in the CIA. It's remarkable how well everything fits once you see it that way. It explains Rukovoi's death, and it explains why Nevelsky exposed Wilson as a Russian agent. It was a frame-up. Classic KGB disinformation."

The M-11 moved again.

Moore said, "If you're thinking of using that on me, I wish you'd make up your mind."

Briggs lifted the gun to firing position and pressed a lever. The foot-long magazine dropped out. He hung it from a hook on his belt.

"Better?" he asked.

"Much."

"You were saying."

"About you and Nevelsky?"

"Right."

Moore studied his former mentor. The trees cut off most of the light from the moon and stars; Moore wished he could read Briggs's expression more clearly.

"One thing bothers me," Moore said. "I don't know if Wilson made all that up out of whole cloth, or if he based it on the truth."

"What truth?"

"That Gherman Nevelsky is your man in the KGB."

"What!"

"Nevelsky works for you."

"How do you figure that one?"

"It's not hard when you have all the pieces. The important thing that Wilson identified for me was the number of interests you and Nevelsky have in common. That was the basis of his argument that you were Nevelsky's agent. But it works both ways. In fact, it works much better if Nevelsky is your agent. Look— Nevelsky exposes Wilson, who really *is* the Walrus, and he justifies it to his superiors because it will destroy Collins and the whole structure he's building, and maybe destroy the whole American intelligence apparatus in the process. That's a plausible argument for sacrificing an agent, even one as well-placed as Wilson. From your point of view, of course, nothing could be better than foiling Collins and stopping his secret reorganization plans. And you figure you'll still be able to put everything back together again, so you're not worried about its really destroying the whole intelligence apparatus.

"As for Nevelsky's having Rukovoi killed, that's the real irony. There I was, worried that Nevelsky wouldn't believe Rukovoi when he said he'd turned me. But in fact Nevelsky did believe him, and that's why Rukovoi is dead. Nevelsky had him killed to prevent his overtaking Nevelsky in the KGB sweepstakes, sure—but that was secondary. The important thing was that Nevelsky was afraid I might tell Rukovoi about Nevelsky's being your man. Nevelsky's official reason for the termination was that Rukovoi was a double agent, but it didn't matter to him whether that was the truth or not. All he could see was the connection between you and me and the possibility that if Rukovoi really had turned me, he would learn about Nevelsky and you."

Moore's mind ran back over the past months, unraveling again the tangled threads. "So there we were— you and me, out of contact with each other, neither of us knowing what the other was doing, and we were both cultivating agents in the KGB. Too bad they were personal rivals."

"Maybe it's too bad, maybe it's not," Briggs said. "Assuming there's any truth in what you've been saying."

"Yeah. Assuming." Moore rubbed his face. "Listen, I'm exhausted."

"I still have some cleaning up to do here. Why don't I have one of my friends give you a lift over to my place? You can spend the night there. We'll need to do some debriefing in the morning."

"All right," Moore said. "That's okay with me."

Relieved of the tensions that had dogged him for months, Moore slept soundly and long. It was almost two in the afternoon when, still bleary, he walked through the house in Alexandria, looking for Briggs. The first person he ran into was Briggs's wife. She had a colorful kerchief over her silver-flecked auburn hair, and she was dressed for gardening.

"Hello, Babs."

"Hello, Greg. How are you feeling?"

"Still a little out of it, but much better, thanks. Been a long time."

"Yes. Too long."

"Is J. P. around?"

"He's in the study; he told me to call him when you got up. Why don't you go sit in the solarium, and I'll send him out."

"Fine."

He sat at a wrought-iron and glass table amidst the tall plants in the glass-walled room. Barbara Briggs brought him coffee and rolls and a plate of eggs. A few minutes later, Briggs came in and sat opposite him.

"I hear you got a little sleep."

"A little."

"Well, you earned it."

"How about you?"

"I got my four-hour minimum. It'll hold me. Funny how you need less sleep when you get old. Some kind of compensation for the things you can't do, I guess."

"What's been happening?"

"The big news is that Martin Wilson committed suicide last night."

Moore stopped in mid-bite. "Suicide?"

"That's right. Shame, isn't it? It seems he was about to be exposed as a Russian spy. Couldn't take it. At least, that's what the suicide note says."

Moore put his fork down on his plate. "Maybe you'd better tell me about it."

"There's not much more. Well, there is one other thing, I guess. He left behind a lot of papers describing a plan he and Collins had to set up a super-secret covert operations outfit, completely immune from oversight,

Congressional or otherwise. There's a bit of a flap about that. It seems whoever uncovered Wilson's papers made several copies before he turned the papers over to the FBI. The way I hear it, the *Post* has a set, and so does the *Times*, and Bill Safire and Jack Anderson."

"So it can't be kept in the family."

"No. It's too late for that, I'm afraid."

"Well, well. That was some cleanup job you did last night. No wonder you only got four hours' sleep."

Briggs's eyes widened, all innocence. "Now, Greg. I don't have the faintest idea what you mean."

Later, they went out into the garden and sat in the sun.

Briggs said, "There's the question of what kind of job you want."

Moore watched a bumblebee surveying roses on a trellis at the side of the house.

"I'll have to think about it," he said noncommittally. "Right now, what I'm concerned about is Vienna."

"The Soviet push?"

"Exactly."

"Don't worry about it."

Moore shaded his eyes so he could see the other man. "Come again?"

"It's not definite, but I think they're going to back off. They've been given some signals that it would be healthier for everybody if they did." Briggs's face brightened. "You'll have to excuse me, Greg. Sometimes I'm a little slow on the uptake. If you want to go back to Vienna for a while . . ."

"The truth is, I'm not sure. I've got mixed feelings."

"About both the past and the future."

"Something like that."

"Think it over. Let me know."

Moore dozed. When he woke up, Briggs was gone. Moore went inside and showered and dressed.

After dinner, Briggs asked him, "You make up your mind about a job?"

"I haven't thought about it, to speak of."

"Well, why don't you? It's a big decision. Take a week's vacation, and really give it some thought."

"Well . . ."

Briggs laughed. "Hell, take two. Go ahead—I insist. We're not going to have things straightened out around here for twice that long."

―――――

In the morning Moore flew to New York. A cab took him to Fifth Avenue and Sixty-ninth Street.

Natalia was waiting for him at the apartment door. For some reason, he felt reserved with her, almost awkward.

She led him into the living room. He was pleased to see how much better she looked. She'd had her hair styled, and she had obviously been out shopping—she was wearing a simple print dress that was the perfect cut for her. She was the picture of a woman of elegance and taste.

They stood in the living room, facing each other, silent. And then, without warning, she came to him, clung to him, her body pressed tightly to his, her face buried in his shoulder.

He stroked her head and back. Her hair smelled of flowers.

She let go of him and stepped back. "I was worried about you."

"I was worried about you, too."

"Your friends have been wonderful to me. I can never repay them properly."

"I'm sure they've been getting their money's worth out of your visit."

"They had a small dinner party last night. They gave only a few hours' notice, but no one refused the invitation. They have planned another party for tonight."

"I told you a countess would be a real attraction in their crowd." He went on admiring her. "You look a lot better."

She smiled. "When you get to be my age, Gregory, you learn the value of sleeping potions and hairdressers and expensive little boutiques. But the thing that did me the most good was hearing you were safe. It was kind of Mrs. Briggs to call."

"I was going to make the call myself, but by the time I got there I could barely keep my head up."

"Will you tell me what happened?"

"Sure."

"Shall we sit down?"

"Why don't we go out and take a walk? It's a beautiful day."

They wandered through Central Park and he told her about the black pickup truck and Wilson and the house by the sea. It was, necessarily, a distorted and limited version of what had happened.

She listened carefully. When he finished, she said, "There are things you are not telling me."

"There have to be."

They walked through an underpass and came out across a broad, green field from Belvedere Castle. Its tiny lake was almost perfectly still; the brown stone castle shimmered on the surface of the water.

"What if Wilson was right?" she asked. "What if your friend Briggs is really the Soviet agent and not Wilson? Is it possible?"

"Yes, it's possible. If you assume that Wilson had Joan killed and tried to kill me only to protect Collins's reorganization plan. That's how Jordie Robbins saw it, God knows. If that's the truth, then what I've done is to put a Soviet agent at the head of the CIA."

"You do not believe that."

"If I sat and brooded about it long enough, I probably would. And I'm willing to bet that from time to time, in moments of doubt, it's going to come back to haunt me. All my life, maybe, I'll be wondering if I handed the country to its enemies. But right now I think I did the right thing."

They were passing the castle. A line was beginning to form for tickets to a free performance of Shakespeare—couples and larger groups with blankets and picnic baskets and bottles of wine.

"Looks like fun," Moore said.

"Yes."

The street at the edge of the park was visible through the trees. They turned around and started back.

"It comes down to this," Moore said. "When you're faced with equally plausible alternatives, you've got to make a choice. At some point, you've got to say—this is the reality I perceive. There may be an absolute reality out there, but I'm not necessarily going to recognize it even if I see it. All I can do is look at the reality I perceive and see if it is moving in a good direction. If it is, I support it. Otherwise, I oppose it. Take Collins and Wilson. Maybe they were a hundred